the kiss

Elda Minger

BERKLEY SENSATION, NEW YORK

THE BERKLEY PUBLISHING GROUP
Published by the Penguin Group
Penguin Group (USA) Inc.
375 Hudson Street, New York, New York 10014, USA
Penguin Group (Canada), 90 Eglinton Avenue East, Suite 700, Toronto, Ontario M4P 2Y3, Canada
(a division of Pearson Penguin Canada Inc.)
Penguin Books Ltd., 80 Strand, London WC2R 0RL, England
Penguin Group Ireland, 25 St. Stephen's Green, Dublin 2, Ireland (a division of Penguin Books Ltd.)
Penguin Group (Australia), 250 Camberwell Road, Camberwell, Victoria 3124, Australia
(a division of Pearson Australia Group Pty. Ltd.)
Penguin Books India Pvt. Ltd., 11 Community Centre, Panchsheel Park, New Delhi—110 017, India
Penguin Group (NZ), Cnr. Airborne and Rosedale Roads, Albany, Auckland 1310, New Zealand
(a division of Pearson New Zealand Ltd.)
Penguin Books (South Africa) (Pty.) Ltd., 24 Sturdee Avenue, Rosebank, Johannesburg 2196,
South Africa

Penguin Books Ltd., Registered Offices: 80 Strand, London WC2R 0RL, England

This is a work of fiction. Names, characters, places, and incidents either are the product of the author's imagination or are used fictitiously, and any resemblance to actual persons, living or dead, business establishments, events, or locales is entirely coincidental. The publisher does not have any control over and does not assume any responsibility for author or third-party websites or their content.

THE KISS

A Berkley Sensation Book / published by arrangement with the author

PRINTING HISTORY
Berkley Sensation edition / March 2006

Copyright © 2006 by Elda Minger.
Cover art by pinglet.
Cover design by Rita Frangie.
Interior text design by Stacy Irwin.

ISBN: 0-425-20681-5

BERKLEY SENSATION®
Berkley Sensation Books are published by The Berkley Publishing Group,
a division of Penguin Group (USA) Inc.,
375 Hudson Street, New York, New York 10014.
BERKLEY SENSATION is a registered trademark of Penguin Group (USA) Inc.
The "B" design is a trademark belonging to Penguin Group (USA) Inc.

PRINTED IN THE UNITED STATES OF AMERICA

10 9 8 7 6 5 4 3 2 1

The Dare JAN 2010

"Any novel that has its two lead characters playing truth or dare is bound to be a lot of fun and that is the case with this book. The story line engages the audience . . . A pleasant story that entertains." —*Midwest Book Review*

"Elda Minger combines humor, romance, hidden fears, and slapstick comedy in a story that will have you laughing out loud . . . A delightful read." —*Readers & Writers Ink Reviews*

"Fan-favorite Minger outdoes herself with this joyous, funny, and warmhearted tale. Filled with engaging people— and animals—*The Dare* is the perfect way to kick back and relax." —*Romantic Times* (Top Pick)

"Sexy and fun . . . Snappy dialogue and hilarious antics . . . Filled with humor and warmth . . . For a romance guaranteed to tickle your funny bone and brighten your day, I dare you to try *The Dare*." —*Romance Reviews Today*

The Fling

"Think of the movie *How to Marry a Millionaire* . . . amusing . . . escapist merriment [for] fans of romantic romps." —*BookBrowser*

"Warmhearted and delightful . . . a very special treat." —*Romantic Times*

"Sexy, fun, light entertainment." —*All About Romance*

"A fun, breezy read . . . The twists and turns of the plot are fun and never overdone . . . *The Fling* is a great summer read." —*The Best Reviews*

*To Kim Kimmel, my writing buddy and good friend.
You were there when this idea was born, over
margaritas and chips, and urged me to go for it!
Your emotional and artistic support over the years has
meant so much to me. Sometimes there are things
only another writer can understand.*

*And to the real Toby, my little terrier with the heart
of a lion. You taught me all I ever needed to learn
about courage in the face of thoughtless cruelty,
and the miracles that can happen if we are tenacious
in having an open and loving heart.*

one

IT IS, THOUGHT Tess Sommerville, with heartfelt apologies to Jane Austen, *a truth universally acknowledged, that a single woman not in possession of a good fortune must be in want of a husband.*

At least that's how her family thought.

"Tess," said her friend Brooke from across the table, "Where are you? Earth to Tess?" She grinned and leaned back in her chair.

Tess blinked, coming back to the present moment with a start.

She and Brooke Matthews, her best friend of twenty-three years, were sitting in their favorite local bar about an hour outside Chicago, trying to celebrate. Only the celebrating part hadn't been going all that well. It was close to ten o'clock this October evening the night before Tess's wedding.

They should've been having a lot more fun than they were, and both of them knew it. This wasn't some dingy, dank bar, blinds closed against the sunlight, all shady and secretive with the various patrons slumped over their scotches.

This was a local hangout, more like *Cheers*, lively and bright, clean and modern. Bands played on the weekend, and the dance floor was packed on a Friday night.

She and Brooke had been coming here for years; it was one of their favorite places. When Tess had said she needed to get out, get away from her anxiety concerning tomorrow, Brooke had suggested they come here.

"Brooke," Tess said, leaning forward and picking up her sparkling water with a slice of lime. *God forbid I put on even one ounce and not fit into that damn dress.* "The truth. Bridal jitters. How scared is scared? How do you know you're doing the right thing? How can you be sure you're not ruining your life by walking down that aisle?"

"You're asking me? *Moi?* Divorced twice and currently not even able to date? A lot *I* know."

"Was it this bad for you, the night before? Either time?"

"Oh, let's see." Brooke set down her vodka martini and gave Tess a sly smile. "First wedding, I was so young everyone thought I was pregnant. Not pregnant, even worse, just young, stupid, and idealistic. I was so nervous I almost hurled walking down the aisle. And then, of course, the highlight was spending my honeymoon sleeping in his car because he hadn't thought to make reservations anywhere. I had the backseat; he had the front."

Tess frowned. "You never told me any of this."

"You never asked. Now, the second time, I knew it was wrong about a month and a half before the actual wedding, but it was like—" She hesitated. "It was like—"

"Heading inexorably toward a train wreck and not being able to stop," interrupted Tess. "Peering over a balcony and having that irresistible urge to jump. Feeling like Bambi staring into the headlights of an oncoming car—"

"You've got the general idea." Brooke picked up her drink and took a sip, scanning the room at the same time. She set down her glass. "Ah, such a vast wasteland. So much time, so few good men. It's no wonder all the fun's gone out of dating."

"But doesn't every bride feel like this the night before?" At her friend's puzzled expression, Tess said, "Not the vast wasteland thing, but back to the train wreck theory. Bambi. Headlights."

"I guess. To some degree. But that's what these little bachelorette get togethers are for, to defuse these fears. Otherwise, Western civilization would grind to a halt."

"Huh?" said Tess. She was so tense, she couldn't seem to follow the conversation.

"If women didn't marry. It would mean the end of Western civilization as we know it."

Tess gave her friend a look.

"Not working, huh?" said Brooke.

Tess had decided to skip the big blowout bachelorette party the night before her wedding and simply hit her favorite local bar with her best friend in the world. And all night, her fears and trepidation had stuck in her throat. She hadn't been able to voice these misgivings or get them out. She had all the classic symptoms of stress—the sick stomach; the start of a headache; the tight, sore throat; the sense of impending disaster . . .

It felt as if a gigantic boxing match was taking place inside her head, the local favorite, *Normal Feelings*, going up against the world champion, *Something's Wrong*, and they were going to battle it out until only one was left standing—

"Maybe this is your starter marriage," Brooke said, signaling the cocktail waitress.

"At thirty? Isn't that for all the *young* twentysomethings?"

Brooke grinned. "Will you stop? You're only twenty-nine, not even thirty, and since when have you ever done anything on schedule?"

Tess had to laugh, but she still felt worried. She'd read the same article on starter marriages, which were simply marriages men and women went into while quite young that averaged between eighteen months and three years. Then, of course, they went through the shock of a divorce and the intense period of mourning, and they parachuted back down into the dating trenches. But the strange thing was, these marriages were considered the marriage you had before you got to the *real* marriage, whenever that was supposed to occur. And whatever that marriage was supposed to be.

Depressing.

It wasn't that she wanted Ozzie and Harriet, or even Ozzie and Sharon. But just when had things become this complicated? All she wanted was a nice, serene little life, free of the nagging fear in the pit of her stomach.

"I guess I have to focus on my future," said Tess.

My future. Which included arriving at St. Anthony's Episcopal Church tomorrow afternoon where a few hundred of her father's and stepmother's closest friends would watch her walk down the aisle toward her future husband, the eminently suitable—meaning, quite well off financially—Paul Atherton.

Tess sighed and took another sip of her sparkling water.

WILLIAM Tremere glanced back at the older couple standing on their doorstep, arms around each other, and raised his hand in a very fond farewell salute. Don and Debra Matthews had treated him like one of their own children during the year he'd spent living with them as an exchange student from London.

The small midwestern town outside Chicago had been quite a change from the cosmopolitan city he'd come from, but he'd thoroughly enjoyed it. His junior year had been one of adventure and cultural change, and Will was the sort of person who relished both. The Matthews had four children, two girls and two boys. They'd all instantly embraced him and made him feel a part of their lively, boisterous family.

Which is exactly why, when his friend Elaine had asked him to drive her van and her dog from the Chicago area back to the West Coast, and he'd found himself back in his old stomping grounds, he'd been sure to stop and see the Matthews family.

Debra had told him that her daughter Brooke was out for the evening at a local bar. Will knew the place; it was a fun establishment. She'd also told him that Brooke was there with her best friend, Tess Sommerville.

Tess. The name brought up very specific images. He had memories of a delicately slender, pretty girl with shiny, straight brown hair and huge, startled eyes hidden behind her tortoiseshell glasses and thick bangs. She'd been terribly quiet the times he'd met her at the Matthews' home, almost as if she were standing well into Brooke's lively shadow.

When Ron, the Matthews son who had become his best friend in the States, had told Will he thought Tess had a major crush on him, he'd laughed. They were ages apart in life experience—four years—and in high school, that had been a huge gulf. While he was a junior, Tess was still attending the upper grade school down the road.

Not exactly dating material. But he'd always liked her and had gone out of his way to treat her well, with gentle respect. He'd sensed the slightest hint of sadness around her, and he'd wondered at that. *Something in her eyes.* The only time he'd really seen her open up and laugh had been around the Matthews' dinner table.

Now, as he got into Elaine's van, started the engine, and then carefully pulled away from the curb, he wondered just how much Tess had changed over the years.

WHY *can't I just settle down and enjoy the future I've se-lected for myself?* Tess thought. *I made all those choices, I'm certainly responsible for them, so now why am I so restless, so nervous, so—*

Unhappy.

Determined to have a good time tonight, Tess pushed the single word aside, picked up her sparkling water, and focused her attention on Brooke, who was—

Staring across to the far end of the bar and smiling.

"What?" said Tess, then she turned in her chair, saw who Brooke was looking at, and felt as if she'd been hit in the stomach with a jumbo medicine ball.

"Incredibly gorgeous guy at the door—" Brooke stopped, squinted, then said, "Oh my God, he's coming this way!" Her green eyes widened, and she whispered, "Oh my God, it's—"

"Who?" said Tess, suddenly desperate to know. The man in question was tall, around six two, and very well built. He moved with a grace that told her he was totally comfortable in his own skin. Dark hair, to his shoulders, and a bit of stubble on his chin completed the picture.

But it was great stubble, like movie idol stubble. It certainly wasn't the common variety of loser stubble like the guy in a chair who hadn't showered for days, wearing a wife-beater shirt and wrinkled boxers, a can of beer clutched in one hand as he searched diligently for the remote so he could watch reruns of *The Jerry Springer Show*.

Gorgeous didn't even come close to describing this guy, stubble and all.

"It's William," said Brooke. "Or Will, as we used to call him." She stood up and waved.

Tess watched as Mr. Gorgeous caught sight of Brooke and smiled. If her first glimpse of him had been a medicine ball to the stomach, that smile went right down to more intimate parts of her body. It felt as if someone had just turned on a light switch deep inside her.

Hel-lo . . .

"Will?" she said to cover her confusion.

"I don't know what he calls himself now," Brooke admitted. "Don't you remember? William Tremere, visiting from England? My brother's junior year? Mom thought it would be a great idea if we broadened our minds and sponsored an exchange student—"

Memory was kicking in as Tess saw him weaving his way through the sea of tables toward their own.

Will. She'd had an incredible crush on him while still in the upper grade school and had come to Brooke's home many times that year just hoping to catch a glimpse of him. It had been everything about him, his looks, that accent—but more than anything, it had been his kindness and consideration, the way he'd always treated her.

He'd never been rough or abrupt like some of her friend's older brothers. He'd never treated her as if she were a nuisance, the little sister they had to watch over whether they wanted to or not.

Mrs. Matthews had told them that Will had a couple of older sisters, so, as she'd said, "He knows how to treat a girl right."

Tess couldn't have agreed more. And now, watching

him walk through the crowded bar, she barely heard Brooke's words.

"My brother stayed in touch with him. Remember, after college, Ron spent the summer in England? He stayed with Will and his family. Hey, you!" Brooke said enthusiastically as he reached their table. Her arms went around him, and she pulled him close for an affectionate hug.

"Brooke," he said. "God, you look gorgeous."

His voice. That voice was the same, exactly the way she remembered. If he still had gorgeous hands—Tess had a thing for men's hands—then she was a goner all over again.

She glanced at them. Just her type. Strong and well proportioned. And more importantly, she saw the way he hugged Brooke back, the way he used those hands, with confidence. Will had developed into quite a man, and there wasn't a tentative bone in his body.

She blinked and came out of her thoughts, as pleasurable as they were, and found herself looking up into a familiar pair of incredible, gray-blue eyes.

"Hello again," he said. But it was enough. What was it about Brits that they could say the most simple words with those stunning, plummy voices and make it sound like you were right in the middle of a *Masterpiece Theatre* production?

Or a Jane Austen movie . . .

"Hello," she said back, slowly standing up, struck dumb by him all over again and feeling like a total idiot. Like she was back in school, a shy girl with coltish legs and thick glasses.

Ugh.

"Will, you remember my best friend in the entire world, Tess. Tess Sommerville."

"Tess of the Sommervilles," he said, a grin tugging at the corner of his mouth as he took her hand. And what a lovely mouth it was, thought Tess. Not to mention that hand, his touch, the warmth and strength of his handshake, which set her off all over again. "Of course I remember you."

Breathe . . . Remember to breathe . . . Think . . .

"What?" she replied. *Oh, brilliant . . .*

"Sommervilles," he said. "D'Urbervilles."

Oh no, so now I get to look stupid as well as sound stupid.

"Never mind," he said, saving the day and winning even more points with her. "Thomas Hardy. English lit. You had to be there."

There had always been the chance that Will might have grown into a man she wouldn't have liked at all. And Tess was glad it just wasn't the case.

"So," Brooke said, "pull up a chair and tell us what you're doing in our neck of the woods."

He did, close enough to Tess that she realized, in the very small part of her brain still functioning, that he *smelled* good.

"I'd lost touch with Ron," she heard Will say, as if through a fog, "and so when the opportunity presented itself to come back to the Midwest, I thought I'd take it and see if he was still here. But your mother informed me that he's living just outside Boulder—which of course, you know."

"I do," said Brooke, teasing him. "But what are you doing here?"

"I'm driving a friend's van, and her dog, back to Los Angeles. She came out to Chicago on a research trip and then had to get back to the coast quickly for another client—an emergency. She didn't want her dog, Sugar, to fly, so I agreed to come out and drive her van back to Los Angeles for her, Sugar included."

"You can take that kind of time off work?"

"All the time," he said. "I find it necessary to have various adventures on a regular basis."

"Nice life," said Brooke. "When do you leave?"

"Tomorrow, six in the morning. I want to beat the morning rush hour, perhaps make it to Nebraska the first night. And now I'm going to try to see Ron when I reach Colorado."

"So," said Brooke, and Tess could tell she was deliberately out to do a little fishing, "is it serious? Is this woman your girlfriend?"

"No, just a good friend." He smiled at Tess and she knew he was making an effort to include her in the conversation. "You'd like Elaine. Both of you would," he said, including Tess in his glance. "She's a very well respected and gifted psychic. Dead accurate. She's had the gift since childhood, and it caused her quite a lot of trouble until she understood what it was."

"You Brits! I love all that stuff. Don't you, Tess?"

She nodded her head automatically, on a sort of emotional autopilot. She couldn't stop looking at him as memories assailed her, all of them good, even though she'd usually been agonizingly self-conscious around him.

"I'll bet my mom was so glad to see you."

"She was," Will said. "As was your father. And then she told me you were still in the area, and at this bar tonight." He leaned back, a hint of mischief in his expression. "So do you two girls come here often?"

Tess sat glued to her chair, so nervous, so attracted to this man that she could only look at him and then look away at Brooke so her staring wouldn't be so terribly obvious. If she'd had a major crush on the boy he'd been in high school, the man, here in the flesh, was absolutely devastating.

"Yeah, we do," Brooke said. "Pathetic, I know. But," she said, raising her glass in a mock toast, "we're celebrating tonight!"

"What?" Will asked.

"Tess's marriage. Tomorrow. Two o'clock."

"Marriage," he said, and Tess realized that the only good thing about the word *marriage,* at this exact moment, was hearing it come out of that gorgeous mouth, with that incredible accent.

"Yes," she said with false brightness. Oh, how the universe had to be laughing at her. Here she was, the night before her wedding, and right in front of her was a man from her past who would've tempted a nun to fling off her robes, forget all her vows, and leave her convent.

"Congratulations," he said, but she detected a somewhat detached tone to that beautiful British voice.

"Thank you," she said.

DAY *late and a dollar short—that's me.*

William Edward Tremere studied the woman in front of him. Tess had matured into quite a beauty. Gone were the glasses and the thick bangs. She didn't seem to be hiding behind them anymore, but he still caught that gently haunted look in her eyes.

What secrets was she hiding? It surprised him, how he wanted to find out. Will had to forcibly remind himself that she was marrying another man the following day.

He'd never know her, secrets and all. This night at this bar would be a moment out of time. She was all grown up, and she fascinated him.

Tess possessed a quiet, serene beauty, in total contrast to Brooke, with her vivid red hair, voluptuous curves, and creamy skin. Tess was slender to the point of fragility, with very long, straight, shiny brown hair the exact shade of a pecan shell. Her eyes, greenish gold with thick, dark eyelashes, were simply stunning. But there was something else . . .

He couldn't figure out what it was. He couldn't even explain it to himself. But he'd thought, when he'd first set eyes on her, all grown up now, that somehow she was going to be significant in his life.

His mother would laugh. She and his grandfather had always told him to trust his intuition, to never try to silence that little voice that tells you things. Elaine had told him the same thing, over and over.

"Everyone's psychic," she'd told him once. "Some of us are just better listeners and taken the trouble to develop our intuition."

Well, his was screaming at him right now. He'd taken one look at Tess and known—something was up.

"Two o'clock?" he said. "Tomorrow?"

Tess jumped and then said, "Yep. That's the plan."

"And you're here for how much longer?"

"We were thinking of turning in pretty soon," said Brooke.

"Well then," he said, improvising madly and hoping Tess wouldn't consider him a total idiot, "Tess, I can't let you go home without at least one celebratory dance."

He'd take what he could get, live in the moment.

And that dance would be his test. That close together on the dance floor, he'd know. But he already had the feeling he was fighting a lost cause . . .

Then Tess surprised him.

"Okay," she said.

* * *

OKAY? said a little voice inside her, the one she usually fought down as she talked herself into doing the right thing, the cautious thing, the sensible thing. *Okay? Have you gone completely nuts?*

But some little demon was driving Tess. If she was getting married tomorrow afternoon and going into a state of deep panic about the whole endeavor, then she'd use this man from her past as a test.

Do not panic, this is only a test . . .

A test. That was it. She'd dance with him, and if that confused her further or made her feel even less like marrying Paul, she'd listen to those feelings.

But for now, she wanted this dance. She wanted this dance, with Will, like she'd never wanted anything in her entire life.

Brooke was looking at her with a very amused expression on her face.

"Go for it, kids," she said, signaling their waitress. "I'm going to get myself a sparkling water for the road."

Will took Tess's hand, and she practically shivered with pleasure. Some guys just had it, and Will, her blast from the past, had it in spades. Unfortunately, most of these guys were the sort you didn't consider marrying, introducing to your friends, or even bringing home to Mother.

Her mother, however, was another matter entirely. Emily Sommerville, now Robards, had divorced her father when Tess had been thirteen. Even at that age, she'd known about her father's affair.

Tess had picked up the phone one morning when she'd come home from school not feeling well and heard the woman who would become her stepmother talking with her father. They'd been discussing their plans, and at that moment, Tess had known that her mother was going to be emotionally devastated.

But Emi, as she liked to be called, had rallied. She'd done everything in her power to help Tess make the difficult transition, yet Tess had looked at her free-spirited mother and seen a woman who put her heart at risk countless times.

A short and bitter custody battle had ensued, with her father, who was the far more financially stable parent, winning custody of all three children, Tess and her two older brothers. Contact with her mother had become less frequent, then nonexistent. It was as if she'd disappeared. It had been the one real heartbreak in Tess's life. Her father and his new wife had settled down to make them all "a proper home," as he had called it. But nothing they'd done had ever taken her mother's place.

Nothing of her mother remained—certainly none of her generous affection or her hugs and kisses. They didn't bake cookies anymore; they didn't laugh in the large kitchen. They simply ate quiet, perfectly balanced and prepared meals in a somewhat sterile dining room. Her stepmother could have been a clone of Bree from *Desperate Housewives* as far as temperament went. Madeline Sommerville was just as forbidding and rigid.

Her parents' divorce had made Tess determined to find stability and security in her own life.

She didn't ever want her world rocked like that again. It was one of the major reasons she'd decided to marry Paul.

"Tess?"

She blinked, then looked up at Will's face. His expression was gentle. He was still holding her hand, waiting for her to follow him.

"Sorry."

The Friday night country-western band had just finished a song and launched into another one, a pretty good rendition of "How Can I Live Without You."

They stood next to each other on the dance floor and, for just a second, Tess felt like an awkward teenager again. Then, Will put his arms around her, and she was lost.

UNBELIEVABLE.

It couldn't possibly happen this way, finding Tess, here, on the eve of her wedding to another man. The little girl he'd known was all grown up. Will never thought he'd see her again, and now she was causing all sorts of havoc in his heart.

Life worked in mysterious ways.

Honor made it impossible to do what he really wanted, which was pursue her with a vengeance.

Will was inexplicably frustrated at the thought of her spending her life with another man. Did he know what he had? And why did she look so—tense? Didn't most brides-to-be go toward the altar with a little more lightness and happiness?

Something wasn't adding up here.

And damn it, Tess felt wonderful in his arms. Like she'd been made for him. He didn't dare rest his cheek against her hair the way he wanted to, or pull her too close. He couldn't disrespect her that way, no matter what he might have wanted. But she felt so soft in his casual embrace and smelled so good—

One song segued into the next, and Will knew he had to do something. When the second song ended, he stepped a little away from her on the dance floor and looked down into those extraordinary green-gold eyes.

She felt it, too. He could tell. Some things you just *knew*.

"Getting married, are you?" he said softly.

She nodded her head, and he had the feeling that the

reason she was biting her full bottom lip was that she didn't want to talk about it.

"Let me give you something, Tess," he said, reaching into his shirt pocket and extracting a pen and a small piece of paper. "I hope you won't think I'm out of line." He wrote down his cell number and gave it to her.

She took the piece of paper, stared at the numbers on it, then looked up at him, puzzled.

For a moment, Will hesitated. He'd never done anything remotely like this in his life. He was flying blind here, with only his intuition as guidance. But it felt right, and he found that he had to go with his feelings.

More than anything, he didn't want to hurt Tess.

"Tess, if anything goes wrong tomorrow, if the wedding doesn't go off as planned, will you please promise to give me a call?"

She nodded her head, and he believed her. There was something off about this whole wedding thing; she seemed like a lamb being led to slaughter, certainly not the happy, radiant bride she should've been. Tess seemed—almost *stunned*.

Intuition told him she wasn't looking forward to her wedding tomorrow. Intuition also told him that, if things went the way he hoped they would, he just might be getting that phone call from her after all.

Well, a man could certainly hope.

"Let's go back to Brooke," he said quietly, his hand resting on the small of her back. Loving the way she felt against his fingers, Will guided her gently toward the small table on the edge of the bar's dance floor.

And hoped this wasn't the end of it.

two

TESS LEFT BOTH the bar and her friend more confused than ever. Will hadn't helped things by showing up and asking her for that dance.

What's the matter with me, that I can be engaged to one man, on the brink of getting married, and be so attracted to someone else?

She remembered something her oldest brother, Brian, had said once, seven years into his marriage. *Just because I'm married doesn't mean I'm dead. You can think whatever you want, but it's what you do, the choices you make, that matter.*

She hadn't cheated on Paul. She'd simply danced with a friend of Brooke's. A friend from her past.

But Will hadn't felt like a friend. And that was what bothered her the most.

Turning right out of the bar's parking lot, Tess started back toward the large house she shared with her financé, Paul. She'd told Brooke she was going to go back to the house and pick up her dog, Toby, so she knew even if her friend went straight home, she wouldn't worry about her being late.

Tess had opted for a very traditional approach to getting married in the morning. She planned on getting ready at Brooke's, so her wedding dress and everything else she needed were already at her friend's condo. About the only thing her stepmother hadn't taken over was getting her ready in the morning; Madeline Sommerville was in charge of every other wedding detail, and reveling in it.

Kim, Brooke's cousin and a makeup artist who worked in Chicago, would be arriving in the morning, ready to help her put on her best bridal face. Tess hadn't wanted Paul to see her before the wedding, so she was taking no chances.

Almost two weeks ago, Tess had partially moved into Paul's elegant house on the lake, but most of her things were still in storage. She'd been living in a small cabin on one of the other lakes and hadn't had room for all her possessions. But the rent at the storage facility had been minimal, so even with that extra bill, her budget hadn't been blown.

As she drove, she still felt far too restless. Tess thought about what it would be like to throw caution to the wind and take off with the man she'd been madly in love with during her early adolescence. What if she just phoned him and said, "Okay, Will, I'd like to hit the road with you and drive out to California." *An adventure.* Something she'd never really had in her life, during her twenty-nine years on the planet.

Spontaneity made Tess nervous.

The youngest of three children and the only girl, she'd been sheltered and cosseted all of her life by her father and brothers. Not much had been expected of her, except that she toe the line. Oh, and look nice while doing it. Be polite, be helpful, be *nice*.

The silent expectation had been that she would meet a man who would marry her and take care of her. And that she wouldn't make any unpleasant waves like her mother had. Though her stepmother had never really come out and said she disliked Emi Robards, there had always been the strange little remarks about her that seemed like compliments but really weren't.

She'd tried her best to sour all three of her stepchildren against their mother, and it seemed to have worked with Brian. He was a lot like their father, conservative and controlling. Charlie had moved away to Colorado with Ron Matthews as soon as he could. Tess could still remember the uproar when her father had found out the two of them had decided to become ski instructors.

"What the hell kind of a career is that?" he'd bellowed, while her stepmother had fluttered around him, calming him, telling him that both boys would eventually come to their senses and stop this nonsense.

Tess had chosen to stay close to home, trying to make sense out of everything that had happened to her family.

She knew the reality of life. She knew every woman needed to be able to make her own living, make her own way in the world.

But not knowing what she really wanted to do with her life, Tess had finally consulted her father and gone to school to become a dental hygienist. Her stepmother and father, as cautious and conservative as they were, had been delighted. People always had to have their teeth cleaned, didn't they? And all of those children they'd produce had to have braces, right? They'd totally approved of her safe career choice.

Tess had thought she would work for Dr. Ackerman for many more years until last month, when she'd given him notice that she was leaving the job. Three days ago, she'd left that office for the last time.

Paul had told her, in no uncertain terms after they were engaged, how he felt about his future wife working.

"I make plenty of money, enough for both of us," he'd said. "Besides, how would it look? If you keep working, it looks like I can't take care of you properly."

Secretly she wasn't all that crazy about her job, so Tess hadn't given him much of an argument. Now, as she drove along through the silent streets, autumn leaves swirling in the late night breeze, she realized she hadn't really thought a whole lot past her wedding day to the actual marriage.

All the focus had been on the *wedding*. So much hoo-ha had built up to that point, and it astonished Tess. Her step-mother had practically been hysterical at the thought of her stepdaughter getting married. This was the only wedding she'd ever get her hands on, which meant, of course, that her *stepmother* was finally able to design the wedding of *her* dreams.

Madeline's own marriage had been rather hastily and furtively accomplished in downtown Chicago; the couple simply signed the necessary documents and returned to work that same afternoon.

Her father was nothing if not practical.

Tess slowed her dark blue Honda at a stop sign and then glanced over the steering wheel at St. Anthony's, a more than familiar sight. The small, beautifully designed church was where she would be married the following afternoon, followed by a lavish reception at the country club. And then the honeymoon—ten days in Barbados with Paul while Brooke took care of her dog.

On a whim, Tess turned into the church's driveway and parked in one of the spaces closest to the front. Suddenly shaky, she headed up the walkway toward the massive double front door.

It was unlocked, as always. Tess let herself in, soothed by the familiar scents of furniture polish and melted wax. And flowers.

There were just a few bouquets of flowers in vases on the altar. Tomorrow, after her stepmother's florist was finished, it would be a riot of roses and greenery.

A few lights were on up by the altar, just enough to see by. Several candles were lit as well.

Tess hesitated and then started down the aisle until she was next to the front left pew. She slid in, knelt down, put her hands together in a gesture of prayer, and rested her forehead against her entwined fingers.

As she wasn't terribly religious, this was hard for her. But she'd reached a low point in her life. She felt so confused and alone. Maybe this would help.

"Okay," she whispered quietly into the scented darkness, "I'm sorry I haven't been here a whole lot, but that was obviously an oversight on my part. Being so busy with the wedding and all. But something's wrong. I can't figure out what it is. I just feel it."

She took a deep breath. It felt like she was blundering badly, but she had to go on. After she got Toby from Paul's house and returned to Brooke's condo, everything would speed up. That would be it. Tomorrow she would become Mrs. Paul Atherton.

This was the last moment she had for a little reflection, some contemplation. Quiet time.

"So I guess . . . what I'm asking for is a sign. *Any* kind of sign. Something that would let me *know* I'm on the right path. So if you're listening . . . Anyone's help would be appreciated at this point, like guardian angels or spirit guides, I'm not picky."

She was babbling, and she knew it.

Wind it up, already. Geez, you're so bad at this . . .

"Okay. A sign. That's really what I want, something super-obvious, you know? Something even *I* can't overlook. A sign, one way or another, that my wedding tomorrow should go as planned. That it's meant to be. And I *promise* I'll do something in return—some good works or something."

She closed her eyes and sighed one more time, as if all the energy and tension were leaving her body, leaving her feeling drained.

A sign . . .

At that exact moment, she heard a small crash from the far back of the church.

Puzzled, Tess opened her eyes.

Her heart started pounding as she remembered an article she'd read the other day in the local paper. There had been a series of small break-ins during the past few weeks, and local police were stumped. They were putting it down to petty thievery for drug money, but they were frustrated by their inability to put these lawbreakers behind bars.

Robbing a church? How low can you go?

She thought of her cell phone, tucked inside her purse, but then realized there wasn't time. If she didn't at least get a look at these guys, they'd probably leave with their loot before the police could get here.

That meant—she had to go and ID them. Not try to stop them, she wasn't that delusional. Just get a good look at them and try to be an excellent eyewitness. She'd be able to help the local police that way, to look at their pictures of various suspects. She'd watched enough *Law and Order* reruns, she knew what to do.

Her heart hammering against her ribs, Tess clutched her shoulder bag in front of her and slid out of the pew. She'd attended services here since she was a child, and she knew the noise came from the direction of the large community room in the far back.

Reverend Wheeler hosted monthly church buffet suppers in that large room, and it was also where the annual Christmas bazaar took place, along with many other church functions. Steeling herself for what was to come, Tess walked down the long, carpeted hallway, soundlessly, in the direction of the noise.

She paused just a few feet from the set of double doors leading to the community room. Small round windows were set high in each door, so she knew she wouldn't have to step inside to get a good look at these guys. She'd just take a quick glance and then get out and call the police on her cell phone.

Taking a deep breath, she stepped up to the door, looked in one of the windows—

And went into shock.

Paul, her fiancé, the man she was marrying tomorrow, totally naked, was having sex with Marti Wheeler, the reverend's daughter, also totally naked, on one of the long tables in the community room. And from what she saw, they were both giving and getting it good.

Shock held her completely immobile, unable to look away from what she was seeing through the small round window. In some part of her brain, Tess knew she had to get away before either of them saw her, but her legs didn't seem to want to work. They felt shaky, rubbery beneath her, as if they were about to collapse right out from under her.

Nausea swept through her, and bile rose in the back of her throat. Her eyes filled, blurring her vision, but she swiped the tears away, suddenly fiercely angry.

Tess took one more long look. She had to make sure, even though a part of her knew it was true . . .

Yeah, it was Paul. And from the way he and Marti were going at it, this probably wasn't the first time. Tess was sure neither of them would've seen her if she'd been standing right next to them. They were both wild, out of control, crazy with lust for each other. As she watched, Paul slung Marti's legs up around his broad shoulders and her head fell back as she moaned. And he just kept pounding away.

Tess's mind raced at high speed as she watched the two of them.

She remembered that Paul and Marti had dated briefly for a while in high school and then again shortly before she and Paul had started going out. And Tess knew at that moment, her intuition practically screamed it at her, that her fiancé hadn't stopped seeing Marti the entire time they'd been dating—or engaged.

These two were *quite* familiar with each other.

A part of her, out of nowhere, still totally reeling, thought, *He never had sex with me that way . . .*

That thought shocked her out of her immobility. Tess moved to the side of the double doors, away from the small round window, and leaned against the hallway wall, breathing heavily. She tried not to hurl right on Reverend Wheeler's relatively new carpet. Her legs didn't seem to want to work.

She concentrated on not throwing up and wondered what the hell she was going to do.

Tess heard them finish in a blaze of guttural sounds, sharp yelps, and screams. The sudden, total silence galvanized her into action. She had to move. They'd be pulling on their clothes and walking out that door within minutes. She had to get out of here. She couldn't let them find her. But before she could move, she heard them again.

Marti spoke first. "Too bad you're getting married tomorrow, babe. I'm going to miss this."

"Hey. Who says it has to stop?" Paul laughed, then said, "And we still have the rest of the night."

Marti giggled. "I'm going to miss you while you're on your honeymoon."

"Come on, let's not talk right now. I know you're still up for more," Paul said.

Tess couldn't stand it.

Paul's reply was the catalyst that finally stopped her shaking, got her angry, and got her going. All she knew was that she had to get away from both of them. As silently as she could, Tess made her way down the hall, through the church, out the front door, and into her car.

On autopilot, she started the engine and backed out of the parking space and then out the driveway. She drove several blocks until her hands were trembling so badly she had to turn off Main Street on to a residential street with huge, bare-branched oak trees and pull over to the curb.

She got out just in time, bending over and throwing up all over the street in front of her. Sick to her stomach and dizzy, Tess leaned against her open car door and closed her eyes, trying to stop everything from spinning.

How long she hung on the car door she didn't know. Slowly, the world seemed to come back into focus. An elderly man she didn't recognize, walking his ancient Basset Hound, was staring at her, concerned.

"You all right over there?" he called.

Ah, the joys of small-town living. She couldn't even have a complete meltdown in private.

"Touch of the flu," she managed to croak out. "Don't get any closer. I'm sure I can get home."

"You go straight home to bed," he called after her as she got into the car and started the engine.

Her stomach totally purged, Tess drove back on to Main Street and knew what she had to do.

Get back to that bastard's house, rescue her dog, pack up her stuff, and go over to Brooke's.

SHE entered the luxurious lakeside house she shared with the rat bastard, as she'd christened Paul, and set down her keys on the small table in the hallway.

Glancing around, still in shock, Tess saw the house clearly for the very first time. It was as if blinders had been ripped off her vision all at once, and she faced stark reality. The place was all Paul's; there wasn't a whole lot of her personality there. With most of her possessions still in storage, about all she had in this house were her clothes, some cooking utensils, a few of her books, her knitting supplies, and, of course, Toby.

She heard dejected whimpering coming from the kitchen and set off at a brisk run.

She turned on the light to the laundry room and opened the plastic dog crate that sat on the tiled floor off the large kitchen. Tess scooped a trembling Toby up into her arms and smelled—

Urine.

As she carried the little Schnauzer mix to the large sink off the washer and dryer and lowered the trembling dog into it, the rage she felt toward Paul threatened to blow the top of her head off. He'd promised to stop by around nine this evening and let Toby out into the backyard to do her business.

The only reason Toby would have peed in her crate was if her bladder was ready to explode. And the only reason that would have happened was if that bastard had conveniently forgotten to let her out.

He'd also left her in the dark. Toby hated being in the dark. Tess had installed a nightlight, and now she saw the small appliance unplugged and on the shelf near the dryer.

The rat bastard was also a *cheap* bastard.

Tess reached for the coconut-scented dog shampoo as she filled the large sink just a few inches up with comfortably warm water. The shampoo was a mild one, with aloe vera, oatmeal, goldenseal, and yucca extracts. Toby had a slight skin condition, a rash, and Tess realized belatedly that it had gotten worse when they'd both moved in with Paul.

"It's okay, Tobe," she said soothingly to the frightened dog. "It's okay. I know it's not your fault. Everything's okay."

The dog stopped trembling and let Tess wash her. Toby was a true Heinz 57, with some Schnauzer and a few other terriers thrown in for good measure. Her coat had a tendency to stick out all over in wild tufts no matter how much Tess groomed her.

Gray and white, Toby weighed about sixteen pounds and the vet had estimated her age at around eleven years old. She had a little bit of a milky film over her right eye, the beginnings of a cataract. Sometimes she barked when she was scared and couldn't see something clearly when it was on her bad side.

And she possessed the heart of a lion.

Tess knew how passionately this little dog loved her, and had loved her since she'd pulled her car over on the side of the road and rescued Toby, covered with mud, during a particularly violent rainstorm last spring.

And Tess loved her right back.

Toby was staring up at her, a concerned look on her doggie face, and Tess realized tears were streaming down her own face.

"It's okay, Tobe. We're getting out of here."

As she finished rinsing the dog and drying her with a fluffy yellow towel, Tess wondered how she could've ever even *considered* marrying a man who hadn't really warmed to her dog.

"Not a purebred, is she?" Paul had said when she'd told him the details of the rescue. Not "How awful" or "How could anyone do something like that to a dog?" or even a simple, "I'm so glad you rescued her!"

Not a purebred.

The next issue had been her age.

"Eleven years old? Come on, Tess, the vet bills are going to start up shortly. There's a lot wrong with this animal; she's practically at the end of her life. Why don't you take her in to animal control, and I'll get you a puppy from a breeder?"

"How," she asked her dog as she rubbed her briskly dry, "could I have *ever* thought he was anything but a turd?"

Toby whimpered.

Tess grabbed the hairdryer she kept in the laundry room for Toby and thoroughly dried the little dog. As cool as it was outside this October evening, she didn't want to chance Toby catching cold.

"Okay, girl, now we pack."

She raced up the stairs, Toby at her heels, and into the master bedroom. Throwing open the doors to her closet, Tess glanced at the bedroom she'd shared with Paul and realized how little of herself she'd really moved into his house.

I knew. Somewhere inside me, I knew. This was what was wrong. He was boffing someone else. And he would've made a shitty, selfish, self-centered husband.

"The only good thing I can say about this," she said to Toby as she dragged out two enormous suitcases and a backpack, "is that better I found out now than later."

She turned when Toby didn't respond. The little dog was standing perfectly still, eyeing the king-sized bed.

A wicked plan began to form in Tess's mind. Toby was not allowed anywhere on the bed. Paul claimed he was allergic to dog hair on the sheets. Before Tess had moved in, Toby had slept on her bed, so there had been a period of intense confusion for her dog.

And Toby had just had a bath, so she would be shedding like crazy.

"Toby," Tess said, walking to the bed, pulling down the bedspread and blanket, exposing the sheets, and patting the foot of the large mattress firmly. "Up!"

The small Schnauzer mix looked at her as if she'd gone insane. The one dark brown eye that wasn't cloudy sparkled beneath a tuft of gray and white spiky hair.

"It's okay, baby. Now, *up*!"

Toby jumped, and Tess laughed out loud as the little dog hurtled through the air, then hit the bedsheets on a roll. And when Toby rolled, she *rolled*.

Especially after a bath.

The little dog rolled and rolled, yipping little barks of pleasure, as she rubbed and rolled all over the light blue bedsheets. Short gray and white hairs began to bloom on those sheets. She looked like a grizzly scratching itself against a giant redwood. And Tess saw, with great satisfaction, the enormous amount of dog hair being deposited all over.

Not that the rat bastard will see it before tomorrow night. He's probably spending the night before his wedding with Marti.

"Well, Marti," said Tess as she reached for an armful of clothing and began to pack in earnest, "better you than me."

SHE didn't rush her packing, didn't want to forget anything, but it only took Tess about two hours to gather all her clothes, her books, Toby's things, her enormous bag of needlework, her kitchen utensils, and a few odds and ends.

Her car, backed up in the two-car garage so the trunk was as close to the laundry room entrance as possible, looked ready to explode.

But the house, even the master bed, looked roughly the same. She'd closed her closet doors tightly so the R.B. wouldn't see that it was completely empty. (He never looked inside.) The same was true for the kitchen cupboards. (He'd never open them because he was a man who didn't know his way around a kitchen—she, his mom, or take-out restaurants had always done most of his cooking.)

He also wouldn't notice her books were missing (he rarely read) or Toby's things (he ignored her dog). Her needlework wouldn't even register in his mind (he thought knitting was painfully old fashioned—had she seriously thought of making the jerk a sweater for Christmas?), and the few other things of hers she'd taken wouldn't be missed (he'd never cared for her taste in furnishings).

In one last mischievous mood, she'd carefully straightened the blanket and bedspread over the hair-filled sheets, so the R.B. would lie down on the bed before he discovered there was dog hair all over it. She also unplugged the nearest bedside lamp. Paul was so lazy, he'd just lie down in the dark.

Happy allergies, you prick!

Tess scooped up her keys from the table in the front hall.

"Well, Toby," she said, glancing down at her dog as she tossed the house keys in the air and caught them, "this is it. We're out of here!"

Toby wagged her stumpy tail so hard her entire backside quivered. Tess laughed as she snapped Toby's leash on to her collar and picked her up. They headed toward the garage.

And freedom.

WITHIN the hour, her car safely hidden away in Brooke's garage, Tess had told her the entire tale.

"Marti Wheeler? That *bastard*!" Brooke said.

"*Rat* bastard," Tess corrected. The first intense level of her anger-fueled adrenaline blast was beginning to wear off, and she found she was tired. But not tired enough to sleep. Yet.

She still had her whole life to plan. Without him.

They were in Brooke's living room, sprawled on her two sofas. She'd improvised some very good quesadillas when she'd heard that Tess had hurled her dinner and also broken out the ingredients for margaritas. Now, after a few, they were comfortably crashed.

"What about the wedding?" Brooke said.

"What wedding?" Tess lay back on the sofa and played with Toby's ears, then Toby sprawled on her stomach, happily panting. Toby loved Mexican food, and she'd shamelessly begged for whatever she could get.

"You really believe your stepmother's going to let a little thing like Paul's infidelity stand in the way of her having the wedding of her dreams?"

Dead silence as Tess digested this.

"Oh *no*! You're right." She sat up, bracing Toby so she didn't go hurtling off her lap. "Brooke, what am I going to do?"

"My cousin. I'll call her. We can drive into Chicago, and you can stay with her until this whole thing blows over. I won't tell anyone where you are." Brooke thought for a second, then added, "Except perhaps the police, so your folks won't file a missing person's complaint."

"Okay." Tess reached into her front jeans pocket. "By the way, can you drop off the rat bastard's house keys—"

She stopped midsentence. In her hand, clutched in her fingers along with her keys, was a small piece of crumpled white paper she knew had numbers written on it. A cell phone number.

Everything inside Tess stilled.

That dance in her favorite bar tonight had felt like it had happened in another lifetime, so much had gone down since then. But all of a sudden, she realized just how many regrets she'd had mere hours ago as she'd left that same bar. And now, since her little detour to the church, things had totally changed.

She stroked Toby's head, and her little dog looked up at her with so much trust and adoration in her dark eyes that Tess's throat closed. Then she cleared it, gave Toby a decisive pat, and decided that the only direction she could go was forward.

She had to make something good come out of this horribly emotionally confusing night.

Now she had some choices to make, some responsibilities to herself and no one else. She had to stand on her own two feet and create a new life, one that didn't include either Paul or a big wedding. And she could think of one very interesting choice right in front of her, symbolized by the scrap of white paper clutched in her hand.

A choice that would buy her time and give her a chance to sort out the mess that was her would-be wedding. A choice that would give her the adventure she desperately needed and a chance to find herself.

A choice that would horrify her stepmother and father.

Tough. She grinned. Somewhere in her heart, an impulsive rebel came to life.

Tess's heart began to pick up speed. She realized she had the power to stop the out-of-control spiral that had been her life. Even better, because of the circumstances of this night, the universe had given her a chance to do her life all over again. Really, how many people ever got that?

She felt like Gwyneth Paltrow in the movie *Sliding Doors*—Tess in two alternate realities—and she knew she had to pick the right one.

Maybe this horrible night had an up side after all.

"What?" Brooke said, clearly intrigued by the expression Tess knew had to be on her face.

She glanced up at her friend. "Brooke, you've always told me that I've been way too nice."

"Ain't that the truth."

"Looked out for everyone's interests but my own—"

"Yep."

"Been a little too much of a nurturer. And truly lousy at self-care."

Her friend nodded.

"Overlooked really bad behavior."

"Which I'm *very* glad you didn't do tonight. If you'd made excuses for that asshole, I would've killed you." Brooke frowned. "Tess, where is this going?"

Tess opened her hand, waved the small scrap of paper in the air, and then spoke quietly, with as much dignity as she could muster after the amount of tequila she'd ingested.

"I'm sick of being the nice little chump. I'm calling him. Will Tremere. I'm driving out to the West Coast with him. Brooke, I'm getting the hell out of Dodge, and for once in my life, I'm finally going to have a real adventure!"

three

THE SHRILL SOUND of the phone cut through the dark, quiet hotel bedroom. Will rolled over in bed, his legs tangled within the sheets, Sugar at his feet. The Keeshond yipped in surprise at all the movement as Will reached blindly for his cell phone, knocking the rest of the bedside table's contents onto the carpeted floor.

"'Lo," he said, his voice husky with sleep. He cleared his throat. "Hello? Elaine?"

Silence. He was about to hang up his cell phone when a feminine voice said, "Will?"

Tess.

"Tess." He reached for the bedside lamp switch and then, as light flooded the room, he almost laughed out loud at the disgusted expression on Sugar's fluffy canine face. The silvery Keeshond was a diva, no two ways about it, and she did not like being woken up at—

He glanced at the bedside clock's glowing face—

Four sixteen in the morning.

He gently stroked Sugar's head and scratched the velvety fur around her ears in just the way he knew she liked it. Sugar sighed and leaned in, clearly deciding to let bygones be bygones. Anything for a good scratch behind the ears.

Will turned his attention back to the phone. Tess wasn't forthcoming with any information, so he decided to take the lead.

"Wedding's not going off as planned, I take it?" *Why else would Tess call?* She didn't seem the type to cheat.

A second of silence and then "Yeah."

"Well, I'm glad you called. Another few hours, and I would've been on the road."

"That's why I called," she said. "I need to—get out of town for a few days, lay low, and I thought perhaps—"

This was going down much better than he'd thought it would, for him at least. He hated the thought of Tess being hurt. He wondered, though, who had dumped who and whether Tess had been the one on the receiving end of a nasty surprise the night before her wedding. She sounded a little shell-shocked.

"You're certainly more than welcome to hitch a ride out of town with me. Where would you like me to drop you off?"

"If you wouldn't mind, I'd like to go all the way to Los Angeles. I can split the cost of gas and everything—"

"Fine." He wasn't about to take her gas money, but no sense in quibbling right now. The main thing was to get her into the van and on the road with him before she changed her mind. Will sensed Tess was nervous, and he knew the only way to deal with a situation like this was to be brisk and businesslike. One of them had to be strong and decisive. Now he knew he had more than two thousand miles to get to the bottom of the mystery that was Tess Sommerville.

"Tess, can you be ready by six?"

"How about six-thirty?"

Her voice sounded wavery.

"Hell, I can give you till seven." What was a little traffic getting out of town? Besides, it would give him even more time to get to know her.

"Thanks so much. Where are you?"

"I'll come pick you up. Give me your address."

She did, they said their good-byes, then he hung up the phone and stared at Sugar. She butted her silky head against his hand, and he continued to scratch her ears. She sighed, in total bliss, and nudged up against him. Nudge, pat. Nudge, pat. They both had the routine down.

"Well," he said after a sufficient amount of ear scratching had put Sugar back into a relaxed state of mind, "this trip just keeps getting better and better."

"WHAT should I take?" Tess said, staring at her jampacked car. Now that she'd committed to getting out of town with Will, the enormity of her decision was beginning to overwhelm her. Adrenaline fueled by rage and hurt had long since left her, and she just felt exhausted.

And unsure of what she was about to attempt.

"Where's your backpack?" Brooke said.

"Brooke?"

"Yeah?"

"I'm kind of fading here."

Her friend gave her a look, and Tess knew what she was thinking.

"No, no, Brooke, I'm not going to go back with him.

It's just—I need someone to help me make some basic decisions, to help me get into that van with Will and hit the road." She put one hand over her eyes, shielding them. "I'm just so damn tired."

"You're sure this is what you want, Tess?"

"I can't stay here." Tess could feel weak tears starting to fill her eyes. Now that the initial rush was over, a rush that had catapulted her from Paul's house to Brooke's and had helped her find the courage to call Will, she found that she was tired. Unsure. Terrified. Everything that she'd counted on was gone. It was as if it had never really existed in the first place.

The sense of safety and security that had always eluded her seemed impossibly out of her reach now.

There was a very small part of her that just wanted to lie down, curl up in a fetal position, and give in.

"Tess," said Brooke. "Sit for a minute."

Her friend guided her over to the steps that led down from the laundry room to the double garage, where her Honda now sat, parked and stuffed to the gills. Tess sat on the cement stair while Brooke knelt down in front of her and took one of her hands.

Brooke's strong grip felt like a lifeline, and Tess squeezed back.

"Okay, let's think this thing out logically. One, you can't marry Paul after what he did tonight. Agreed?"

Tess nodded. Toby, leaning against her legs, nervously wagged her stumpy tail, whined, and climbed into Tess's lap and tried to lick her face.

"Two, Will is giving you the perfect way to get out of town and disappear for a week or so, until you can get things under control emotionally. Right?"

"Yeah."

"And you know I wouldn't let you get in a car with just

anyone. I lived with Will for a year, and he's a great guy. My mom adores him. You're safe with him, you know that."

"Okay."

"Three, I know your stepmother, and she's the kind of person who'd rather see you unhappy and married to Paul than have to go through the embarrassment of calling this whole thing off. You know I'm right about this. I hate to say it about her, but you know I'm telling you the truth. And Tess, I also know you usually cave when it comes to both your dad and stepmother's wishes, so drastic measures are called for in this case, right?"

"Yes."

"So with all that to think about, packing is the least of our worries. Besides, I love to travel so I know how to pack, and I can do it for you. Now, how about if you go upstairs with Toby and lie down, and I'll pack."

"You'd do that?" Tess said.

"I'd move a goddamn mountain if it meant you weren't going to marry that bastard!"

Tess laughed, then suddenly found herself crying, with Brooke's arms around her as Toby whined and anxiously licked her face.

After a few moments, Brooke said, "Tess, I'm so sorry your heart was broken tonight. I'm going to walk you upstairs, you're going to wash your face and get into a pair of my pajamas, and you and Toby are going to catch an hour or two of sleep. I'll pack and have a quick breakfast ready when Will gets here, okay?"

"You," said Tess, her voice shaky, "are the greatest friend anyone could ever have."

"Right back at you, sweetie. Let's go."

* * *

WILL pulled into the condo complex right around seven that morning, and Brooke met him at the door before he could ring the bell.

"She's in the shower," Brooke said as she ushered him and Sugar inside. "Let me get you a cup of coffee and fill you in."

Swiftly, succinctly, she told him the details of what had transpired the previous night.

"What a bastard," Will said softly, not wanting his voice to carry. "Good thing she found out before she married him."

"Yeah, but the deal with Tess is, she has this very rigid, unemotional family, especially her stepmother, that always does the right thing. 'How would it look to the neighbors?' is the motto on their family crest. So you're a godsend, Will, getting her out of town before her stepmother can convince her to carry on, consider their standing in town and all her father's business buddies, and go ahead and marry that bastard."

"She would actually do that?" The idea seemed totally inconceivable to Will.

"Her stepmother would not only do that, but by the end of the day, she'd have Tess convinced the whole thing was her idea. You have no idea, Will. Just get her out of town."

"I can certainly do that."

"She's probably going to crack up somewhere along the way—"

"I grew up with two sisters. I can handle it."

"Just, whatever you do, *don't let her come back.* At least not for a week or so. Tess needs some time. No matter what she says, Will. Trust me on this."

"You have my word."

He was draining the last of his coffee when Brooke said,

"One last thing. I saw the way you were looking at her last night in the bar."

He had to grin. Brooke was like the pesky little sister he'd never had. Both of his sisters back in England were older. Not much had gotten past Brooke during the year he'd lived with her family, and he was pleased to see the status quo hadn't changed when it came to her superb instincts.

"Not the time or the place," he said. "I'd never take advantage."

"Glad we understand each other."

"Perfectly," he said. "She's safe with me."

Brooke glanced upstairs as she heard the water turn off. "Let's get her stuff into the van before she changes her mind."

"I didn't know how much room you had," Brooke said as Will walked her out to the van, Tess's backpack slung over his shoulder, a large cooler in his arms, and Sugar at his heels. "So I packed her kind of light. The backpack has essentials, and the large tote bag has her knitting and a few good paperback books. Anything else she needs, she can stop and buy. This will be a much-needed vacation for her."

Will had to grin. Brooke, like her mother, thought of everything.

"I made you guys some sandwiches for lunch, and there's a cooler with fruit, veggies, cheese, and some ice, soda, water, and juice. That should make up for the time you lost this morning 'cause you won't have to stop to eat today until dinner. And then there's Toby's crate, her leash and bowls and food—

"She has a dog?" Will said.

"Is that a problem?"

"No. I'm glad. I imagine her dog will be a great comfort to her. What kind?"

"A real mix, some terrier and Schnauzer in there somewhere. Just think Toto in *The Wizard of Oz.* I think it would be traumatic for both of them if Toby was left behind at this point."

"I understand and agree with you."

Will positioned the cooler directly behind the driver's seat and slung the backpack into the back of the van. He took the large tote out of Brooke's hands and deposited it behind the front passenger seat. Then he shut the van's sliding door.

"Show me where Toby's crate is," he said.

When all of Toby's things were loaded, Will stepped back from the van.

"I'm going to leave Sugar here in the car just until I see Toby and then the two dogs can meet out here on the lawn, on leashes and neutral ground. How's that?"

"Sounds good to me," Brooke said, and they headed back into the house.

TESS was standing in the kitchen, dressed in well-worn jeans, scuffed boots, a pink ribbed T-shirt, and a hand-knit cardigan sweater made of a kaleidoscope of colors. The first thing Will noticed was that she looked as if a stiff wind would blow her right over.

He could empathize. No one enjoyed having their heart broken or having their trust betrayed in such a profound manner. Especially right before their wedding day.

"Tess," he said, holding out his hand. She took it, her fingers cold, and he squeezed her hand briefly, gently, and then let her go. She seemed almost out of her body. Still in emotional shock. Her skin looked so white against her dark, waist-length hair.

She'd pulled it off her face and braided it into one long severe French braid down her back. The style made her features stand out in stark relief, and he noticed distinct shadows beneath her eyes. She couldn't have gotten much sleep.

"This must be Toby," he said, seeing the small salt-and-pepper-colored terrier mix hovering protectively at her heels, her dark eyes desperately worried.

"Yes, but she—" Tess began.

He knelt down, put out a hand, and looked indirectly at the little dog, somewhere in the vicinity of the top of her head. Never make direct eye contact the first time you met a dog, because they take it as a challenge, he'd heard. He had no desire to scare this little one.

Will smiled as he encouraged her to come closer. As she did, he noticed the cloudy eye and the slight trembling in the back legs and realized Toby was an older dog.

Her spiky terrier hair stood up haphazardly all over her head, but the one good eye, a beautiful dark brown, suddenly twinkled, as if she'd made up her mind, and Toby cautiously sidled over and sniffed his outstretched hand.

"—doesn't really like men," Tess finished.

Will was gently scratching Toby just behind her ears. The dog, while frightened and trembling, was letting him touch her. That was enough for today.

"She's a wonderful dog," Will said as he gave Toby a final, gentle pat and stood. "Where did you find her?"

As Tess told the story, he could see her visibly become calmer.

"That was a good thing you did," Will said. "She wouldn't have lasted long at a shelter. People rarely adopt the older dogs."

"I know."

"She must have had some kind of a home," Will mused. "Perhaps they tossed her when she became too old. Or the kids wanted a new puppy. Or the vet bills became too much. It amazes me, what people are capable of doing to a dog. Or a cat. Any animal, really."

He caught her eye, and Tess seemed to relax even more. *Good.*

"The muffins!" Brooke said suddenly. She ran to her oven and pulled out a cookie sheet.

"You bake now?" Will said, impressed.

"Hell, no! These are courtesy of Marie Callendar. Pumpkin spice with really good icing. I just thought I'd warm them up for you. Have some coffee, Tess. It'll keep you from falling asleep too soon today."

"Good idea." Tess reached for a mug.

THEY got into the van by seven-forty that morning after introducing Sugar and Toby to each other.

The two dogs had strained against their leashes, and then Will said softly to Tess, "Unhook Toby so she doesn't feel she has to protect you."

She did as he requested, and Toby shot toward Sugar, clearly interested in making a new friend.

"Be good," Will said sternly to Sugar, but the Keeshond's curly Nordic tail was wagging so madly, it was clear Sugar thought Toby was a delightful new development in their trip.

"What kind of dog is that?" Brooke asked. "She's gorgeous, and that fluffy silver fur is stunning. She looks just like a little Husky!"

"A Keeshond," Will said. "They're Dutch dogs. They

used to be watchdogs on the barges on the canals in Holland. And on farms. They're good family dogs, very friendly. We shouldn't have any trouble—"

As he said the words, he unsnapped Sugar's lead. The two dogs, after thoroughly sniffing each other, began to play, front paws splayed out in front of them, butts in the air, tails wagging. Toby gave a little yip and turned, and Sugar gave chase.

"Let them run around a little," Will said. "They'll be in the van most of the day."

He caught sight of Tess, noticed the brightness of her eyes, the beginning of tears.

What was she thinking?

AS Tess watched Toby play with Sugar, she realized how lonely her little dog had been for a playmate. She'd thought about getting another dog from the local shelter, and had almost done so. But then she'd met Paul, and she'd known without any discussion that another dog was out of the question.

So Toby had spent the time, when she wasn't with her, inside her crate and alone. Not that there was anything wrong in crating a dog. The security of a crate made many dogs feel much better about being left alone for short periods of time. But Tess knew Toby probably would have been happier if her crate had been facing another dog's crate. If she hadn't been all alone.

Now, watching the two dogs, she decided that as soon as she got back from this trip and found a decent place to live, she was going to get Toby a dog.

The thought made her strangely happy until she thought about what still had to happen today.

"Brooke," she said to her friend. "What are you going to do about the wedding?"

"Leave it to me," said Brooke.

"That's what I was afraid of."

"Don't worry," said Brooke. "I won't do anything you wouldn't do."

"Promise?"

"Swear to God."

Tess glanced up at Will, shaking off any remaining reservations.

"Let's get this show on the road."

BROOKE watched as the van backed out of her driveway, and she waved at Tess until the vehicle turned the corner toward the main gate and was out of sight. Her friend's face had looked small, pale, and a little uncertain, yet Brooke knew Tess was doing the right thing.

And she knew her best friend in the world was safe with Will. In a world of nonexistent manners and even fewer morals, Will was one of those rare men who would always do the right thing. And more importantly, he had a big heart.

The one thing she'd known was that she had to get Tess out of town before her controlling stepmother tried to convince Tess to continue on with the wedding of her dreams—*her* being Madeline Sommerville—not Tess.

Brooke wasn't sure *she* would've been able to face down the onslaught that was Tess's stepmother. It would've been comparable to weathering a hurricane inside a child's play tent.

No, the best thing was to get Tess out of town for at least a week or two until this whole mess blew over.

Brooke hated seeing Tess hurt so badly. But she'd never really felt right about Paul for Tess. She had to admit she was relieved they weren't getting married.

This trip would be good for Tess. It would allow her to step out of her life for a short while and see what parts of it still fit and which parts would never be right and should be discarded.

As Brooke stared out toward where Will's van had been mere moments before, she reached into her jacket pocket for her cell and called her cousin in Chicago.

As the phone rang, she thought about what she'd promised Tess.

I won't do anything you wouldn't do . . .

Well. Tess was leaving town with a sinfully gorgeous man, even though Brooke did think of Will as more of an honorary brother than actual dating material. Tess was blowing off the wedding of any girl's dreams, if you took Paul the Rat Bastard out of the equation and replaced him with someone like Orlando Bloom or Johnny Depp. Tess was kicking up her heels and finally doing something for *herself* for a change.

And now Brooke had to figure out a way to break it to the hundreds of guests, to Tess's and Paul's families, that there was to be no wedding. And they had to know *exactly* why . . .

She smiled as her cousin Kim picked up the phone. The two of them shared more than their vivid auburn hair and green eyes, courtesy of the English and Irish sides of the family. They both loved a good practical joke, especially when it was well deserved.

And this one certainly was.

"Kim," she said, and quickly filled her in on what had happened in the last few hours.

"My God!" said Kim. "Do you still want me to come out?"

"Do I ever. I have this plan . . ." And with that, Brooke told her cousin exactly what she thought they should both do.

four

AS WILL DROVE down 173 East early in the morning, he glanced at his traveling companion. Tess kept her attention out the window, riveted to what was surely familiar scenery, corn fields, and farmland. They passed the occasional rusty red barn, with trailers and cars parked outside.

The fall foliage, glorious in its intense coloration, the crisp fall air, and the vivid blue sky all reminded Will of some of the happiest times he'd had in the States as a teenager. Nothing could beat autumn in Illinois.

Sugar had laid down in her crate on the middle seat of the van, securely strapped in. Toby seemed settled for now. The nervous little dog sat in her crate beside Sugar's, every muscle alert, her ears perked up, looking a lot less frightened than she had just an hour ago.

What a motley crew. What a trip. He knew Tess's feelings had to be fragile right about now, less than twenty-four hours after such a massive betrayal. So Will decided that the best thing to do was to simply drive, put some distance between her and her afternoon wedding, and perhaps attempt some conversation when they were a little farther west of the Chicago area.

Like maybe Boulder, Colorado.

BROOKE let her cousin Kim inside her condo, knowing she had to look a sight with her hair all covered in dye, in a mint green terry robe, fluffy bunny slippers on her feet.

"Tess get out of town okay?" Kim asked as she came in the door, setting down two enormous makeup cases.

"Yeah. They should be well on their way."

"I remember Will. Is he still as yummy as he was as a teenager?"

"Even better."

"Damn. Wish I could've checked him out. Ah well, maybe he'll come back another time. I always loved that accent."

"I know. Makes you think of Hugh Grant, Colin Firth, Colin Farrell, Ewan McGregor, and Hugh Jackman all rolled up in one."

Kim had to laugh. "You've just mixed up English, Irish, Scottish, and Australian accents. There *are* subtle differences, you know!"

"Whatever."

They headed into Brooke's large bedroom, and Kim began to unpack her arsenal of makeup—her "bag of tricks" as she liked to call it.

"I know you love a challenge," Brooke said as she headed downstairs to fetch them both fresh cups of coffee and what was left of the pumpkin muffins. "So I figured this one was a real doozy!"

"Brooke," Kim said as she carefully set out brushes, pots, palettes, and tubes, "I wouldn't have wanted to miss this for the world!"

* * *

TESS had fallen asleep, exhausted from the night before. Her head had drifted back against the comfortable headrest in the front passenger seat, so when she lolled awake, she glanced over at Will. And found herself incredibly thankful that she hadn't been caught drooling out the side of her mouth. Then she looked back at the dogs.

She frowned. Something was wrong with this picture. Toby was gazing at Will as she sat scrunched far over in her crate. Her furry head was resting on the plastic lip by the metal grid door, her dark eye watching everything around her.

Her nervous little dog didn't seem nervous at all.

"Sorry," she said, straightening up in her seat and feeling strangely vulnerable.

"Not to worry. You don't have to apologize for sleeping, Tess. If you're tired, go ahead and sleep some more. You could even lie down on the backseat of the van if you want." He smiled. "It's all cornfields for most of today."

The temptation was overwhelming. Last night she'd been running on sheer adrenaline, and this morning she felt all tapped out. The thought of some uninterrupted sleep, just crashing for a few hours, felt wonderful. Even the cup of coffee she'd had at Brooke's this morning hadn't been enough to keep exhaustion at bay.

"I think I might—if it's okay."

"It's fine. Toby will help me with directions."

The idea struck her as funny, and she smiled.

"Okay." She hesitated. "Thanks a lot, Will. For all of this."

As the van ate up the miles, distancing her from her ill-fated wedding, Tess carefully maneuvered her way to the back of the van, where she stretched out on the very backseat, pulled a red and black plaid blanket over her, and was asleep within three or four deep breaths.

BETTER *this way,* thought Will as he drove. *She won't be tempted to give in to second thoughts, call the louse, and try to make it back for the wedding.*

Though he didn't think that was a possibility. Tess seemed like a woman who'd made up her mind. There couldn't be any other choice after a betrayal on that scale. She didn't seem terribly confident about the future, but who would after an evening like she'd had?

He continued driving at a leisurely pace, all thoughts of meeting any personally imposed rushed deadline forgotten. He couldn't call Elaine about the change in plans. It was still too early on the West Coast.

But Elaine had told him to take all the time he needed, and now, with Tess along for the ride, he decided to take it easy and see how things unfolded.

As he drove, he thought about what Brooke had told him Tess had seen last night, about how she'd reacted. And he wondered about this guy she'd wanted to marry, how he could have been stupid enough to go out looking when he'd had someone like Tess at home.

"WHAT do you think?" Kim said, turning the chair so Brooke could see herself in her bedroom vanity mirror.

"Oh my God! You're *such* a genius!"

"Thank you, thank you," Kim said, picking up her coffee mug and taking a sip. "I don't suppose I can give out any of my business cards at this little shindig?"

Brooke had to laugh. "Nope. But I think once we pull

this off, we're heading out to your place in Chicago for a few days. I don't know how welcome we'll be anywhere in town after this is all over."

Kim eyed her cousin's face with a professionally critical eye. "Small towns have very short memories. They'll be talking about someone else before next weekend." She grinned slyly at her cousin. "But that doesn't mean we shouldn't do our best to give them something to talk about tonight!"

TESS woke up as the van slowed and realized that Will had turned off into a rest stop. The bathrooms were clearly marked, along with picnic tables and an inside area visible through a large glass window with vending machines, a large state map up on one wall, and various pamphlets to help travelers on their way.

Toby barked sharply once, then twice. Sugar whined.

"I'll get you guys out first," Will said as he deftly maneuvered the large van into a parking space.

"I can help," said Tess, sitting up and pushing a few stray strands of hair off her face.

"Great."

They leashed up Sugar and Toby and took them, along with plastic bags, to the area designated for dogs.

Tess had to laugh as Toby careened along. Her little dog had seemed to discover a new lease on life. Her black nose fairly quivered with excitement as she sniffed all the strange new smells, and after she did her business she furiously kicked up twigs and dirt in a flurry, as if to say, *So there!*

"Okay, Tobe, okay," Tess said as she cleaned up after her dog and found a trash can. She had to laugh as her furry little sixteen-pound tornado bounced along beside her.

"She seems to like the open road," Will said as he fell into step beside her, with Sugar on a long lead, exploring.

"We've never really traveled before." Tess thought of what Paul would've said at the idea of traveling with a dog and didn't even want to contemplate such a thing. She glanced up at the sky. The sun was bright and almost directly overhead.

"How long did I sleep?" she said.

"A while." Will ambled along, and Tess had the feeling he was the sort of man who enjoyed every moment. "We just crossed into Iowa. This rest stop might be a good place for an early lunch. It's right around noon."

"Sounds good." She'd only had half a muffin this morning at Brooke's and now found herself hungry. Though how she could still eat was beyond Tess. She'd never been one of those women whose appetite went into a decline when it came to heartache. She had the metabolism of an athlete and simply enjoyed food.

"Can you keep an eye on Toby while I use the bathroom?"

"Sure," he said, taking the leash she offered.

And as Tess walked toward the bathroom, she glanced back and realized that Toby wasn't panicking at all. Will had sat down at one of the picnic tables beneath a large tree with the two dogs, and they were both prancing around him, delighted to be out in the sunshine on such a spectacular autumn day.

WILL brought the cooler out to their picnic table, and they feasted on ham and Swiss cheese sandwiches on good French bread, celery and carrot sticks, bunches of red grapes, crisp Granny Smith apples, and soda. Brooke was quite a good cook, and when she packed a lunch, she packed a lunch. Even though she'd been in a hurry, she'd paid a definite attention to detail.

"A day like this is a gift," Will said as he cut one of the apples into pieces with his pocketknife. They'd finished most of their lunch and were lazing in the sun. The dogs had enjoyed some of the ham, cheese, and carrots, along with a few gourmet dog biscuits.

Will handed a slice of apple to Tess, then gave one piece each to Sugar and Toby, who crunched away enthusiastically.

Tess paused, apple slice halfway to her mouth, and suddenly remembered that today was the day she was supposed to be getting married. For a short time, when she'd been sleeping and now while sitting out in the sunshine during their impromptu picnic, she'd completely forgotten.

"I'm sorry," Will said quietly. "That was thoughtless of me."

"No," she said. "No, it's a gorgeous day, and just because it was supposed to be my wedding day doesn't take away from how beautiful it is." She glanced over at him, still holding the remainder of the apple. "Please don't feel bad about what you said, Will."

He nodded and then looked away. She took a bite out of the slice of apple, chewed, and wondered what was going on back in her hometown.

Less than two hours to showtime, she thought. But Brooke had probably already called her stepmother and told her that the wedding wasn't going to go off as planned.

"YOU owe me big for this one," Kim muttered as she put the finishing touches on Brooke's hair.

"How about an entire weekend, on me, at your favorite spa?" Brooke said, sitting in front of the mirror, watching her cousin work with appreciative eyes.

"That should just about cover it." Kim paused in the midst of her work. "We can't get in big trouble for doing this, can we?"

Brooke started to laugh. "You mean as in go to jail kind of trouble?"

"Well—yeah."

"Nope." As Brooke met her own reflection in the mirror, she couldn't believe the transformation her cousin had achieved. "But I do think we should have your car ready to get out of town the minute everyone finally figures out what's going down."

"I did want to say," Will said as he disposed of the trash and packed up their cooler, "that I'm very sorry things didn't go off the way you wanted them to, primarily because I'm sorry you were hurt."

"Thank you," Tess said, deciding to take the kind words in the spirit they were given. She liked the fact that he didn't treat her as if she were made of china and came right to the point. And that he didn't let this thing fester between them so he felt he had to walk on eggshells around her at all times.

There was no point in pretending he didn't know what had happened. She'd told him last night, in the bar, that she was getting married.

Now she wasn't.

He had to know something was really off.

She was thankful he was enough of a human being to be understanding about the whole thing and not pry. She knew she wasn't up to talking about it yet, and she didn't know if she'd ever want to talk to him about it.

She barely knew him, after all. One year in high school, while she'd been at the middle school, didn't put her in a position to know a whole lot about him, other than her tremendous crush.

Actually, most of what she knew about Will was from what Brooke had told her. But just these few hours on the road told her that he was kind, thoughtful, a great driver, loved animals, and was able to think and feel beyond his own life and world. He could offer empathy, see into another person's situation, and in Tess's opinion, that counted for a lot.

And of course, there was that whole physical attraction thing. She wouldn't think about that right now, or any of the implications that attraction had down the road. For now, she just wanted to get through today, the day that was supposed to have been her wedding day.

TWO in the afternoon, Will thought as he glanced at the dashboard clock. That was the time Brooke had told him Tess's wedding was scheduled. It was now about ten to two, and Tess had retired to the back of the van to sleep a little more. He'd thought that a wise move on her part, far better than glancing at the clock and torturing herself with what might have been.

Knowing Brooke as he did, he wondered how she planned to tell Tess's family and the hundreds of guests that this particular wedding was not going to go forward as planned . . .

* * *

ONE of the things, Brooke thought as she headed toward the church with her cousin in tow, *that was so cool about having a cousin who was a makeup artist, was that she had no trouble getting her hands on various costumes in the nick of time.*

Like, oh, say, a simple little bridal gown.

She never would have fit in Tess's dress. It was hanging in her closet, back at the condo. They had totally different bodies and wore different styles. But this dress was similar enough to Tess's original dress that no one would question it. And she wasn't *that* much bigger than Tess. Nothing that a couple of strategically worn super-control undergarments with a little bit—okay, a *lot*—of spandex couldn't flatten out.

And as far as the veil, they'd simply doubled it, so until her veil was raised—at what she hoped was a very strategic time in the ceremony—she'd go unnoticed.

But her hair, now a glorious dark golden brown, was in the same elegant upsweep that Tess had wanted to wear, and Kim had done wonders with her makeup, sculpting her face to look like Tess's—from under a veil and at a distance.

Kim had the same sort of body she did, voluptuous and curvy, so she'd had no problem fitting into Brooke's matron of honor dress. So now, with Brooke dressed as Tess and Kim dressed as Brooke, they headed toward the church and the showdown that was sure to follow.

TESS wondered if she was fooling Will into believing she was asleep. But he was British enough, and well mannered enough, that even if he suspected, he'd let her get away with it.

She glanced at her watch while lying on the very backseat of the van. Almost two. Twenty-four hours ago exactly she'd thought she was getting married. Twenty-four hours ago, she'd started having all of those doubts, which had culminated in her evening out with Brooke—and then her little discovery at the church.

And now here she was, in a different state.

She'd turned off her cell phone. Tess rummaged through her purse, being careful not to make any noise that might alert Will to the fact that she wasn't sleeping. Cell in hand, she checked her messages, sure that her stepmother would have left a frantic and accusing one by now.

Nothing.

What had Brooke told her?

Sighing, Tess shifted position on the van's long seat, tucked her cell into her purse, closed her eyes, and tried to sleep.

But she couldn't help wondering what Paul was going to think when their wedding didn't go off as planned.

THE wedding had officially begun.

The measured and familiar notes of "The Wedding March" could be heard coming from the organ, an elderly man expertly playing the instrument in the far corner of the church. All heads, several hundred of them, were turned toward the back double doors as people craned their necks for a first glimpse of the blushing bride.

And in back, behind those doors, Kim gave her cousin's hair and veil one last check.

"Remember," Brooke muttered, "When I start to run, just follow me."

"Got it," Kim muttered back. "We're parked out front, aren't we?"

Brooke nodded. "I didn't want to get trapped in the lot. Just keep me in sight and follow me. And if we get blocked by any people, throw the damn bouquet and create a distraction."

Kim nodded, then busied herself with straightening out Brooke's elaborate train.

Tess's father, Richard Sommerville, looking very distinguished in his tux, had been talking to a business acquaintance, but now he approached them and took his daughter's—really Brooke's—arm.

"Ready, Tess?" he said, barely glancing at her, his tone more businesslike than gruff with emotion. This was just closing another deal to him.

Brooke nodded her head, not trusting her voice to sound like Tess's.

"Then let's get this show on the road."

AS Will drove through the Iowa countryside, Toby kept careful watch, Sugar dozed in her crate and Tess tried to sleep on the backseat of Elaine's van.

Back in Illinois, Brooke started down the aisle of St. Anthony's church, her footsteps measured and in time to the music.

She wasn't worried about the moment when any normal father would have lifted the veil and kissed his daughter a symbolic and heartfelt good-bye. Richard Sommerville was as cold a fish as his second wife Madeline was, so he'd probably just hand her over, happy to have made a marriage as advantageous as this one promised to be.

And if he did raise her veil and recognize her, well, they'd just run with it. Start the fun a little early. Improvise.

She reached the altar without incident and gazed at Paul through the heavy veil, thinking, *What a total shit.* Of course he was fooled, as he'd never really looked at Tess closely, and her veil was quite the little handy-dandy disguise. Brooke felt, more than saw, her cousin Kim come around to her side as the matron of honor. Tess's father, ever predictable, didn't even kiss her, just handed her over to Paul, aka the rat bastard.

Checkmate, you asshole. Maybe you'll think twice about hurting another woman the next time.

Everything was in place, and she couldn't help being rather pleased at the smug, satisfied expression on Paul's face. She couldn't wait to bring him down.

Buddy, have I got a surprise for you . . .

She handed her bridal bouquet to her cousin and took the rat bastard's arm.

"Dearly beloved—" began the reverend.

The ceremony droned on, and Brooke took a few deep breaths, centered herself, and glanced at Kim as the minister reached those crucial words—

"Is there anyone here who has any reason to believe that this man and this woman should not come together in holy matrimony?"

Kim turned toward the gathered guests, right on schedule. "*I* do!"

"What?" said the reverend, puzzled. He clearly wasn't used to the matron of honor speaking up. "What's the matter with you?"

"He *can't* marry her!" Kim cried out in her best soap opera sweeps-week voice. "He *can't* marry her because the woman in that wedding dress *is not Tess!*"

Horrified gasps all around as Brooke pivoted toward the assembled guests and flipped up her veil.

The congregation began to buzz. Before the noise could get any louder, Brooke called out, "Tess isn't here because we *all* know who *Paul* was with last night—and it *wasn't the bride-to-be!*"

She faced Paul, who was turning an unbecoming shade of scarlet. But he wasn't going to break.

"Not going to say anything, are you?" Brooke called out in a strong, clear voice that could be heard by the guests in the pews farthest back. "Well, in that case, *I will*." She turned and faced the puzzled crowd. "Last night, when *Tess* came into *this very church* to offer up a *prayer* for a happy marriage, she heard a strange noise."

Brooke paused, very briefly, for effect, and felt the audience right with her every step of the way.

"What could it be, Tess wondered? So she followed that noise back to the community room and found *that* man"— she pointed to an enraged Paul—"giving it good to *Marti Wheeler,* the reverend's daughter! Both of them *starkers,* and her *butt* on one of the very tables where a lot of you have *eaten your church suppers!*"

"That's so *gross!*" piped up one of the guests.

"Oh my *God!*" screamed Marti, actually quite fashionable in a stunning dark blue suit complete with a darling little hat. She turned fuschia with embarrassment and then slipped out of her pew and ran out the back door of the church, almost breaking a heel in the process.

Brooke went in for the kill.

"And *so,*" she said, with a touch of melodrama, "this morning, after our bride-to-be spent a night in deep spiritual contemplation, I drove a brokenhearted Tess to Our Lady of Perpetual Sorrow and supported her in her decision to give the rest of her shattered life over to God!"

"What?" screamed Tess's stepmother, Madeline, holding the sides of her perfectly coifed head as if this were all too much for her.

"There will be no wedding! Ever!" Brooke called out to the confused mob. "This man *cheated* on his bride-to-be, and she *caught* him! Paul *destroyed* her life, and now everyone knows what a rat bastard he really is!"

With that, Brooke whipped her train up over her arm and started down the aisle in a move worthy of Katharine Ross in *The Graduate.*

Kim, hot on her heels, was almost blocked by a beefy man who got in her way, when she yelled out, "Here comes the bouquet, girls!" She tossed the extremely expensive bridal bouquet of more than eleven different types of roses straight into his face, and he was promptly attacked by all the single women in town. As modern as the rest of the world was, tradition died hard in a town this small.

While he was overpowered trying to disengage the desperate singletons, Kim slipped around him and high-tailed it after Brooke.

They raced for the back of the church, Kim getting her car keys out of her bridesmaid's gloves. They burst out the main entrance and leapt down the cement stairs to the car parked on Main Street. Kim unlocked it, and they both dove into the front seat. She started the car, and they peeled out like bad bridal versions of Luke and Bo Duke of *The Dukes of Hazzard.*

Total pandemonium erupted behind them. Chaos ensued, with emotional bombshells just starting to detonate.

"I love a good wedding, don't you?" Brooke managed to gasp out between fits of laughter, her eyes streaming and her stomach cramping.

"Ah, nothing comes close," said Kim, catching her breath and then grinning.

"For Tess!" Brooke said. "In honor of Tess, and for women everywhere who've been cheated on by their own rat bastards!"

"Amen, sister," said Kim, her eyes on the road as she sped out of town.

five

WILL WAS A man who had gone far in life by using his intuition. It rarely steered him wrong. So when he sensed, several hours after they'd stopped for lunch at the rest stop, that Tess wasn't doing very well emotionally, he decided that they'd had enough driving for the day.

He'd planned on going a lot farther on the first day, but then he hadn't counted on Tess coming with him. And if he had to take a few more days getting out to the West Coast than he'd originally thought, it was a small price to pay for helping Tess get out of town.

He'd put aside all thoughts of the two of them having a relationship. Even though he was still immensely attracted to her, she'd been so emotionally devastated by the whole experience last night that he would have had to have been a total idiot to think she was ready for anything remotely resembling a relationship with another man.

No, Tess needed time to heal. It had to be painful, to have put your trust in someone you thought you were going to spend the rest of your life with only to experience that kind of betrayal.

Will knew he wouldn't have handled it well.

As soon as he'd sensed she wasn't in the best shape, he'd started searching for a hotel. They reached Des Moines at close to six that evening, and he found what he was looking for—a Super 8.

"Stay right here with the dogs," he told her as he got out of the van. "I'll take care of everything."

TESS sat in the front seat of the van. She'd let Toby out of her crate, and the little dog perched on her lap and stared out at the chain motel as Will walked toward it.

The early evening weather was starting to kick up, the wind blowing dried autumn leaves around in little whirls and eddies in the street. She knew Will could have probably driven for quite a few more hours, and she wondered if he was stopping because of her.

She didn't feel well, and she was sure it showed. Two in the afternoon had come and gone, and even though she knew Paul wasn't the man for her, there was still that residual emotion. Those horrible feelings that kept consuming her, that went along with the fact that her entire life, as she'd carefully planned it out, had come to an end.

The future, *her* future, as she'd hoped it would be, was over. And she had nothing left to replace it with.

Brooke had been right about one thing, though. Tess knew she was far better off on the road with Will, as opposed to still being in town and subjected to pitying looks and stares. And of course, the gossip.

The Midwest could still be an extremely sexist place, with the whole "boys will be boys" mentality easily making excuses for what Paul had done. She would be the object of pity, and people would even wonder why she hadn't been able to keep him "interested."

It would have been pure hell at home, at least until the locals found someone or something else to gossip about.

At least here, out on the road, she was a virtual stranger. For this short week with Will, she could start over, pretend to be someone else. Other than Will, no one really knew all that much about her past. And even he didn't know all the dirty details.

Tess leaned her forehead against the coolness of the van's glass window and closed her eyes. She'd given up so much for Paul, and she'd given it up willingly, out of love. She didn't have a job to go back to. She didn't have a place to live. Her entire life with Paul, the promise of it, had been a sham.

All she had back in town was a large storage locker and her car—stuffed to capacity—in Brooke's garage.

Her father and stepmother would be furious at her for not going through with the wedding. She knew she wouldn't be able to talk to either of them, especially her stepmother, for at least a week. And Tess didn't know if seven days was enough time for her stepmother to start feeling better.

Or if she ever would . . .

No doubt she would call tonight and give her a huge piece of her mind. Madeline Sommerville never missed a chance to give anyone her opinion on anything.

Tess didn't want to think about that right now.

She sighed. She'd messed up her life, no doubt about it. She'd messed up her life by making some pretty stupid choices. The number-one choice, the real doozy, had been trusting a man like Paul.

Her father and stepmother had been over the moon the evening she and Paul had announced their engagement at the country club, and Tess could remember basking in their wholehearted approval. For a short time that evening she'd felt she'd finally made them proud of her.

For just an instant, she wondered if her life would've been better if she'd never gone to the church last night, if she'd never seen Paul having sex with Marti.

You would have found him out sooner or later, a weary little voice in her head insisted. *Men like that don't hide their true characters for long. You would've been much more unhappy married to him, and your parents would've been much more scandalized by a divorce.*

If she'd even had the courage to go through with one. Her stepmother would've tried to talk her out of it. Appearances were everything to her.

In a way, the whole ordeal left her feeling like a fox snared in a trap, gnawing off its leg to escape. Though it was a grisly image, Tess knew that no matter how much it hurt now, she'd done the right thing by escaping.

A blasting noise made her open her eyes and turn her head. Nearly thirty men, dressed in black leather and all on enormous motorcycles, came careening down the main street in front of the motel, the combined noise of their powerful engines deafening.

Sugar began to thrash around in her dog crate, while Toby barked and, terrified, tried to burrow closer into Tess's lap.

If she found the noise deafening, it had to be pure misery for both dogs.

She slipped back into the middle seat and let Sugar out of her crate, holding both dogs close. At around thirty pounds, and incredibly fluffy, Sugar was easily twice the size of Toby. Both dogs shivered as she held them close, sitting on the van's floor.

She heard the van's door open, and then Will slid into the driver's seat.

"There's some kind of motorcycle convention in town," he said. "I asked for two rooms in back so we could be spared most of the noise."

The idea of collapsing in a hotel room, lying across a soft bed in a quiet room, sounded like heaven to Tess. She'd been going and going and going, a real Energizer Bunny, and she needed a place to crash, to burrow in for a while, to get her equilibrium back.

"Thank you," she said as he started up the van and backed out of the parking space.

"OUR Lady of *Perpetual Sorrow*?" Kim said to Brooke as they prepared an early dinner in Kim's spacious Chicago apartment. Free of their wedding finery, clad in jeans and comfortable sweatshirts, they'd ordered in a Chicago-style pizza. Kim was tossing a salad in her well-equipped kitchen.

Brooke, pouring red wine and then taking the two glasses to the breakfast bar, said, "Hey, I thought it lent the proceedings a very nice touch. Spiritual, you know what I mean? And on the practical side, it'll keep Tess's stepmom from calling her for a few days. I think nuns have to give up their cell phones."

"Like you would know!" Kim carried the salad to the table along with two bowls. "But what would Martha Stewart say?"

"I don't know, and I don't care. Hey, she served her time. I just know I'll never forget the look on Paul's face!"

They were both still laughing when the pizza delivery guy came to the door.

* * *

WILL was worried about Tess, so he'd done one thing that could be misconstrued as being a bit out of line.

He'd asked that the two rooms be adjoining, and he'd asked for the door between them to be unlocked.

"She's going to have a meltdown soon," he told Sugar, coming out of the shower, a towel around his waist. "And I'm afraid we're all she's got at the moment."

Sugar wagged her plumed tail and whined.

TOBY stayed right by her side on the bed, up until the time Tess sat up, swayed dizzily, and then ran to the bathroom and proceeded to hurl her lunch into the toilet bowl. The small dog paced back and forth in front of the bathroom door, whining worriedly.

"Not good," she muttered to Toby after she rinsed her mouth and felt her forehead. It seemed kind of warm. "Not good at all."

Tess managed to stagger out of the bathroom and then her legs gave way. She sat down on the carpet in front of the bathroom door, pulled Toby close to her, and began to cry.

This is it, she thought. *Meltdown.*

WILL heard her crying and didn't even hesitate.

"Tess?" he said through the closed adjoining door.

No answer. Just crying.

"Tess?"

Still crying. More muffled, now.

To hell with it. He opened the adjoining door, knelt down, and took her into his arms.

* * *

TESS didn't know it was possible for a person to cry so much, so hard, and for so long. And somewhere in the midst of all that crying, she felt a pair of strong, comforting arms come around her, and she knew she wasn't alone. She clung to those arms, those strong shoulders, as if they were all that kept her from falling into total chaos.

Safety. Security. A solid place amid all this craziness . . .

"Sorry," she managed to get out when she could finally talk. "So sorry—"

"Stop it," came that crisp, British voice. "Come on, let's get you to bed."

He was as good as his word, depositing her on top of the soft bed, then asking her if she wanted a 7Up from the cooler.

"That would be—heaven," she said, getting beneath the covers.

He brought her the soda in a small glass with some ice, and then he sat down at the foot of her bed.

"I'm thinking of walking over to that restaurant just next door. Perkins, I think it's called. It looks like regular diner food. Would you like me to bring you back some soup? Maybe some crackers?"

She took a slow sip of her soda, cautiously testing her stomach, and then set it down on her bedside table.

"I'm really sorry, Will."

"For what?"

"This can't have been what you thought was going to happen when you agreed to let me come with you."

He smiled down at her, and she noticed how really beautiful and kind his eyes were.

"Tess, believe it or not, I don't generally go around

thinking about how things are supposed to turn out. Most of the time, I just try to keep up with what happens."

"Hmmm."

"Soup? More soda? Crackers? Toast?"

"Chicken soup," she said softly. "And some toast. White. No butter. And another 7Up."

"You got it." He glanced back toward his room. "I'm going to leave Sugar loose, out of her crate. She's very sensitive and was quite concerned when she heard you crying."

That touched Tess.

"Is that all right?" he said.

"Of course."

And then he was gone.

She went to her window and pulled back the drapes. A soft rain had begun to fall outside, ticking quietly against the glass.

She glanced over to the adjoining door that Will had left open. Sugar was peeking around it, into the room, with a concerned expression on her fluffy face.

"Come on, then," Tess said, patting her mattress as she sat back down on it.

Sugar didn't need any more encouragement. She raced for the bed and jumped gracefully up on to it, circled around a few times, and lay down with a sigh right next to Toby.

Tess couldn't believe how comforting it was to have both dogs on her bed. She snuggled beneath the covers, put her head down on the pillow, and decided to rest just a little bit more . . .

WHEN she woke, the rain was coming down in earnest.

The bed was empty; the dogs had deserted her. The only light in her room came from the bathroom. The light was on, but the door had been almost completely closed so just the merest sliver of light came out into the main room.

Just beyond the adjoining door, she heard the soft sounds of a television and Will talking to one of the dogs.

Smiling, Tess stood up, felt dizzy, and sat right back down. Within seconds, Toby appeared in the open doorway.

"She's up?" Will said, following the small dog.

"I am," Tess said, rubbing the side of her head. "But I'm not all that steady on my feet."

"Stay in bed. We'll bring your food to you."

Her chicken rice soup, in an insulated container, was still warm, and that was good enough for Tess. She managed to eat half of it and two pieces of dry toast.

"I should be all right in the morning," she began before Will cut her off.

"Don't put any time constraints on it, Tess. You've been through a hell of a lot emotionally. I don't have any particular timetable to be back in Los Angeles. We can take an extra day or two. It's all right."

"Thanks," she whispered. Then she smiled.

"What is it?" he said softly.

"You're like some—like Mary Poppins. You take care of everything and make me feel so safe. Thank you, Will."

"My pleasure," he said, clearing away the soup container and giving the rest of her toast to Toby and Sugar.

MARY Poppins. Great.

Although he'd resigned himself to the fact that he wasn't going to have a steamy fling with Tess anytime soon, Will had certainly not expected himself to be compared to perhaps one of the most sexless characters in all of children's literature.

Next thing you know he'd be gathering up all their luggage while proclaiming, "Spit-spot, off we go!"

The thought made him smile. Will glanced at the clock by his bed. It was only ten twenty-three at night. He'd turned in early and already decided they would spend the day here tomorrow and leave the day after that at the very earliest.

He hated seeing her in such shape. He knew how it felt to be that ill, that helpless. He'd gone through his share of heartbreak, and he knew how awful the emotions were right at the start. And there was nothing for it. You just had to endure it, get through it, and keep going.

His cell phone rang, and he answered on the first ring.

"Hey, am I calling too late?"

Brooke.

"No." He hesitated and then said, "Dare I ask what happened today?"

"Will, you know me too well!" And she proceeded to tell him all about the wedding that wasn't.

Their laughter felt good. Brooke had always been up for a practical joke as a child, and he knew she loved pulling off such pranks.

"I'm glad you embarrassed the bastard," he said when Brooke had finished. "He deserved it."

"How's Tess?" Brooke said.

Not mincing any words, he told her.

"I had a feeling she was going to need some time to have her own little breakdown," Brooke said. "She was wound up pretty tight the night before the wedding."

"How did her parents take it?"

"Not well. Paul's a big deal in our little town, and her parents were crazy for this wedding to take place. Sometimes I think that's the main appeal he had for Tess, that her dad and stepmother really liked him."

"She was looking for their approval?" he said, wanting to make sure he understood the situation.

"Big time."

"So she's never really figured out what it is she wants to do with her life."

"Nope. She's been too busy letting everyone else tell her what to do. She's a big-time people-pleaser, Will."

"I see."

"Do me a favor, will you?"

He sighed. "I'm going to be cautious and ask you what it is before I commit myself."

"This one's easy. Take Tess's cell away from her so her stepmother doesn't call her and wake her up in the middle of the night. She needs to sleep."

"That I can do. Brooke?"

"Yes?"

"Give me a call every few days and let me know how things are at home. Tess's parents, the bastard, that sort of thing."

"You got it. That is, if I'm even allowed back in town!"

When Will hung up the phone, he got up quietly and walked across his motel room then through the door into Tess's room. She lay curled up in bed, beneath the covers, both dogs positioned protectively around her. Will smiled at this and then picked up her purse and found her cell inside.

Taking it with him, he placed it next to his own on the night table by his bed, lay back down, and stared at the ceiling, determined to fall asleep.

Within the hour, he did.

THE ringing seemed to come from a long way off.

Will came awake slowly, then one of his hands made a

groping effort toward his night table, where his fingers closed around a cell phone. He glanced at the clock—almost three in the morning.

Brooke. Calling late. An emergency.

He answered the call, anything to stop that sharp ringing. Emergency or not, he didn't want to wake Tess.

"'Lo," he said, his voice low and raspy.

"Hello!" said a hard, feminine voice. "Who is this?"

Now he was annoyed. "Who is *this?*" His voice still sounded sleepy to his own ears.

"Madeline Sommerville, and I want to speak to Tess, at once!"

Will considered this. First of all, he didn't like the woman's tone. Second, he thought it beyond rudeness that she would choose to call at this late an hour. And third, it appalled him that there was so little actual concern for her stepdaughter and what she'd just been through in the woman's—her *stepmother's*—voice.

What a complete and utter narcissist. A devious little plan flashed into his mind. This woman deserved it.

Putting just the right amount of subservience into his tone, Will said quietly, "Just a minute, Mrs. Sommerville, and I'll get someone who can help you."

"It's about time!"

He took a moment, remembering what Brooke had mentioned about the convent, then, calling up his best imitation of a thick, German accent, he said, "Hello, madam. Ah yes, the little girl, Tess. The one dat is broken-hearted."

"You know my stepdaughter?" said the abrupt voice on the other end of the line.

"How could I not? She joined our convent early dis morning. She took all her vows and renounced all earthly possessions, including dis little phone."

"Listen, you—"

"Father. Father Vilhelm. And you are?"

"Madeline Sommerville, of the Philadelphia Sommervilles. And I *must* talk to my stepdaughter! *Immediately!*"

Will fought to control his laughter. "It is you who does not understand, madam. Your daughter is over the age of twenty-one, and she has taken her preliminary vows. For the next thirty days, she will remain at our convent and vee will see if she is truly able to carry out the promises she wishes to make to *Gott*."

And *he* hoped to God Madeline Sommerville wasn't terribly religious, or she would know that what he was making up on the spot had nothing to do with what nuns actually did—whatever that was.

The woman hesitated, then said, "She really took her vows?"

"*Yah,*" said Will. "My own opinion? I tink dat seeing dis *oaf* she loved, dis *foolish* boy, slipping his *wiener schnitzel* to another woman—and a *reverend's* daughter! *Ach, mein Gott!* What it would do to an impressionable young girl! And in the sanctity of the holy church! You see, madam? It did something to her mind. How do you say— she is not herself."

"You bet she's not! I want her to come right home, right now, *tonight*—"

"Madam, please," Will said, in what he hoped was a soothing tone. "There is not a chance of dat. Surely you must understand? Your daughter has made a commitment. Thirty days. Legally she is in her right mind and has made her decision. Now, if you or your husband insist on coming here and harassing her, I will have to have you both thrown off the premises."

Madeline didn't answer. He thought wildly.

"And she could not speak to you even if she came to the

phone or you traveled up here, for your little girl has taken a vow of silence. It is a matter of penance, for the horrific spectacle she saw in her church on dat table."

"Where exactly *are* you?" Madeline demanded. "What part of Wisconsin?"

He wondered if he'd gone too far with that bit about the vow of silence.

"You don't know?" he said. "Then *Gott* tells me not to tell you, because your daughter needs time to heal her broken heart. And I suggest, good woman, dat you stop thinking about yourself and start thinking about your daughter and all dat you have put her through these last few years. Now good night, madam, and *Gott* bless you."

And with that, Will hung up. He studied Tess's cell phone in his hand. Brooke would probably be the only person who would call her during their time on the road, and she could just as easily reach both of them on his cell.

For safety's sake, Will decided that he'd have to do a little work on Tess's cell phone and be sure he tinkered with it just enough so her stepmother wouldn't be able to get through. Though he didn't want to treat Tess like a child incapable of making her own decisions, she was in no shape to go up against this woman.

He wondered what her ex, Paul, was like. Probably not much better.

Tess's phone rang again. Curious, wondering if her mother dared to call the convent back and mess with Father Vilhelm, Will answered.

"Tess?" said an edgy male voice.

"Who is this?" Will said cheerfully, really enjoying the moment.

"Who the hell are you?"

"Is this Paul?" Will said.

That stopped the bastard dead in his tracks.

"Just get me Tess, goddamn it!" Paul said, and it sounded like he was talking through gritted teeth.

Will hoped he was clenching his jaw so tight it hurt. Obviously Madeline had gotten a hold of this Paul, her little lapdog, somewhere along the line and demanded that he fix things.

To both of their advantages, of course. Their selfishness was beyond belief.

"She's rather tired at the moment," Will replied. "You know, what's good for the goose and all that?"

"Listen, smart-ass, just get her on the phone—"

"Really? At this time of night?" he said, his voice deliberately very clipped, very chilly, and *very* British. Bond. James Bond. Early Sean Connery, shaken, not stirred.

"Damn it, get her on the phone—"

"I think *not*," Will said, with a touch of Mary Poppins thrown in for good measure. "You can call her back in the morning at a decent hour when she isn't so exhausted by all her—exercise. And by the way, Paul, *quite* a charming little wedding yesterday afternoon, wasn't it? I particularly enjoyed the part *you* played."

"Why, you—"

Will hung up, eyed Tess's cell phone in his hand, and then silenced the ringer.

Dismantled. Disconnected. Destroyed. He'd think of something. All he knew was that he would protect her from those people with everything he had.

He'd do what he had to do to make sure Tess never received their calls. Because he was going to make sure she had a few glorious days on the open road all to herself.

Time to heal—at least a week, maybe two. A week or two of freedom he was beginning to sense she'd never known. Tess needed the freedom to be herself, but her old self would have to surrender.

Well, he'd see to it. The Mary Poppins thing, after all. He'd simply take care of her, whether she wanted him to or not.

He wanted to see her smile, and he wanted that smile to reach those glorious green and gold eyes. It seemed to him—a complete outsider and, therefore, he considered his opinion impartial—that she'd grown up surrounded by a bunch of self-serving narcissists. No one in her immediate family seemed to genuinely care about her well-being.

Only Brooke, and she wasn't even a family member.

No one in her family seemed to care about how Tess felt or what she needed. It was enough to make a person completely crazy.

In a sense, it already had.

Will came to his decision quickly. He'd go along with whatever Tess wanted and needed for the duration of this road trip. If she wanted a breakdown, so be it. Hell, she probably *needed* one.

And by God, he was just the man to give it to her!

six

TESS CAME SLOWLY awake, and for just a moment, she didn't know where she was. The bed felt unfamiliar, the room looked strange, and she felt completely out of it. About the only familiar presence in the room was Toby, curled up tightly against her beneath the covers and snoring softly.

Within her next breath, it all came back. The wedding, or lack of one, and her horrible discovery about Paul and Marti. The haste and furtiveness with which she'd packed her belongings and headed to Brooke's condo, and from there the quick decision that had led to Will's van and out of town.

And here she was, somewhere in Iowa without a clue as to what was to happen next. Every single thing she'd counted on, every single plan she'd made had been blown to smithereens in a matter of seconds. Just as long as it had taken her to look through the church door and discover who was really making all that noise.

She glanced up as Sugar came around the adjoining entrance that connected her room to Will's and stopped in the doorway, her furry face anxious. Within seconds, Will was standing next to the Keeshond.

How did dogs do that? You barely made a sound, and they knew you were up and about.

"Hi," she said, smoothing her hair off her face and feeling totally awkward. She felt bad for Will. He hardly knew her, yet he'd agreed to take her along and help her out of a jam. She was sure a crazy woman's complete emotional breakdown had not been on his preferred travel agenda.

"Hello," he replied. "How are you feeling?"

She almost lied and told him she'd take a fast shower and they could take off, but Tess felt as if a vast weight had settled over her in the vicinity of her chest. She was just barely sitting up in bed, and even that felt like too much of an effort. Her entire body felt heavy, as if a large weight were pulling her down, overwhelming her.

Why lie? He'd already seen so much of the worst.

"Like crap," she admitted.

"It's pouring outside," he replied and then said, "I thought we'd take a day off from the trip and just settle in. How does that work for you?"

She glanced at the window, and the sounds of the rain finally registered. She hadn't noticed them at first; she'd been so caught up in her feelings and all her regrets, her doubts. She had no idea what she was doing or where she was going. Lost. Completely lost.

She couldn't meet his eyes. They were too . . . kind. Empathetic. He knew. She didn't know how or why, but he knew. He knew she wasn't up to a day on the road.

"Perfect," she managed to whisper and then she glanced up at him.

They kept looking at each other, she in her bed with Toby by her side, Will standing in the doorway with Sugar.

"Well," he said finally, breaking the silence. "I took the dogs out for a long walk this morning during a break in the rain, and I'll probably make a quick run to the nearest store and maybe the diner again for some lunch. Soup?"

It sounded wonderful. She glanced down at the hotel bedspread, grateful for his understanding and compassion. "The same as before would be great."

"Tess?"

She glanced up at him.

"Take it easy today."

She nodded.

"Tess, there's really nothing you have to take care of right now. Brooke handled things beautifully. Why don't you rest?"

She slid down farther beneath the comfort of the bed-covers while Toby gently wheezed and adjusted her position beneath the bedspread.

"Okay," she said finally. "What time is it?"

"A little after eleven. Why don't I go get lunch in about an hour and you can get up then?"

"Sounds like a plan," she said and then yawned. As he moved to leave she called out, "Will?"

He turned toward her, his blue eyes attentive.

"Thanks. So much. For everything."

SHE managed to snooze for another forty-five minutes but then woke up and couldn't get back to sleep. It was a great escape, sleep, the only refuge she could think of at the moment from the total mess her life had become. She had never been one to take a lot of drugs, but at the moment she was tempted to start. Reality had never looked so unappealing.

Sitting up, she put her feet on the carpeted floor and her head in her hands.

Tess had no delusions about what it would take to put her life back in order. Following the chaos of the last thirty-six hours, there would be a lot of hard work involved in getting back on her feet emotionally.

If her life had been a wall, it would have been a decimated, shattered pile of rubble. The image that came to mind was that of picking up each brick and starting to rebuild the basic structure, one at a time.

It would be a lot of work, and it would take some time. But she also knew that if she didn't get to the bottom of how her life had become so totally unmanageable, she'd end up building another unstable wall and watching it crash down around her again.

What had happened? She'd never been one to cast blame elsewhere and wouldn't blame her parents or even Paul. After all, she was an adult and had made every single choice herself. They might not have been the most conscious choices, but they had been hers. She had to own them, as painful as that might be.

With this thought in mind, she padded toward the bathroom, changed direction, and went back to her backpack and pulled out a clean change of clothing. After she'd grabbed clothes and her toiletry bag, she headed for the shower.

Twenty minutes later, showered and toweling off, she felt marginally better. Toby had come into the bathroom with her and stayed by the closed door, squinting at her through the damp, warm steam.

Tess had unbraided her hair, brushed it out, washed it during her shower, and was now working her way gently through the tangles with a wide-toothed comb.

"I think I always took the path of least resistance," she said to her dog, who wagged her stumpy tail in answer. "I didn't do the hard work, Toby. I let everyone else make my decisions for me." She hesitated and then attacked a particularly nasty knot, easing it out. "I know that's not an admirable approach to life. Maybe that's why the whole thing blew up in my face."

"Tess?"

The sound of a masculine voice caused her to tighten the white towel around her naked body.

"Yes?"

"Brooke's on the phone for you. Shall I have her call you back?"

Suddenly she wanted to talk to her friend. She wanted to know what had happened, what everyone's emotional reaction had been, especially Paul's.

"I'll take it," she called and stepped to the bathroom door and opened it a crack.

He handed her the phone and had the grace not to look at her too long. Not that she would've been freaked out by it—she was wearing more than she'd have on at the lake. No biggie. She shut the bathroom door.

"Brooke." She sat down on the side of the tub and reached down to scratch Toby's ears with her free hand. "What happened? Tell me everything."

"First, promise not to be mad at me. Or at Kim."

"What did you guys do?"

Briefly and succinctly, Brooke told her what had happened at the church.

Tess couldn't speak.

"Tess? Tess, are you okay? Speak to me, I'm getting worried! Please don't be mad—"

Tess couldn't control the laughter that bubbled out of her throat, first a smothered snort, but then she started *re-*

ally laughing, great big deep belly laughs at the mental picture she had of Paul's face as the veil had literally been
lifted and he'd seen Brooke.

He was a man obsessed with what people thought, with
how he appeared to others, and as she laughed, she realized
Brooke had devised the punishment that had served him
best—total humiliation on a grand scale.

Yes, small towns had short memories. What happened
on the weekend was always a source of local gossip to be
thoroughly dissected on Monday. But what had happened
at St. Anthony's yesterday afternoon would be worthy of
rehashing for at least a month if not longer. And some people, no matter how many years passed, would always look
at Paul when he entered the local drugstore or market and
say, "Hey, remember when—"

A truly fitting punishment for the man she'd thought
she'd loved. He'd thought of himself as so much better
than other people, and he'd been brought down to reality
with quite a thud.

She laughed and laughed, but as she laughed, something
seemed to release in her chest and all of a sudden she was
crying, great big sobs, gasping for air, all the hurt and
shame and embarrassment coming to the surface, tears
pouring down her face. Toby scrabbled into her lap, whining and pressing close.

"I'm so sorry, Tess," Brooke said softly.

"It's okay," she said, still in the middle of crying, taking
some tissue from the box on the sink, blowing her nose,
and then tossing the tissue into the nearby waste basket. "I
actually . . . feel better. It sucks, holding all that in. But
now," she said, her voice wobbling, "the million-dollar
question is, what do I do with the rest of my life?"

"I don't think you need to figure that out right now, Tess."

"It feels like I do. It feels like I just wasted my entire life and everything I ever knew or planned just exploded. Or never really existed."

She wiped her eyes, switched the cell to her other ear, and said, "Tell me something funny."

"Marti screamed and ran out of the church."

"That'll do for starters."

"Your stepmother was literally holding her head like she couldn't process what was going on right in front of her eyes. Like her head might explode."

Tess chewed on a nail, then patted Toby. "She's going to be furious."

"Forget her. It wasn't her wedding, it was yours, and I for one am glad you found out that Paul was a cheater and a liar before you walked down that aisle."

"I know. I keep telling myself that. I keep telling myself that things could've been worse. I could've married him and then had a few kids and found out he was cheating and then—"

She stopped.

"And then?" Brooke prompted gently.

"I could have been in a situation just like my mom was. Oh, God."

"I think sometimes we just have to roll with the punches and make the best of it, and this is one of those times."

"Just tell me what to do, Brooke. Just for today. I feel like I used up every bit of energy I possess just taking this shower."

"Okay. I don't want you to do too much. Have you got food in the room?"

"I think Will just went out and got me some soup."

"Good man. Eat your soup. Maybe go back to bed. But if you feel bad, talk to Will. He's easy to talk to, and he's not judgmental. Don't hold it all inside, Tess, or you'll make yourself sick."

"He'll think I'm stupid."

"No, he won't. You're not the only one who's ever had their heart broken. But you *are* the most recent."

"Thanks." Tess reached for another tissue, blew her nose again, and tossed the tissue into the trash. "I needed that little bit of perspective."

BY the time she got dressed, headed out of the shower, and knocked on the open door to Will's room, he'd already laid their food out on the small round table located in front of the large window in his room. He'd drawn the curtains against the rain, put out the plastic flatware, and filled their glasses with ice.

"This is very nice," she said, surveying what he'd done.

"Don't let the pooches fool you," he said, indicating both dogs now sprawled on his bed, tails wagging, eyes hopeful. "They've been fed and had several biscuits besides. So you can eat your late lunch knowing they aren't starving."

She sat down, put a paper napkin in her lap, and reached for her soup, her usual chicken and rice. He'd ordered fish and chips, and they ate in a companionable silence for a short while.

Tess knew she looked haggard. Red, swollen eyes, chapped red shiny nose, blotchy skin. One thing she knew was that she wasn't cute when she cried.

"You talked to Brooke?" he said once she finished her soup and reached for her dry toast.

"Yep."

"Pretty good stunt, what those two pulled off."

"Amazing."

"Thank God the two of them aren't in government. The world wouldn't be safe."

She laughed.

"How are you doing?"

She liked the way he came straight to the point.

"Surviving." She took a bite of toast, chewed, swallowed. He poured her more 7Up and then set the bottle down.

"Can I ask you a question?" she said.

"I'll see if I can come up with an answer."

"Why do men cheat?"

WHY *do men cheat?*

Will studied her across the table. She'd taken his breath away when she'd opened the bathroom door with her hair wild and loose and wet down around her shoulders. Even in the midst of personal pain, Tess looked fantastic. Her skin had glowed, her bare shoulders had looked smooth, she'd been so unwittingly sensual—

He had to shake that mental image—now.

"Why do men cheat?" he said, stalling for time. "Well, some don't."

"But when they do? Why? I mean, you're a guy, so enlighten me."

Will thought about what he wanted to say, but before he replied, she asked him, "Have you ever cheated on anyone?"

"No."

"Me neither."

She was suddenly so still that he knew, even though she'd obviously cried in the bathroom while she was on the phone to Brooke, that she was filled up with emotion again and was holding herself very still so it wouldn't come out.

"You can cry again. I won't be upset with you."

Tess glanced up at him, her eyes teary, but she shook her head and glanced down.

"He's not worth it," she whispered.

"That's the spirit."

She was quiet for a moment longer and then said, "I'm not very good company right now."

"Back to bed?"

"Could we sit here a little longer?"

"Of course."

She took a small sip of her soda, and he admired the valiant effort she was making to pull herself together. "What do you do out in Los Angeles?"

"I play guitar."

"In a band?"

"Yes."

"Really?"

"Yes."

"I remember you used to play when you stayed with the Matthews. You wrote some songs."

"That I did,"

"Does it pay the bills?" she said, then stopped as if the question had seemed too personal to ask.

"I do all right."

"Your own material?"

"Mostly."

"That's great. I'd like to see you perform sometime."

"I think that can be arranged." It touched him, how she was trying so hard to make things normal, to make this a meal with everyday conversation when it was so clear that her heart was still thoroughly broken.

He pushed a small container across the table toward her. "I thought you might like some dessert."

Tess opened the container and found the generous slice of rich chocolate cake he'd bought for her, heavy on the frosting. Classic American diner food, the best of the best.

"They say chocolate's always a good choice for a broken heart."

"That was . . . very kind, Will." She picked up her fork, took one bite, then another, then—

"Will, I know I'm awful company, but I feel as if I'm just about ready to . . . fall apart."

He could almost literally feel her shame. "Want some privacy?"

She nodded.

"Come on." He helped her out of her chair and walked her back to her room. "Keep in mind it's only been a couple of days. You're still pretty raw emotionally. But if you need anything, any time, three in the morning, *any time* Tess, just wake me up."

Now she was crying but trying not to let him see. "You're a very good person, Will."

He helped her into bed, pulling the covers up and tucking them gently around her. Toby and Sugar had followed him and now hopped up on the bed with Tess, snuggling close. Then he went into her bathroom and grabbed the box of tissue and put it at the head of her bed, close to her.

As Will approached the door that opened between their two rooms, he turned back toward Tess, huddled beneath the covers.

"Why do men cheat?" he said. "Because they're too damn stupid to know when they have something wonderful at home. Because they think they're entitled to more. Because it's easier to keep a few women dangling on a string than to try to truly get close to one. Because they need numerous conquests to shore up their very shaky egos. Because they have some deranged idea of what masculinity is. And because they're incapable of loving anyone but themselves."

"I could give you countless other reasons, Tess, but the only thing you need to know for certain is that you deserve better, so much better, than *any* man who cheats on you."

"Thank you," came the muffled reply from beneath the bedding.

"Don't thank me for something that's a basic truth and that you should have in your life, Tess. And by the way, I watched the Weather Channel, and it's going to rain all day tomorrow. I don't fancy driving in that kind of a mess, so I think we'll be here for another day, at least."

"Okay," she said, sounding tired.

"Sleep well," he said, his voice low, and then he turned and headed into his room.

WHERE *did that outburst come from?*

He'd realized he was angry at Paul, not the least for breaking Tess's heart in such a cavalier manner. He didn't even know the man and he was angry with him.

His middle sister had dated a man like Paul, a real egotist, and Will had spent hours with her, reassuring her, listening to her as she cried, trying to make her believe that she deserved a better man. He was fiercely loyal to his family, and he had hated seeing his sister hurt. He had no respect for any man who didn't have the courage to call it quits with one woman before he began seeing another.

The Weather Channel. Now that was a good one.

He hadn't watched the television station. For all he knew, tomorrow promised to be a glorious day. But he knew Tess needed a little more time.

Picking up his cell phone, he called Elaine.

"Hi, hon," she said, and Will could picture her in her spacious Encino home out in the San Fernando Valley, sitting outside by the pool with some sort of frosty concoction in hand. Her other dog, a Golden Retriever named Bear, was probably curled up by her chaise longue.

In her early fifties, Elaine was one of those people who were pure fun and had a great heart to match. He'd gotten to know her through his band; the drummer's girlfriend had been into metaphysics at the time. She'd dared anyone in the band to have a reading with her favorite psychic, and Will had been intrigued.

Elaine had told him stuff about himself he hadn't even suspected, things just on the tip of his consciousness, but the minute she'd said the words he'd known they were right. And damned if she wasn't one hundred percent accurate. It was a little joke between them that she never, ever missed.

"Well, it's taking a little longer than I thought," he began, jumping right in.

"You're doing the right thing, and you know it," she said.

"That's good to know." Briefly, he filled her in on his new traveling companion and how her wedding day had been shattered.

"Poor little thing," Elaine said, and he could picture the genuine concern on her face. Elaine was a very petite woman, with dark curly hair, but she had a smile and a presence that filled the room and made you forget she was only five feet tall. And her dark, expressive eyes didn't miss much.

"Is she coming all the way to Los Angeles with you?"

"Yes."

"Does she know what she wants to do with the rest of her life?"

"Not a clue."

"That's all right. She just needs some time."

He could feel her hesitation over the phone.

"Out with it."

"You're very attracted to her, aren't you?"

He sighed. "Elaine, is it obvious?"

"All I'm going to say is, give it time. Give her time. You're very intuitive, Will, and you'll know when the time is right. But I do have the feeling that she's going to be a very important person in your life. A turning point."

"That's exactly right."

"There's something else that's bothering you, isn't there?" she said.

Briefly he told her about the phone calls he'd taken from both Tess's stepmother and Paul, and the whole lie about Tess joining the convent. He also told her he'd taken Tess's cell phone again after her call from Brooke. He'd justified it by the fact that Tess desperately needed the rest, and her stepmother and Paul would be hunting for Our Lady of Perpetual Sorrow and wouldn't stop calling and harassing her. He'd considered it an act of protection.

Elaine loved the convent story. She laughed so hard she almost dropped the phone, but when she could speak again, she said, "You know me, I love a good joke! Those self-centered jerks—they deserve what you did and worse! Seriously, Will, I think you did the right thing, keeping her from talking to the two of them. She's very weak now. Not exactly physically, but emotionally. That's not me as a psychic telling you, that's me as a woman. There's not much worse than a broken heart at her age."

"Tell me about it."

"You take your time, whatever time the two of you need. I'm in no hurry to get the van back, and I know Sugar's having a wonderful time with you. She loves driving in the van. Just give me a call from time to time and let me know where you are and how things are coming. And how is my Sugar?"

"Fat and sassy. And she has a new friend." He filled her in on Toby.

"That little one's coming through loud and clear. She doesn't mind my reading her. Oh, she hated that man, the fiancé, but she was afraid of him. Oh no—"

"Don't tell me—"

"Oh Will, she's showing me that he hit her when Tess wasn't around. Toby tried to hide behind the couch, but—Will, I wouldn't tell her this, not now—maybe not ever, Tess will beat herself up over it. It's over. I don't believe she'll ever go back to that man, and strangely enough, this darling little dog is one of the main reasons. I think she realized that this man never cared for her dog, never treated her right, do you know what I mean?"

"Yeah," he said, thinking of Toby and the scared look he'd originally seen on her face—and disliking Paul the jerk more than he'd ever thought he could. Now he had no trouble with lying to this man about Tess being in a convent, safely locked away.

"Toby loves you. She loves you for taking Tess away in the van and away from that man. She loves you because she can see that you care for Tess, and this little dog adores the ground she walks on. When she found her—she's showing me mud and—and it's so sad, Will."

"It was a bad story with a happy ending."

"A very happy ending. I'm glad you got Tess and Toby away from that man. What was his name?"

"Paul."

"Paul. Not a nice guy. He's a total user. He would've used her to move up to where he wanted to get to, like social climbing, do you know what I mean? But now that's over."

"So give her time."

"She needs time. I don't know how much. Her spirit

needs time to heal. Shamans used to say that when some-one went through a traumatic event, they suffered from soul loss. It's what she's going through. Just make sure she eats and sleeps and laughs, and let her get some sunshine. And nature. It's very healing for where she is right now, and you're going through some beautiful country."

"I'm looking forward to it."

"Give my furry girl a pat for me, and give Toby a pat as well and tell her I was very pleased to meet her. She's a lit-tle doll."

"I'm sure you'll meet her in person when she gets to the coast. Tess, too."

"I'm looking forward to it."

Will hung up the phone and sensed a presence by the connecting door. Glancing down, he saw Toby standing in the doorway, staring at him.

"She enjoyed meeting you," he said.

The little dog bounded over and jumped up on his bed, came close, and licked his hand quickly, once, then twice, then turned and raced out of the room back to Tess.

And when Will lay back down on his bed, he couldn't stop smiling.

seven

WILL WOKE TO the sound of steady, heavy rain. He rolled over in bed, then sat up, glancing down to the foot of the queen-sized bed where Sugar usually slept.

Aside from him, his bed was empty.

He had to grin. Sugar was sleeping with Tess, as was Toby. Trust a dog to know who needed comfort and support.

When he checked the clock, he realized both dogs probably needed to go out, and neither would want to do so in this weather. Thank God the motel had a roof that hung over the sidewalk in back, so there was a dry area they could walk on. He'd just have to be very careful about cleanup, as always.

He picked up both leashes, jingled the hardware softly, and was rewarded by the sound of two sets of paws hitting the carpeted floor in the room next door. He grinned as the furry friends came around the door, eyes bright, tails wagging, ready for another adventure.

And as he pulled on his jeans, sweatshirt, socks, shoes,

and jacket, he noticed that the door between his room and Tess's now stood open. They'd even stopped knocking before entering each other's space.

It was certainly progress. Bit by bit, she was coming to trust him. And like Elaine had told him last night, she needed time.

With both dogs leashed up, he glanced in the adjoining doorway toward Tess's bed and saw masses of tumbled dark hair at pillow level. She was fast asleep, even the slight noises the dogs made not enough to wake her.

Leashes in hand, he headed toward his door. All things considered, he felt pretty good. Even the weather was cooperating, and Will took that as a good sign.

PAUL Atherton hadn't slept at all last night. He'd thought his troubles were over after that fiasco and huge embarrassment of a wedding. He'd never liked Tess's friend Brooke, had never trusted her. The way she'd looked at him it had been clear she hadn't been thrilled with him either, but he'd never thought of her as the type capable of the stunt she'd pulled at St. Anthony's. The woman was out of control. And how in God's name could Tess have been involved in something like that?

He'd been mad as hell at Tess for that little debacle, especially last night when he'd pulled into the local gas station to fill up his car and caught the cashier laughing with a friend as he was looking at Paul. It seemed like everyone in town was caught up in remembering his so-called wedding, and he didn't like it. He didn't mind being the center of attention, but not as the butt of a huge joke.

And Madeline Sommerville had been on his ass from the moment total pandemonium at the church had died down, demanding to know what was going on and insisting he get a hold of Tess and bring the girl back to her senses. Hadn't Tess understood how advantageous this marriage would have been to both of them? What was wrong with her? And how the hell had she gotten wind that he was seeing Marti?

None of it had gone according to his plan, and he was pissed.

No use even trying to pretend he was going to get any sleep. Getting heavily to his feet, he stumbled into the bathroom, turned on the overhead light, and stared at himself in the large mirror, disbelieving.

He'd come in late last night, exhausted and pissed as hell after a huge argument with Marti. She'd been hysterical, screaming that she refused to be the center of some huge joke and telling him she was leaving for a couple of weeks, to her sister's a few towns over. Easy for her to do—the woman had never worked a day in her life.

He'd been angry. First Tess had disappeared, and now Marti. Why couldn't either woman see what she was doing to him? He'd come home, stripped down to his underwear, and practically passed out on the bed, he'd been so stressed.

Now he stood in his master bathroom, staring at himself in the mirror in disbelief. His Calvin Klein navy blue boxers and T-shirt were covered, completely covered, in that damn dog's hair!

He looked like a Wookie. A Wookie with a hangover.

"Goddamnit, Tess!" he said to the empty house and then strode back into the bedroom and tried to turn on the bedside lamp. No go. Grabbing a flashlight out of his closet, he found the electrical socket in back and plugged in the bedroom lamp, turned it on to the highest setting, and examined his bed.

Dog hair everywhere, all over the sheets, the distinctive

salt and pepper color of that old wreck of a dog Tess had insisted on picking up off the street.

"Dammit," he whispered between gritted teeth as he started to strip the bed. His fury escalated into a full fledged tantrum as he wadded up bedspread, blanket, sheets, and pillowcases; wrestled them into a huge ball; and threw them into the corner with considerable force. Breathing heavily, he saw that a considerable amount of the dog hair had drifted down on to the dark carpet, where it seemed to silently taunt him.

He'd managed to keep that damn dog at bay by telling Tess he had allergies. Even though it wasn't true, the lie had worked, and he'd gotten his way—until now. What the hell was wrong with her? And where the hell did Tess keep the vacuum?

She'd officially screwed up his day. She'd officially screwed up his *life*. And he was angry he hadn't seen this coming and prepared for it.

Paul stood silently in the large master bedroom, taking deep breaths, trying to calm down. He'd planned on calling Greg and playing golf today. With Tess out of the picture and Marti high-tailing it to her sister's like the little coward she was, he'd decided to indulge himself with a game of golf at the club, with maybe a massage afterward.

Nothing had turned out the way he'd planned it, and he was a man who planned carefully for his own future. He knew Madeline, they certainly understood each other, and she wasn't the sort to give up. The only solution was to find out where Tess was hiding and try to talk some sense into her.

He could pretend he was contrite about what had happened with Marti, even deeply regretful, though he still couldn't figure out how in God's name Tess had found out.

Who would have dared tell her? He'd always been good at covering his tracks before. And she wasn't exactly the sharpest tack in the box. For him, that had definitely been part of her appeal. He'd considered her a girl who would be easy to control, who would assist him in leading the life he wanted to lead.

And if she'd gotten out of line, he'd trusted in Madeline's help in getting her right back in line. That was part of why the whole wedding fiasco had been such a shock.

He stared at the wadded-up ball of dog hair–infested bed linen in the corner of the master bedroom. He'd never really cared for animals in the house, and hair was only a small part of the reason. Once he got Tess back and she came to her senses, he'd insist she dump that damn dog at the animal shelter.

She wasn't going to get the best of him.

He knew Tess, knew how to manipulate her. He could always write off the thing with Marti as pre-wedding jitters. He'd made a mistake, so what? It wasn't that uncommon, wasn't anything that countless men hadn't done over the years. Tess would get over it.

And once she was back in town and they were married, people would stop laughing at him and he'd have his life on track again, right where he wanted it.

But first he had to find her.

TOBY seemed in particularly good spirits as Will walked both dogs. The rain had stopped pouring, but it was coming down steadily as he jogged with the dogs along the side of the motel protected by the overhanging roof.

What to do today? He'd been thinking about Tess as he'd walked and decided that his goal was to get her outside the room and to a restaurant to sit down to a decent meal. She couldn't live on chicken and rice soup forever.

Then maybe they could rent a movie from the collection in the motel lobby and take it easy. A comedy would be good. Elaine had suggested making her laugh, and that seemed like good advice.

His cell rang, and he flipped it open. Brooke.

"Hey, you," he said as he opened the door into the motel's hallway, the dogs hot on his heels. Neither of them cared much for the rain.

"Just calling for a progress report."

He filled her in, including his plans for the day, and she said, "Tess loves breakfast, especially pancakes. If you can find a place that makes great pancakes, she'll be in heaven."

He thought of Perkins, right next door. Excellent.

"Still at your cousin's?" he said.

"Oh, yeah. I work in Chicago, so I normally take the train in. This is a lot easier for the time being, and as Kim and I wear the same size, I can borrow clothes from her. Hey, the way things are going, I may never come back."

He could hear her cousin's laughter in the background.

"Stay there for a while," Will said suddenly, though he had no idea where the thought had come from. Over the years he'd known Elaine, she'd always encouraged him to trust his intuition. "From what you've told me about Paul, I don't like the sound of this guy."

"I know what you mean."

Will thought about what he was about to ask Brooke and then decided it was better to ask while he was in the hallway, outside their rooms so Tess would have no chance of overhearing him. Both dogs were lying at his feet, happily panting and, glad to be out of the rain.

"Do you think there's any chance of him coming after her?" he said quietly.

Brooke was silent for a moment, thinking. Then she said, "I think it's a distinct possibility."

"Does he love her?"

"Paul Atherton only loves himself. That's something I'm absolutely sure of."

"Is he dangerous?"

"Not in a Lifetime Movie of the Week kind of way. He's more dangerous in that he's one of those guys who can talk women into things. Do you know the type I'm talking about?"

"Unfortunately, I've met a few. Tell me this, Brooke, does anyone but you know she came on this trip with me?"

"Just Kim. I didn't even tell my mom. There was so much to do before the wedding went off and then we had to get out of town. I haven't talked to her yet."

"Has Kim told anyone? Anyone who could get the information back to Paul? Or that stepmother?"

He waited as he heard her asking her cousin, and then Brooke said, "No one. Neither of us will breathe a word."

"I think that would be best. Do me a favor, and don't tell your parents where Tess is. If they genuinely don't know anything, there's no way they can be harassed by those two." He was silent for a moment, gathering his thoughts. "So then the only way he can find her at this point is if she takes one of his calls and lets him know where she is. Agrees to meet him. And she might need that emotional closure in this matter."

"Right. Hey, did you dismantle her phone?"

"I have it with me, but I don't want to do that, Brooke. I don't want to treat her like a child, no matter what might happen. I get the feeling that Tess has been told what to do for most of her life, and I have absolutely no desire to join that particular group of people. I'm going to talk to her over breakfast."

"Good idea. And if she won't listen to you, tell her to call me."

MADELINE Sommerville turned the corner and headed down one of the frozen food aisles at the market. Glancing up, she saw another shopper, a woman in her forties, put some nonfat frozen yogurt in her shopping cart and then turn away to hide the grin on her face.

Madeline knew what that grin was all about, and her perfectly made-up lips compressed into a thin line.

How Tess could have been so ungrateful after all she'd done for her! She'd unselfishly arranged for her to have the wedding most women dreamed about all of their lives, and this was the thanks she got? To have to maneuver her way through her small town, avoiding knowing looks and sly smiles?

If someone had told her even a week ago that this was what was going to happen to the incredibly beautiful wedding she'd planned down to the smallest detail, Madeline wouldn't have believed them.

Tess's selfishness knew no bounds. Her stepdaughter clearly had no idea of the anguish she was putting her through. And it had all been so unnecessary. Paul had had a momentary lapse in judgment, but nothing worth canceling a wedding and a lifetime together. She could have helped Tess get her husband in line.

She rounded another corner, lost in her angry thoughts, groceries almost forgotten, when she caught sight of Debra Matthews, Brooke's mother, pushing a grocery cart ahead of her.

"Debra!" she called out and then began to walk briskly toward the woman, her heels clicking against the linoleum floor.

"Hello, Madeline," Debra said, and Madeline noticed there was nothing in the woman's expression that made Madeline think she thought this whole mess was amusing. Thank God for small favors. Maybe she could get the information she wanted out of the woman.

"Debra," she began. "Where is your daughter, Brooke? I have to talk to her."

"I've been leaving messages on her machine at her condo, but she hasn't called me back."

"She's probably afraid you're going to tell her what you thought of what she did. Absolutely disgraceful."

"Have you heard from Tess?" Debra asked, changing the subject. "Is she allowed to make calls from the convent?"

"I haven't even been able to find this convent, it's so isolated, let alone make any calls. Tell me, do you have any idea where it is?"

"I don't."

"If you hear from your daughter, will you tell her to call me?"

"I'll pass along your message."

"I want you to know, Debra, that I certainly do not hold you responsible in any way for what your daughter did. I don't want this to have any affect on our women's group at church."

"I appreciate your thoughtfulness, Madeline."

"I just want to do the right thing. You know what I mean?"

"Yes, I believe I do."

"So we're in agreement then?"

"How do you think Tess is taking all this?" Debra asked

suddenly, and Madeline was confused once again by the sudden change of subject. When she wanted something, she was single-minded in her thought process.

"What do you mean? Taking what?"

"It has to be just devastating, emotionally, to find out that the man you'd planned to marry, to have this dream wedding with and spend the rest of your life with, turns out to be someone you didn't think he was."

"I'm sure they could have worked things out. These little things have a way of blowing up out of proportion—"

"Madeline, infidelity and lies before a wedding are *not* little things."

"Yes, but you can't blame a man for the rest of his life for one little mistake—"

"It's *not* a little mistake. By doing what he did, Paul let Tess know he didn't have any respect for her or the vows he was taking in the church the following morning. Now I know you and your husband adore Paul, but I've known Tess since she was a little girl, and quite frankly, I think she's better off becoming a nun than marrying a man who would cheat on her the night before her wedding."

Madeline stared at the woman. Debra's face was flushed with color, a delicate pink tinged her cheekbones, and her eyes were full of emotion. And Madeline knew she would get no help from this woman.

This was going nowhere. Why did Debra keep taking *Tess's* side in all of this? What about what Tess had done to *her?* Why couldn't she see how the girl had ruined everything? Madeline pursed her lips in disgust as she gazed at Debra. She was as difficult as that daughter of hers.

"Would you let me know if you hear from Tess?" Madeline finally asked.

"If I hear from her, I'll tell her you're concerned and would appreciate a call."

And Madeline knew this was as good as she was ever going to get from this woman. Glancing up, she saw Trudie Evans, another member of her church's women's group, heading her way. Trudie was a notorious gossip.

"I have to run, Debra. Thank you for your time."

"Take care of yourself, Madeline. And don't worry about what people might be saying. These things happen in any family, and you'll get through it."

"Thank you," she muttered absently, already intent on getting away from Trudie.

WHEN Will let himself in the door to his room, he could hear Tess moving around in hers. She was up out of bed, and that was a good sign.

"Good morning!" he called out, unsnapping Toby's leash so the small Schnauzer mix could shoot into Tess's room, tail wagging furiously.

"They were right about the rain," Tess said, coming to the adjoining door, Toby in her arms.

"Not a good day for driving, but they say it may clear up tomorrow." He had no idea if this was true, but from the way she looked, they might get in some actual travel time tomorrow.

"What are you up to today?" she said.

He thought she looked fantastic in jeans, boots, and a soft green T-shirt with a V neck. She'd braided her hair back once again, off her face, and she'd even put on a little makeup. This was a good sign. She was making a real effort.

"First on my agenda is breakfast. I was thinking of feeding the dogs, then taking them out one more time, crating them, and then walking over to Perkins for some pancakes. Care to join me?"

He could see warring emotions playing out on her face, the comfort and emotional safety of staying in bed as opposed to the absolute pleasure of eating a plate of pancakes.

He'd bet on carbs every time.

And pancakes won. "Could I come with you?"

He grinned. "I'd be delighted to have the company. Just let me get these guys fed and another quick stroll outside, and we'll take off."

eight

THE TORRENTIAL RAIN died down briefly as Will and Tess walked over to Perkins, the diner next to their motel. Tess loved the way the air smelled right after a good rain, and today was no exception. Gray masses of clouds scudded along in the sky, and a cold, damp wind blew briskly against her face, so she knew they were in for more of the storm. But the brief respite was nice.

The last real meal she'd had was the picnic their first day on the road, so she had an appetite. Pancakes were sounding better and better.

She caught sight of a bird—a little nondescript, brown-feathered bird—flying furiously. But because of the force of the wind, it seemed to be staying in one place. Its small wings worked rapidly, but the bird couldn't make any headway.

Will saw the direction of her gaze and watched with her.

"I feel like that," she said quietly, watching as the bird struggled to fly forward.

"But the point is, she's flying," said Will. "And think about this—maybe you're meant to stay in one place for now, not really move ahead, but to be poised in place, waiting for something."

"I never thought of it like that." She gave the gallant little bird one more long look, turned, hunched her shoulders against the cold, and headed toward the diner.

WHEN the phone rang, Paul picked it up before the first ring tone even finished. He'd given Madeline's number its own particular ring, so he knew who was on the line.

"Hello," he said, lying back down on his bed. Even with new, clean sheets, he wasn't sleeping well. His life was too upsetting. Everything was deteriorating. All the stress he'd been under was taking its toll. Couldn't Tess have understood what this would do to him? How could she have been so selfish?

"Have you had any luck finding that convent?" Madeline demanded without preamble, without even a "How are you?" No one seemed to care what all this craziness was doing to him.

"No. I can't find anything called Our Lady of Perpetual Sorrow."

Madeline sniffed. "Then Brooke gave us the wrong name. She's deliberately trying to mislead us. Have you driven past her condo and figured out if she's home yet?"

"I was going to go over today."

"Don't forget! The longer we wait, the colder the trail gets."

He sighed. "Madeline, it isn't like this is a murder, and we're in an episode of *Law and Order*."

"No excuses, Paul. We have to find her and talk some

sense into her. It's the only way to get everything back on track. You still want to marry her, don't you?"

He thought about this for a second and was surprised that for once in her life, Madeline didn't push him for an answer once she'd asked the question.

He was angry with Tess, no question. No one humiliated him and walked away. Oh, he'd marry her all right, even if after a few very brief years he asked for a divorce. He'd marry her just to show everyone that he was the one who was still in control. He wanted that upper hand. That was paramount at this time. One way or another, he had to get back in control of this whole situation.

"Of course I want to marry her." He thought for a moment and then added "I love her" for good measure.

"Well then, here's what I think we should do. As well as looking for this convent and for Brooke, start talking to anyone you can find, nosing around. Someone has to know where Tess went. Maybe she's not even in a convent. Maybe she's somewhere nearby, maybe outside Chicago staying with a friend. You could ask the other bridesmaids."

"Give me their names," he said, reaching for a piece of paper and pen from his nightstand. *Yeah, like "maybe outside Chicago" isn't vague enough.*

"Paul, I did find out one bit of information—Brooke has a cousin in Chicago named Kim who's a makeup artist. I'm sure this is the girl who helped her pull off that whole fiasco on Saturday."

"What?" He was tired and having a little trouble following this conversation.

"The wedding, Paul. *The wedding.* This is the girl who helped Brooke dress up like Tess and make fools of both of us."

"Right."

"Anyway, I managed to get her address. If Brooke isn't at her condo, I want you to drive to this Kim's place and see if Brooke is hiding out there. And have you been calling Tess on her cell?"

"She doesn't answer. I've been leaving messages."

"Well, keep doing that. I want to find that girl by the end of this week. We've got to move fast and not give people a lot of time to talk."

One of the bonuses of having Madeline Sommerville as a mother-in-law was that she thought the way he did. Their goals were closely aligned; they were the sort of people who operated the same way, wanted the same things. It just made life easier when people shared his values.

"Give me that cousin's address," he said. "I'll find Brooke today."

THE diner smelled wonderful, the cozy heat felt divine after the cold wetness outside. As Will pushed open the door and guided her inside, and as the smells of cooking breakfast foods teased her senses, Tess realized she was ravenous.

A cheerful college-age girl showed them to a booth by a large wall of windows. The place was packed with bikers, a veritable sea of black leather. The men and women were obviously part of the weekend convention. It didn't seem like weather to ride a motorcycle in, but these people looked tough and were putting away gargantuan amounts of food.

Their waitress, a gangly brunette with too many teeth for her mouth, quickly and efficiently poured two cups of coffee, handed them plastic-coated menus, and gave them a friendly smile.

Tess smiled back and shrugged out of her jacket. She fixed her coffee the way she liked it—two sugars and a generous dollop of half-and-half—took wonderful first sip, and picked up her menu.

"I already know what I want," she said.

"You do?"

"Yep. There's always something called a pancake sandwich or a special, the one with the works. That's what I want."

"Sounds like your appetite's back."

"Yeah. I can't quite believe it, but it is."

"It's the therapeutic value of a day of sleep, a day off from life," he said, setting down his menu and reaching for his coffee. "Everyone needs a major time-out once in a while."

"You were right." And she glanced outside as the rain began to come down again, gathering speed until it was pouring in earnest. She wondered if the little bird had gotten to its nest and hoped it had.

"She'll be all right," Will said, and Tess could hear the smile in his voice. "They have terrific instincts."

"I hope so." She took another sip of coffee, comforted by how well he could read her.

"And the dogs are fine."

"I know. Normally I'd be worried about Toby, alone in her crate with a storm outside. But she has Sugar with her, so I'm sure she's all right."

"Sugar doesn't really mind storms, not even thunder. It's getting wet that she can't stand."

Their waitress reappeared and took their orders, saying "Good choice" when they both opted for the special— eggs, pancakes, bacon, and sausage.

She'd just walked away when Tess's cell phone rang. In Will's pocket.

"Ah. This is yours, I believe." He seemed slightly embarrassed as he handed it to her.

"You had my phone?" She checked to see who was calling, didn't answer, turned off the ringer, and slid the cell into her purse.

"While you were sleeping. I didn't want it to wake you up. You needed the rest."

She considered this and then said, "It's okay. Thanks, Will."

"No problem. Do you mind my asking who it was?"

"Paul."

He reached for his coffee.

"Okay," she said. "What was that look about?"

"I was just wondering what he possibly thinks he can say to you to make things right."

"Knowing Paul, he'll come up with something to justify it and to convince me he was right." She was surprised at the slight sarcasm she gave the words and realized that one of the things she'd always disliked about her ex-fiancé was how judgmental and self-righteous he'd been.

And one of the reasons she could react this way was that Will was exactly the opposite. He wasn't as tiring as Paul had been, because Will was easy to be with. He just let people, herself included, be who they were.

And he liked people. She hadn't realized it until she was away from Paul, but he'd always operated from the assumption that he was slightly better—okay, make that a *lot* better—than anyone else in the room. He'd always had a tinge of superiority, almost a sense of entitlement, of being local royalty.

Tess realized that her ex hadn't liked people a whole lot. She couldn't imagine Paul with her at this diner, surrounded by bikers, diving into a simple plate of pancakes.

Will was much more live and let live. She had a feeling that not much fazed him.

"Are you going to talk to him eventually?" Will said, breaking into her thoughts.

"I suppose so—but not right now. I was thinking of leaving a new message on my phone, something along the lines of 'I'm out of town for the next few weeks, but please don't worry. I discovered I wasn't supposed to get married after all.'"

He grinned. "Might not be a bad idea."

"But after breakfast," she said.

"Of course."

"Actually, I don't want to talk to either of them, Paul or my stepmother. I could see both of them trying to make me understand what a huge mistake I'd made and talking me out of the whole thing—not getting married, I mean. They'd both want to talk me back into it, to save face in town if nothing else."

"You've *got* to be joking." He leaned forward. "When you do call this Paul, I'd be rather curious to know how he's planning on justifying his behavior. Or even explaining it."

"I'll let you know what he says. But for now, I just want to eat." She took a generous sip of coffee, loving the way both the warmth and the caffeine spread throughout her body. She felt as if she were waking up, coming back to life after a long sleep—and she didn't mean the marathon nap she'd taken yesterday.

"Any thoughts about the rest of the day?"

"I don't feel like sleeping. Maybe just hang out in the room, read, knit. I'd like to relax."

"Good plan."

Their food arrived, and she attacked her pancakes first,

piling them with butter and syrup. Was there anything more wonderful than pancakes and good coffee?

"How do they do it?" she said.

"What?"

"I can never get my pancakes to come out this good."

"You cook?" he said.

"I love to. I guess I'm something of a foodie."

"Do you watch the Food Network?"

"I do. How do you know about it?"

"Elaine told me. She suggested that if I had to leave Sugar crated in any hotel room, that I turn on that channel so she'd feel comforted hearing voices. Her vet told her it's the best bet, because people are always either explaining things in a reasonable tone, or exclaiming delightedly over what they've just made and how good it tastes. Both tones of expression are ideal for a dog alone."

"That's a fantastic piece of advice. And the good thing is, neither Toby or Sugar are alone." Will had crated both dogs in his room, with the grilled fronts of both crates facing so the dogs could see each other. That, the snugly drawn drapes and the Food Network humming away in the background, and both dogs were probably snoozing the morning away.

"I was thinking of a movie," Will said. "Popcorn, soda, the whole thing."

"At a theater?" She wasn't sure how she liked this idea. Though she didn't feel that fragile, Tess wasn't sure she wanted to be around a whole lot of people. But on Monday morning, who would be at the movies?

"No, not going out. Getting a movie from the front lobby, playing it in the room, and purchasing one of their microwave popcorns. Keeping it simple. Something light, a comedy."

She considered this. "Yeah. I'd like that."

* * *

PAUL drove steadily on the expressway through the drizzle to the outskirts of Chicago, the directions to Kim's apartment building on the seat beside him, courtesy of one of his computer programs.

He hadn't found Brooke at her condo, and he didn't expect her to be at her cousin's place this morning. Both of them would be at work. But he wanted to do a clean sweep of the neighborhood, check it out, and be lying in wait when both women arrived home this evening.

The element of surprise always worked in his favor, and today would be no exception.

He'd get answers out of both Brooke and Kim and find out where the hell Tess had disappeared to once and for all. How smart could either of them be?

Pretty smart, an uneasy little voice nagged, *to have pulled off that whole wedding stunt on such short notice . . .*

AS their waitress handed them their bill, Tess studied a woman in another booth. She liked the way her hair looked and found herself unconsciously fiddling with the long braid that hung down her back.

Change was a good thing. She could embrace change. It was practically the one constant in her life right now.

"I'll get this," Will said, indicating their bill, and she nodded.

"I'm just going to the bathroom," she said and then added, "I'll cover dinner, okay?"

Will nodded and headed toward the cashier. Tess watched him move away, liking the way he walked, before she turned her attention back to the woman with the glorious haircut and headed toward her booth.

* * *

"I have one little thing I want to do before we watch our movie," she said as she walked back toward their motel with Will.

"What's that?"

"Could you drop me off about six blocks that way for about an hour?"

"Now I'm curious."

"A salon."

"Ah. Okay. Do you trust me to pick out the movie?"

"Yeah." She hesitated. "Just nothing too bloody."

"Something light."

"Exactly."

"Well then," Will said, "let's get you dropped off, and I'll go back and attend to the dogs."

THE salon was clean and cheerful, with a peach and green décor that was soothing. Tess walked in and headed toward the front desk.

"Can I help you?" The girl behind the counter looked about seventeen, with gorgeous skin and golden blond hair.

"I'm looking for Mary Anne."

"My mom."

"Yep. Is she here?"

"Yeah, she's just finishing up with a customer."

"Do I need to schedule an appointment?"

"No, there's no one for the next hour. She can fit you in."

"Great." Tess headed toward the comfortable chairs and a pile of current magazines on an end table. It felt right, what she was about to do. She wanted to make some major changes in her life, and as every woman from the beginning of time has always known, those changes could start with a brand-new makeover.

WILL scanned the shelves of movies in the small lounge off the motel's front desk. Something light, funny, and uplifting—and not too bloody. And nothing about weddings, he thought as he caught sight of *My Best Friend's Wedding*.

He kept looking, all the while mentally cataloging the various movies' strengths and weaknesses, until he found what he was looking for. Pleased, he slid the two movies off the shelf and headed toward the front desk to buy the microwave popcorn.

"WHAT kind of style are you looking for, hon?"

Mary Anne was a comforting sort of woman, gently rounded, with the same beautiful blond hair as her daughter and a calm, confident manner. You looked into her blue eyes and knew you could trust her. She just seemed to generate calm. Tess envied her daughter, just for a moment.

She'd come to the right place for her hair. From the way the last satisfied customer had looked as she walked out the front door, Mary Anne was a fantastic stylist. And Tess had loved the style of the woman at the diner.

"A change."

"Hmmm." The older woman looked thoughtful.

Tess watched the stylist as she carefully studied her for a moment and then said, "Something upsetting you?"

"In a way."

"I always advise my clients not to do anything to their hair in a rash state of mind. How are you feeling?"

"I think," Tess said, "that this is a change I've wanted to

make for a long time. Only I didn't know it until recently."

"I understand. You have beautiful hair," Mary Anne said. She'd unbraided Tess's French braid and was brushing her hair, all loose around her shoulders.

"It's not what I want," Tess said. "It's what—other people wanted for me."

"You mean for *them*," Mary Anne said, continuing her brushing. "So you're sure you want a change?"

"Yes."

"How short?"

"What do you think would look good?"

Mary Anne considered this and then said, "If we cut off about eight or nine inches, you could donate the braid to Wigs for Kids."

"What's that?"

"Donations of human hair that are given to some really wonderful people who make wigs for children who have cancer and choose to go through radiation or chemo. I can't tell you how wonderful it is when they get their 'hair' back. It changes their lives."

Tess closed her eyes for a moment. All of her problems, every single one, didn't seem so overwhelming.

The end of my life as I know it is nothing compared to the end of a life, period.

She opened her eyes. "I'd like that," she said softly.

"How about if I braid you back up and we cut the braid off first, and then I'll shampoo you and we can do the final cut."

"That sounds about right. And bangs. But not the straight-across, little-girl bangs. I want wispy and sexy."

"You got it."

As the stylist began to braid her hair, Tess closed her eyes one more time and breathed in, then offered up a silent prayer of thanks that fate had led her to this woman and to this realization.

Things weren't so bad. She still had her health. She still had people who loved her and she loved them. And in a strange twist of fate, she'd been given the open road and several more days to figure out what she was going to do with the rest of her life.

She wasn't staring death in the face. She was facing a sort of death, though, a death of her previous self. But that was nothing compared to the real thing. And what made the thought of actual death so frightening was that she knew, deep inside, that there were so many things she hadn't done, so many things she'd wanted to do, and she hadn't come close to doing any of them. She'd been scared and had let that fear, both her own and of what other people would think of her, get squarely in her way.

No more. Ever. Life was truly too short.

"Ready?" said Mary Anne, and Tess opened her eyes to see that the stylist had finished her braid and held her scissors in her hand.

"Make sure to cut off enough so those kids can have their wigs," she said.

"I will. But are you ready, Tess? Are you sure you want to do this?"

She took a deep breath and couldn't stop the smile that spread over her face as she contemplated this newest leap into the unknown.

"Yes. I'm ready."

nine

"LET ME GET you a hand mirror so you can see the back," Mary Anne said, but as she turned away, Tess knew she wouldn't need a mirror. She loved her new haircut. It was as if the weight of the world—and her hair—had been taken off her shoulders.

Her dark brown hair fell just below her shoulders, her bangs were perfection, and Mary Anne had also cut in subtle layers so now it seemed that her hair really moved. She turned her head from side to side, watching the way her hair fell, loving everything about this new look.

When the stylist handed her the mirror and turned her chair so she was facing away from the main mirror, Tess studied the back of her hair.

"I can't thank you enough!" she said, jumping up out of the chair and handing Mary Anne the mirror.

"I think it looks fantastic, hon. And thanks so much for donating your braid."

"I'm glad to do it," Tess said as she headed toward the front desk to pay her bill.

* * *

PAUL slumped in the front seat of his car, furious at the time he was wasting. But he knew that if he didn't come home this evening with at least some idea of where Brooke had gone, Madeline would be all over him. And that wasn't something he looked forward to.

He'd taken a brief break and gone for an Italian beef sandwich and a soda, but now he was stuck here, in his car, in the rain. Thank God he'd had the foresight to bring a couple of newspapers and a magazine.

Sighing with frustration, he picked up a copy of the *Wall Street Journal* and began to read the front page. He glanced up, suddenly aware that someone's eyes were on him, and saw a police car cruise slowly by. The cop's eyes met his, and Paul made a conscious effort to smile. He certainly didn't want to look like he was loitering in this neighborhood with bad intent.

He wasn't going to hurt Brooke. He just wanted some answers to his questions.

TESS walked a few stores over to a drugstore and went inside. In the cosmetics department, she carefully picked out two lipsticks and some eye shadow, all in brighter shades than she would normally wear. She also selected a creamy, vanilla-scented body lotion and a bag of mini chocolate bars.

After she left the drugstore, she bought a latte at a small coffeehouse and sat outside at a table. Though the weather was still brisk and the sky still gray, the rain had let up for a while. It felt good to sit outside and just relax.

She called Will to let him know she was ready to be picked up, then, studying her phone, decided to change her message. After giving it some thought, she recorded her new message.

"Hi, this is Tess. Well, I decided not to get married after all, so I'm taking some time off, kind of a mini-vacation. Unless it's an absolute emergency, please don't leave a message. I'll be back in town by the end of the month. Thank you. Oh, and all of you will get your presents back, don't worry."

Satisfied with her message, she turned off her phone and slipped it back into her purse, leaned back in her chair, and took another sip of her latte.

PAUL couldn't concentrate.

How could he read about other men's business successes when his own life was in such a shambles? He took his cell out of his jacket pocket and tried Tess once again.

"Hi, this is Tess. Well, I decided not to get married after all, so I'm taking some time off, kind of a mini-vacation—"

He listened to the rest of the message in a kind of shock, then once he heard the beep, said, "Damn it, Tess, this isn't funny anymore! Would you do me the courtesy of giving me a call and letting me know what the hell is going on!"

He petulantly flung the phone onto the passenger seat beside him, then stared out the windshield, thoroughly pissed.

He shouldn't have yelled at her. He should have made more of an effort to be sweet. He wasn't going to get her back by throwing a tantrum.

It was just that no woman had ever rejected him this way. He was used to being the one doing the rejecting. And in a perverse sort of way, it made him want Tess back more than ever.

* * *

WILL was walking toward the coffeehouse where Tess had said she'd be waiting when he caught sight of her.

She looked fantastic.

Gone was the French braid, which had been a rather severe style for her. In its place, her hair looked much softer, easier. She smiled at him, and he realized something else was different about her. A heartbeat later he realized she had more color in her face. A new lipstick perhaps. Or maybe she was just happier.

"I like it," he said as he sat down across from her.

"Really?"

"It's immensely flattering."

He was touched when she told him about Wigs for Kids, and agreed that it was the right decision. There was so much he liked about Tess, much more than just the initial attraction he'd had for her that first night at the bar. That attraction would have been enough to make him explore the connection between them if it hadn't been such an awkward time for her.

But now Will realized that he really, really liked her. She was a sensitive person, and he suddenly wanted a better life for Tess than what she'd been prepared to settle for. And he realized he could be instrumental in making sure she achieved it.

He knew what it was like to have your heart broken, to think that life would never be the same. You couldn't reach a certain age without a few hard knocks in love. But what he adored about Tess was that, even with what she'd been through, she was making the effort to bounce back up, to make the best of things.

He was curiously moved by her courage. Will had the feeling that even though she'd lived a rather quiet life, she hadn't had a whole lot of help in figuring out what she wanted in her future.

"Okay, what movie did you get?" she said.

"Now I hope I made the right choice, but you can exchange them both if you like—"

"Tell me."

"*Rush Hour* with Jackie Chan and Chris Tucker. Both one and two."

"I love Jackie Chan!"

"You've seen them, then?"

"I saw the first one, but I'd love to see it again. I never saw the second one."

"Good. That's settled. Do I have time for a coffee?" he said, "Or should I get it to go?"

"Have it here. I think we have a little more time before the rain comes back."

"Tess, your hair really does look amazing."

He went inside then, after promising to bring her back a cookie.

SHE watched him walk away, liking just about everything about him. And for a moment she wondered why it couldn't have been Will she'd been engaged to, Will she was going to marry.

Just the few days she'd spent in his company had convinced her that she'd never really known what it was like to be comfortable with a man, to have this easy rapport with someone, to share a sense of humor.

He was so much more than the boy she'd had a crush on as a teenager, someone she'd thought she'd loved from afar. She found she *liked* Will, the man, immensely. And he was no strain on the eyes, with his terrific build and easy stride. She even liked the way he wore his hair today, just below shoulder length and tied back with a thin strip of leather. The jeans and dark blue sweatshirt were casual, along with his boots and brown leather jacket.

He came back out with coffee and a huge chocolate-chip cookie for her.

"You really do look completely different," he said, still studying her as he sat down. "It suits you so well, Tess."

"Thank you."

"How did you know to come to this place?"

"I saw a woman at the diner who had a great cut and asked her where she'd gotten it."

"Good thinking."

They sat at their table, and even though the sun wasn't shining and toward the end raindrops began to fall, Tess couldn't remember an afternoon she'd enjoyed more.

THE ring of Paul's cell jerked him awake. Reaching for his phone, he blinked rapidly, coming back to the present moment.

"Hello."

"What are you doing?"

Madeline.

Briefly he described where he was and his plan for the evening.

"So Brooke wasn't at her condo?"

"No. She's got to be here with her cousin."

"Just don't let her out of your sight until she tells you where my stepdaughter is!"

"Of course." He hung up before she could say any more, turned off the ringer, and settled back in his seat to finish his nap.

He'd be awake long before Brooke and her cousin got home. And then he'd deal with both of them.

* * *

TESS couldn't remember the last time she'd laughed harder.

They popped the popcorn in the microwave by the breakfast bar, poured themselves sodas, and settled down on Will's bed. The movie began, and Tess forgot her troubles as she became involved with the story of a little girl's kidnapping, laughing all the while at Chris Tucker's antics and astounded at Jackie Chan's fighting skills.

Both dogs curled up on the bed with them, and even when the rain started coming down harder, they all continued to watch. When the first movie ended, they went right into the second, stopping only to order a pizza for dinner.

Will was so easy to be with. She'd hesitated just a moment before getting on his bed, but she knew he was the sort of man who would never, ever take advantage of a situation.

Maybe you want him to . . .

The thought had slipped into her consciousness so easily, and she realized she was that attracted to him. It seemed strange, thinking this way when just a few days ago she'd been planning to marry Paul, but Tess knew it was true.

Ever since she'd been spending time with Will, she'd come to understand what being really at ease with a man entailed. It wasn't that there was no attraction between them, no little spark. She wasn't sure about Will—he was being a perfect gentleman because of circumstances—but she knew her heart sped up a little when she'd catch him looking at her.

She just really liked him. It touched her, how he'd gone out of his way since this trip had started to be there for her, to make things easier for her. He was a good and kind man, and right now, she'd take those qualities over Paul's incredible salary and his gorgeous house on the lake.

She didn't even know where Will really lived, except that it was somewhere in Los Angeles. She didn't really know what he did, other than play in a band. For all she knew, the band was something he did on the side, with a real job somewhere else to take care of the bills.

He seemed really flexible at the moment. After all, he'd taken this job Elaine had given him, to drive both her van and her dog back to the West Coast.

But right now she didn't want to think too much. She just wanted to enjoy the moment and laugh and not even worry about what lay ahead. Watching movies and eating pizza with Will had pointed out to her how little fun she and Paul had really had.

Tess didn't want Will to be a rebound romance after her failed wedding. He deserved better. But she would always be thankful that he'd been there when she'd fallen and that he'd cared for her as tenderly as if she had been the most important woman in his life.

DUSK had fallen in Chicago, and Paul was uncomfortably aware that the cop had seen him now several times as he made his rounds.

One time, just to make sure there were no misunderstandings, he'd rolled down his window and motioned the policeman and his partner over.

"I'm just waiting for an old college buddy to come home," he explained, attempting a sincere smile.

"Well, be careful," one of the cops said. "We've been having a rash of home robberies around here."

"That's why you're patrolling?"

"We're keeping an eye out," the cop said before their car glided away.

One good thing about this whole mess, Paul thought. *At least I'm as safe here as I would be at home.*

Just as he finished the thought, he saw a car coming down the street and then recognized Brooke in the passenger seat.

Showtime, he thought. He opened his car door and got out, shutting it behind him. Now he'd finally get some answers. He wasn't leaving without them.

THE credits were running on *Rush Hour Two*, and Tess felt comfortably stuffed with pepperoni pizza and popcorn. Sugar and Toby had done their share of begging for bits of popcorn and the smallest taste of the pepperoni. Now, with the almost empty pizza box on the small table beneath the window and their sodas on either end table, Tess turned toward Will.

"I had a wonderful time."

"Me, too," he said, smiling down at her.

"I'll be ready to leave tomorrow, weather permitting."

"Okay. Actually, I wanted to get out the map and show you the route we're taking."

Which he did, and when she noticed they were headed so near to Boulder, Tess said, "If I called my brother and let him know we were in the area, do you think we could stop for a little while and visit?"

"Better than that," Will said. "I wanted to see both him and Ron, so I thought we could have dinner with them."

He showed her the rest of the route, which included Utah, Nevada, Arizona, and finally California.

"Las Vegas," Tess said. "I can't remember the last time I was there. I think I was around fourteen."

"A lot's changed since then."

"I'm looking forward to it. I realized while I was sitting out with my coffee that I haven't had a vacation in a couple of years."

"Yearly breaks should be mandatory," he said, teasing.

She laughed.

Will began to clear away the pizza box when Tess said, "I changed the message on my cell."

"What does it say?"

She told him, and he laughed, obviously approving.

"I don't really want to talk to either of them."

"You could call them when we reach Los Angeles. That gives you a few more days to really think about what you want to tell them."

"A good plan."

BROOKE had just gotten out of her cousin's car when she felt a strong hand roughly grip her elbow and yank her backward. Acting strictly on instinct, she reached for the small pepper spray on her key chain, readied it, turned, and pointed it directly into her assailant's eyes and delivered the goods.

"Auuuuugggghhhhhhh!" Paul screamed, fury in his voice as he let her go and dropped to his knees, rubbing his eyes with his fingers and then reaching for Brooke, angry.

Acting in self-defense, Brooke took the heavy textbook she was holding and hit him on the head with it.

Paul fell like a stone.

"Oh, shit! Paul! I didn't mean—I mean, I thought you were—oh, damn it—"

"What was he *doing*, grabbing you like that?" Kim demanded, coming around the side of the car and putting a comforting hand on Brooke's arm. "What ever happened to saying hello and approaching someone before you just grab them?"

"What are we going to do—" Brooke said, but the red flash of cop car lights and the short blast of a siren interrupted her words. The police car double-parked next to Kim's car, and both officers stepped up onto the sidewalk and looked down at Paul, lying perfectly still on the cement.

"What's going on?" one cop asked.

"I don't—I mean—"

"Is this man your friend from college?" the other cop said.

"No!" Brooke said. "I mean, I know him, but he's my best friend's ex-fiancé and she ran away and I think he just wants me to tell him where she is—and—"

"Was he bothering the two of you?" the first cop asked.

Brooke hesitated.

"Yes," Kim said. "He grabbed my cousin pretty hard and almost pulled her off her feet."

Both cops looked at each other.

The second cop said, "You know, I didn't like the looks of this guy when we saw him this morning."

"He was here this *morning*?" Brooke said, her voice coming out in a weak squeak.

"Yep. Claimed he was waiting for an old college buddy. But he was here to cause trouble for the two of you girls, right?"

"Yes," said Kim, giving her cousin a look Brooke recognized that said, *Go along with this!*

"One of those stalker types, huh?" The other cop smiled grimly. "Well, if one of you will consent to file charges—"

"I will," both women said simultaneously, and Brooke grinned.

"Like I said, if you'll take the time to fill out a minimum of paperwork, we can hold him for a little while."

"Wonderful," said Kim. "And what do you know, his car's on the side of the street that gets cleaned tomorrow morning."

"He'll get a nice, fat ticket," the cop said.

"Okay, let's get him off the sidewalk," the other said.

Brooke watched as the cops got Paul to his feet, dead weight between them. They dragged him toward the police car and flung him into the backseat.

"Are you sure we should do this?" Brooke whispered to her cousin as they watched.

"You want him to come back to my apartment, demanding to know why you blasted his eyeballs with pepper spray and gave him a big lump on his head?"

"Ah—no."

"Just as I thought. Even going down to the station and filing the report, we can be back here, packed and to my brother Matt's house before midnight."

"He and Alicia will be cool with it?"

"They'll think it's hilarious. And we should call Tess and tell her what Paul's been up to. He's just not giving up."

Brooke kept her eyes on the police car as both cops got inside and started the engine. Several of the neighbors had come out of their homes and were gathered around watching the show—or what was left of it.

She frowned. "I know. He won't give up until he finds her." And although she hated to call Tess and create more worries for her, she knew she had to.

WILL had opened a bottle of red wine with dinner, and Tess, after two glasses, felt totally relaxed.

"I should probably tell you what really happened," she said. She and Will were still in his room, though she'd moved to one of the chairs by the small round table while Will still lay on the bed with the two dogs.

"You don't have to tell me anything."

"It's okay. I want you to know. I mean, you're the reason I'm feeling as good as I do." She could feel her face warming with a blush. "That came out wrong. What I meant was, you gave me the opportunity to come on this trip with you, and it's made a huge difference."

He nodded.

"To make a long and very depressing story really short and concise, I went to our church to pray and ask for a sign as to whether or not I should marry Paul.

"I heard a noise in the community room, and when I went back there to investigate, I saw Paul with the reverend's daughter. They were having sex—" She hesitated and then said, "I knew I couldn't marry him."

"I can absolutely see why not."

"So I packed up and drove over to Brooke's, and as I went to get my keys out of my pocket, I found your number and, well, it—"

"Seemed like a good idea at the time."

"Exactly."

"Are you still happy you decided to come on this trip?"

"Yes!" She studied him. "You aren't sorry you asked me along, are you?"

"Never."

"I just wanted to thank you again, because it's been this lovely little moment of time, completely off to the side, out of my regular life, and—"

"You don't have to keep thanking me!" For some reason, Will sounded annoyed.

"Sorry."

A short silence, then—

"No, Tess, I'm sorry. It's just that—I'm enjoying your company immensely, and I hate for you to keep thanking me over and over. You have a lot to offer, and I want you to know that—"

His phone rang.

"Go ahead and get it," Tess said.

She watched as he answered, as his facial expression changed, hardened slightly, as those gorgeous eyes narrowed.

"I see," he said, and his tone was one Tess hoped he'd never use with her. Who had called, and what had they told him?

"For you," he said, handing her the phone. "Brooke."

She took his phone.

"I tried calling you, but you must have your ringer turned off—"

"I'm sorry—"

"No, it's okay. But I had to tell you—Tess, I'm so sorry, I wanted you to take this trip with Will and just relax—"

Tess went very still as Brooke told her what had happened with Paul that evening. She listened carefully to every detail, trying to ignore the sick feeling in her stomach.

"I'm so sorry," she said when her friend finished. "I'm sorry you and Kim had to go through all that. I wish to God I'd never met Paul!"

"I know the feeling," Brooke said.

"I have to call him," Tess said. "I have to tell him to leave you both alone. It's me he wants, and I can't have him harassing my friends."

"No! That's not why I called! I just wanted you to know that he's really intent on finding you. I wanted to warn you and let Will know so you'd be safe—"

"What's he going to do to me, Brooke? He can't force me to walk down the aisle!"

"I think Paul could make things very unpleasant for you if he put his mind to it. It's like he's deranged or something, like he can't believe you wouldn't want to marry him. Why else would he still insist on coming after you?"

Tess could feel panic curling her insides and shame suffusing her stomach. What was *wrong* with Paul? How could her judgment have been so faulty?

"Need some help?" Will asked.

She nodded her head.

"Let's make this a conference call," he said. "Between the three of us, we can work things out."

THEY talked for about an hour and came up with a plan.

"Vegas," Brooke said. "You're right, Tess, that's the place. What happens in Vegas stays in Vegas! I'll fly out to give you support, and with me and Will there, you can face anyone. And if Paul knows you're going to meet him there at a specified time, he'll stop harassing everyone else!"

"It should work," Tess said. "I don't know why I didn't see it before, but he's a massive, massive control freak. If I give Paul a date and a time when we can meet, he'll feel like things are in control again, and I'll let him think he has the upper hand."

"I'm glad you put the bastard in jail for a night," Will said. "Not that he doesn't deserve worse!"

"Okay," Tess said. "We've got the date set. Brooke, you're going to get your plane ticket. Where should we meet?"

"The Hard Rock?" Will suggested.

"Perfect," Brooke said.

"And I want to meet Paul in a public place," Tess added.

"Like one of those famous Vegas buffets with lots of people around."

"Good idea," Brooke said. "Just remember, Tess, you're not alone in all this. Will and I are going to be right with you every step of the way."

She could feel her throat closing. "You guys—"

"Now don't go all weepy on me," Brooke said, but she sounded as if she were almost in tears herself.

"You're both just the best," Tess whispered.

"We aim to please," Will said.

"You think this will work?" Tess said.

"Yes," Will and Brooke replied in unison.

It has to, Tess thought.

ABOUT fifteen minutes later, Tess put the first stage of their plan into effect. She called Paul's cell phone and left a message, knowing that he wouldn't pick up because he was sitting in a jail cell without access to his phone. Quickly and concisely, she told him the time and date she'd meet him in Vegas, and the place.

Will had remembered a massive buffet, one of the most popular in the city, and she'd decided it would do. They'd called the hotel to get the exact address, and now she gave Paul the information carefully, speaking clearly, also telling him that if he harassed Brooke again, she would not meet with him, ever.

"Nicely done," Will said as she disconnected the call.

"Thanks," Tess said, but the delight in their evening had left her. All she wanted was to crawl back into bed and sleep.

"We can hit the road tomorrow," she said. "As early as you like."

"Sure you're ready?"

"Yeah. The sooner we leave, the sooner we get to Vegas." Tess paused, the details of their plan running through her mind. "And the sooner that rat bastard is out of my life."

THE night stretched out before her, and Tess knew she wouldn't sleep. Exhaustion would probably catch up with her on the road tomorrow.

Shame was her constant companion, eating away at her self-confidence. She went over the past year in minute detail, wondering how she'd let herself get caught up with a man like Paul. She'd ignored so much of his basic character because she'd wanted to win her parents' love.

Love shouldn't have to be earned, Tess thought as she stared at the ceiling. *Love shouldn't be something you're constantly afraid of losing.*

Tired of tossing and turning, she finally willed herself to sleep, determined to settle things with Paul once and for all. And most important, make wiser choices in the future and never let anything like this happen to her ever again.

PAUL woke up in a jail cell on a thin mattress that smelled of disinfectant. He glanced around at his surroundings, incredulous.

Then he leapt out of bed and banged on the bars, furious.

"What the *hell* is going on here?"

"Well from where I sit," came the voice of a policeman, "it seems you were a little disorderly with a young lady, and she decided to press charges."

He opened his mouth to dispute this but then realized the futility of it all.

·

"I want a phone call—or a lawyer. Now."

"Sure thing, hotshot," the policeman said, his voice laced with amusement.

WILL lay in bed. He couldn't sleep, and his gaze strayed to the door separating his room from Tess's. She had taken the news about her fiancé—ex-fiancé, he corrected himself—better than expected. Will's phone rattled gently against the surface of the side table. He picked it up, opened it, and answered the call.

"Will?"

Brooke.

"What's up?" he said softly, not wanting to wake Tess.

"I think we need a backup plan. Just in case."

"I know. I've been running through the whole thing in my head, over and over. I've never met this Paul, but I think we're dealing with a nasty piece of work here. Far worse than any of us suspect, even Tess."

"I think you're right." Brooke hesitated and then said, "I didn't tell Tess the worst of it. When he grabbed me, he *really* grabbed me. With the intent to hurt. I think that, if the police hadn't stepped in, he was planning on inflicting some bodily harm, if you know what I mean."

"Exactly. And by the way, good work with that pepper spray. Couldn't have happened to a nicer guy."

"Thanks."

"There's something else I've been thinking about." And he told her about Elaine and her psychic abilities, how she had read Toby, and what the little dog had told her Paul had done to her.

"Don't tell Tess, whatever you do," Brooke said. "She'll go off the deep end. It's too much."

"I know. I wasn't planning on it. I just told you because

I think it shows what this man is capable of when no one's watching."

"Good point."

"We cannot leave her alone with him," Will said. "Ever."

"I know. But I have this idea, Will, just in case things escalate and get as bad as I think they might."

"What?"

He heard her take a deep breath and then she said, "You could marry her."

"What?" He wasn't sure he'd heard her correctly.

"You could marry her, Will. A quickie Vegas wedding. That way the bastard wouldn't have a leg to stand on. Then, after a certain amount of time and after Paul's forgotten all about her, the two of you could quietly get the marriage annulled."

Silence as he digested this idea. "Wouldn't a restraining order be more effective, not to mention less extreme?"

"I'm afraid even that might not stop him," she said. "Not when he has her stepmother on his side."

Will frowned. "I hate the thought of those two ganging up on Tess."

"Will, I know it's a lot to ask, but—"

"Desperate times call for desperate measures. I know," he said.

"It may be our only hope. I don't think even Paul would go up against another man. If you were in a position to protect Tess, I think he'd leave the two of you alone."

"I know he would. He's a coward at heart, preying on women and small dogs. What a man," he added sarcastically.

"A total jerk. And you might not even have to marry Tess. Just the sight of you and a ring might do the trick, just to get him off the scent. I think Paul and her stepmother should be easy to fool."

"It's a good alternate plan, Brooke."

"So we'll keep this just between ourselves for now, all right?"

"Good idea," Will said quietly. "We'll just have it as an option in case things get out of control."

"I knew I could count on you, Will."

He hung up and then stared into the darkness and finally smiled. Well, when Elaine had said Tess was going to be significant in his life, she hadn't been kidding.

Once again, she'd been dead on with her reading.

IN the end, Paul gave up and called Madeline.

She bailed him out of jail very early the following morning, bitching the entire time. He was tired of hearing it, and when the cops gave him his phone back, along with his wallet and other possessions, he took the opportunity to check his messages.

Tess had called.

"Be quiet!" he said brusquely to Madeline as he listened to the message. Then he played it again for her and watched as a smile spread over her calculating face.

"Las Vegas, in just a few days," she mused. "I won't tell her father about this. You know, Paul, we may actually be in time to do some damage control after all."

"What do you mean, we?" he said. "I'm the one she wants to see!"

Madeline rounded on him so fiercely he took a startled step back.

"You think I'd let you do something like this by yourself and botch it up like you did that wedding? A man who couldn't keep it in his pants until the deal was sealed?"

He didn't dare tell her that he thrived on such excitement, that having sex with Marti the night before his wedding, and in a church besides, had added to his satisfaction, made him feel more alive.

But he hadn't counted on being caught by Tess.

"Let me go alone, Madeline. I can get her back in line. Just let me—"

"Oh no, this time we're going to work *together* and make things right. I want everything to go back to the way it was before that girl left town and created this whole mess."

"Fine." It didn't matter. Madeline or no Madeline, he'd be flying to Las Vegas in a few days and bringing Tess back home. Then his new life could finally, officially begin. And if Tess had a brain in her head, she would never interfere with any of his plans again.

ten

THE FOLLOWING MORNING while Tess took a shower, she thought about all the tiny steps, the choices that had led to her engagement to Paul. And she realized, as she soaped up with her favorite peach mango bath gel, that, for better or for worse, she'd made the decision to marry him on her own. Whatever pressure she'd received from Paul or her parents was irrelevant. *You grew a backbone a little too late, Sommerville,* Tess thought. Instead of living happily ever after, she'd ended up a one-woman episode of *Dr. Phil.*

Tess knew her parents' divorce had deeply affected the way she viewed her own life. Perhaps another person, someone with a different temperament, would have escaped emotionally unscathed. But Tess never managed to leave that unhappy piece of her childhood behind.

She wanted, more than anything, a happy home and family. Tess never really had huge career ambitions, but now as she washed her newly styled hair—much easier with all the length cut off—she realized how much she'd invested in making other people happy.

No one had been happy in her family for the longest time. Her brother Charlie had hit the road as soon as he could. Her father had thought his divorce would make him happy, but it hadn't. He and Madeline fought, but her stepmother seemed to handle him better—really, the correct word was *manipulate* him—with far more ease than her mother ever had.

But they never seemed content. She couldn't remember an occasion when her father and stepmother had actually seemed *happy*. It had felt as if whenever they achieved something or reached a goal, they were already on their way to the next *thing*. Their life had been utterly outer directed, they were both obsessed with what other people thought, had, or did.

She'd wanted to make them happy. She'd wanted them to be proud of her. She'd yearned for a connection to either of them, had wanted that closeness that was in the best of happy families. And she'd finally figured out a way.

Paul had made her father happy. He'd made her stepmother ecstatic. Perhaps the only person in this entire scenario who hadn't been overjoyed had been Tess. And Toby. But she'd deliberately overlooked Paul's various flaws because she'd seen the marriage as a way of making her parents happy. Talk about denial. She'd crushed down her feelings, even toward the end, the night before the wedding when they'd been screaming at her to wake up and see what she was about to do to her life.

Thank God Paul had provided the ultimate wake-up call. Even pleasing her father and stepmother couldn't justify infidelity.

Tess had wanted so much from her father and from Madeline, and now, as she rinsed her hair and reached for her conditioner, she realized how incredibly tired she was from constantly trying to anticipate what they might want and deliver it up to them. Bone tired. Exhausted. She'd set herself an impossible task, because the more she gave up of her life to please them, the more they would want.

Tess turned beneath the shower stream and rinsed the conditioner out of her hair, running her fingers through the slippery, shoulder-length strands. The one thing she was certain of was that her parents hadn't given her a whole lot of experience in making decisions on her own. She'd been told, through much of her childhood and into young adulthood, what was expected of her and what they wanted her to do.

So don't be too hard on yourself—how could you be expected to know what was right for you when no one ever helped you even articulate it? Feelings were avoided in her family at all cost, even laughed at. She'd learned early on to keep her head low, just do what she was told and run for cover. Stay off their radar and out of sight.

Horrible preparation for picking a marital partner. She'd given little to no thought about what she wanted and picked the perfect person for her father and stepmother. They'd been so proud of her, and for what? Picking an emotionally constipated, unfaithful, and conventionally successful man who would make the two of them look good in their community, never mind how he treated her.

The thought made her stomach knot.

And then, of course, there was Paul himself. From the beginning, as she finally had the time and distance to look back on their whole courtship honestly, he'd been just a little too charming. Without revealing a whole lot about himself, he'd encouraged her to tell him all about herself, to initiate a sort of false emotional intimacy that she'd mistaken for the real thing. Their relationship had been—at his insistence—in the fast lane from the start, even though she'd sometimes had the uncomfortable feeling that neither of them had that much in common.

She closed her eyes, the hot water pounding down on her and helping ease the tension from her shoulders. She'd been guilty of overdisclosure right from the start, so eager to believe that he found her interesting. Hindsight being twenty-twenty, she could see how she'd been so eager for emotional closeness and acceptance, for talking about feelings—which had never been present at home—that she'd jumped at the first false signs of it from Paul.

In essence, she'd been a sitting duck. A *crippled* duck. With her background, she'd been putty in his clever hands. Oh, she'd made the choice to be with Paul, but now she could see how her background had primed that choice, almost made it inevitable. She would have had to possess extraordinary insight into her life to resist him.

And suddenly she knew that these few days with Will, on the road, were a lifeline to an entirely new way of being. That piece of paper with his cell phone number had been the push she'd needed. If she took this chance to strike out into uncharted territory, her life might just take a whole new direction.

Tess turned off the shower and stepped out, reaching for a towel. Throughout their entire engagement, Paul never once made her feel the way Will had that night at the bar. He was so easy to talk to. He was charming but always sincere. The two men were complete opposites. Will was everything her ex-fiancé could never hope to be.

Pathetic, that she hadn't seen through Paul's act sooner.

Tess pulled on a clean bra and underwear, then jeans and a cotton hand-knit sweater she'd made from a deep indigo yarn. It was soft and comforting, with a rolled neckline and long sleeves, one of her favorites. She combed her wet hair and blew it dry and then applied sunscreen, mascara, and some lipgloss. When that basic grooming was finished, she headed out of the bathroom to find her shoes.

Will was just coming in his door, both dogs on their leashes, Toby and Sugar looking decidedly windblown.

"No rain so far this morning," he called out. "I think if we get going in the next hour, we can beat the storm."

"Give me fifteen minutes," she called back. She'd packed up the night before, and it was just a matter of stowing her toiletries in her large tote.

"Dogs are fed and emptied out," he called back, and Tess almost laughed. Here they were, working together like a well-oiled machine, an old married couple. Will was so easy, so—*uncomplicated*, for lack of a better word.

"Don't you want to shower?" she said.

"I'm heading toward my bathroom as you speak," he called back. "I left *M*A*S*H* on for the dogs."

She had to grin as she stowed her stuff in her bags. Sugar was a relentless television watcher; she loved dramas best of all, especially *Law and Order* and the original *CSI*. Toby had quickly learned what fun it was, but she had more of a leaning toward comedies. *M*A*S*H* filled the bill for both of them. And they barked furiously whenever Klinger came on in one of his outfits.

She heard the shower come on and sat down on her bed, ready to leave.

Will was a good man—and a great friend. But how much longer would he be in her life? Their roadtrip would eventually end, and she'd have to start over on her own.

Thinking about the past—and facing Paul in Las Vegas—Tess felt utterly and incredibly alone, as if every single relationship she'd ever had was a fraud. Her father, her stepmother, and especially Paul. None of these relationships had any true foundation. They'd only worked as long as she'd pretended to be exactly what they wanted her to be. And in a very real sense, none of them even *knew* her. Her mother had simply disappeared.

She sensed, rather than saw, doggy eyes on her. Glancing toward the door, she caught sight of Toby staring at her, a concerned look on her furry face.

Suddenly Tess couldn't speak. She knew if she did, she'd cry. So she simply patted the bed and Toby came hurtling toward her, bounded onto the bed and, with one solid bounce, landed in her arms. She hugged the little dog to her tightly, feeling such life and warmth and love in the wriggling body.

So you have your dog, she thought as tears welled and she blinked them furiously away. *And Brooke. And you have Will and Sugar. Even if you barely know them, you've been authentic with them from the start. And Charlie— you'll be seeing Charlie soon, and he always cared for you . . .*

Toby struggled in her grasp, and she loosened it enough so her little dog could swipe at her face with her pink tongue.

"I'm never going to lie to you again, Toby," she whispered. "I've been such a coward. I knew things were screwed up with Paul, but I closed my eyes and ignored it and thought it would all go away. And it made it worse."

Toby cocked her head, and her one good eye sparkled warmly, a deep and wise brown.

"So I don't know where we're going or where we're going to end up, and at this moment I don't care. But I will promise you that whatever happens, we'll stick together and no more Pauls for either of us!"

Toby wagged her stubby tail and barked.

"Ready to go?" Will said in his crisp British accent as he appeared in the doorway. She liked the clothing he'd chosen for the day: comfortable, well-worn jeans, a dark green turtleneck sweater, and his boots. His hair, freshly shampooed, fell damply around his shoulders.

"Yeah," she said. "I am."

"WANT to drive?" Will asked.

Tess hadn't considered this.

"Would it be all right with Elaine?"

"I'm sure it would be fine."

They'd enjoyed coffee and excellent doughnuts in the motel lobby before checking out and taking off. Now, about two hours into their trip, Will had stopped at a fast-food restaurant, and they'd ordered breakfast. They'd run the dogs around before eating and now fed them bits of French toast strips and egg sandwiches. The coffee, Tess thought, was surprisingly good.

"I think I'd like that," she replied. The van was automatic, and she'd driven vans before. Maybe driving would be a way of getting her mind to settle down.

"How long do you think it will take to get to Boulder?"

Will scratched Sugar's head and moved his breakfast out of range. "We'll be in Nebraska for another day, but we should be in Colorado by tomorrow."

"Great. We should phone Ron and Charlie—"

"Already have. They've picked out a steak house for dinner."

"Typical."

He laughed. "When was the last time you saw your brother?"

"Charlie?" She thought. He hadn't been home in— "Maybe five years. Six?"

"He didn't come home a lot? Was he planning to attend your wedding?"

"He was busy." But she knew it was more than that. He hadn't wanted to face their father's relentless criticism. The one thing she admired in her brother, more than anything else, was the way he was determined to live his own life. Brian, her other brother, was a clone of their father.

Where did she fit in? She'd tried to become a clone, but more and more she was starting to see herself as closer to Charlie.

"I can't wait to see him," she said, crushing her food wrappers and tossing them into the main food bag.

"I know. It's been a while for me, too. So," Will said, feeding a pleading Sugar and hopeful Toby his last French toast stick, split in half, "Why don't you drive for a while and we'll try to make some real time today?"

"Is that a comment on my driving?"

"Whatever made you think that?"

She had to laugh. "You have a tendency toward a little pedal to the metal yourself."

"Me? Speed?"

"Huh." She grabbed the large fast-food bag and swung the passenger side door open. "I'm headed for the bathroom, but I'll be back."

"I'll take the dogs out for one last walk."

SHE liked driving. It filled her mind, relaxed her. It was peaceful, as Nebraska was a rather flat state, the only hills the rolling variety. There weren't many cars on the road, but it was still very early in the day. Each state had a beauty all its own, and in Nebraska, Tess knew it was the vast, endless sky.

The skies were glorious, still storm-washed and filled with incredible clouds. High winds whipped leaves into the air. She could feel that wind against the van as she drove.

Birds wheeled frantically through the crisp fall air, seemingly determined to get somewhere else but not making much headway. And Tess realized that Will had been right—they were outracing the storm. She kept the vehicle firmly within the speed limit but drove with determination, feeling that it was absolutely essential that she do her share.

They'd bought coffee with their meal, and now she sipped it as she drove and realized with a start that she was happy. Right here, right now, in the present moment, her life in utter and complete shambles, she was happy. She had no real idea what she was going to say to Paul when she saw him in Las Vegas—other than the very obvious statement that they were over—but even that didn't bother her.

For the longest time she'd lived her life on tiptoe, wondering what Paul wanted or liked, wondering what she could do to make his life easier. Now she had no one to please but herself, and she was looking forward to dinner with her brother.

She had the window down, and the cool morning air filled the van. Glancing in her rearview mirror, she saw both dog's noses come up, sniffing the breeze, taking stock the way only a dog could. Toby was like a little Zen master to her, reminding her to stay in the moment, love with all her heart, and offer that unconditional love whenever possible. Dogs made things seem so simple. Why did humans have to complicate life so much?

Both Toby and Sugar had gotten to the point where they whined if they caught sight of a rest stop. She couldn't blame them—Tess found herself enjoying the long walks she took with the dogs and Will. It helped allievate the tension. If she had one wish in the world, it would be that this period of her life had happened a few months ago and she had a new perspective and a little more understanding about the whole thing. But she was in the midst of it, up to her neck.

Tess felt a yearning, a desire for her life to be profoundly different from what it had been. She remembered something she'd once seen in a woman's magazine, about faking something until you were comfortable with it. Like trying on a new personality and playing with it until you felt as if it fit you or not. And she found that she didn't want to be this painfully shy, earnest little thing anymore, this person who always looked to others before she spoke up. She wanted to be someone who started conversations, who opened things up, who dared to make things happen.

So she'd try it on, see if it fit. This was as good a chance as any, especially dinner tomorrow night with Charlie and Ron. As she glanced at Will, she realized with a start that he would accept anything new she threw his way. And she wondered if he was really as easygoing and uncomplicated as he seemed.

Somehow, she doubted it.

WILL tilted his head back against the passenger seat headrest and closed his eyes, pretending to rest. But what he really wanted to do was think. And he was grateful Tess couldn't read his mind.

She seemed to be healing at lightning speed—which introduced a whole new set of dilemmas. How did one ask a woman to kind of keep him in mind, not that she was ready for a relationship within the shadow of her last one? Impossible. But maybe he could ask her if, when she felt ready for another emotional involvement, she'd call him again.

Ridiculous. Lame as hell. He had no idea of how to go about making sure he stayed on Tess's emotional radar. He had no idea if he even had the right to bring up something like this, what with her broken heart.

But damn it, she didn't look as if her heart were broken. Yes, there had been a few bad days at the motel, but Will had a feeling that Tess's subconscious had already known that the relationship with Paul was a bust. She'd gone into that church and asked that question for a reason; she'd known that the whole thing was wrong, wasn't going to work, was going up in flames. She'd sensed it, and thank God Paul had seen fit to destroy any illusions she might have held about him once and for all.

The only thing Will knew was that he didn't want to miss this opportunity with Tess and hear from Brooke, a year or two later, that she'd hooked up with some nice guy and was married and having babies.

He was shocked by how strongly he wanted to be that guy.

Stranger things had happened in relationships. Stranger things happened every day. He'd gone out enough, had enough relationship experience to know when there were possibilities between two people. He'd had two serious relationships with women he'd genuinely liked and loved, and he knew you couldn't always predict how you'd find the next significant woman. This had to be one for the books.

And the other thing that amazed him was how strongly he wanted Tess to be his final relationship. He thought about her a lot, and he knew he'd met his match. Will was a man who accepted what life threw his way. How could he know this in just a few days, meeting her again after all these years. He didn't know how; he just knew it felt right and he didn't want to mess it up. But how was he going to proceed?

His cell rang, and he fished around for it and flipped it open.

"Yes?"

"How's my girl?"

"Elaine—great to hear from you. Sugar's fine. She ate almost all my French toast this morning, begging shamefully. She's loving all the new sights and smells and has created quite a little friendship with Toby."

"I'll have to meet that darling little dog. And the van? It's running all right?"

"Doing fine, running well, nothing out of the ordinary. We're in Nebraska, about a day and a half from Boulder."

"And Tess?"

"What do you mean?" Even though Elaine was an old friend, he was on his guard, especially as the woman in question was mere feet away from him.

"How's she doing?"

"Much better," Will said.

"Excellent. I was thinking about you this morning and had this feeling—"

"Yes?" Elaine had always been right before, and he was curious as to what she'd come up with.

"Are you by any chance getting married in the near future?"

"Perhaps," he said, remembering the conversation he'd had with Brooke. If worst came to worst in Vegas with Paul, a marriage between him and Tess was their last resort to get this man off their collective backs.

"Does it have anything to do with that man she was engaged to? I think he's a stalker, Will."

"Really." This was not good news.

"Don't say anything to Tess. She's doing well, but she needs time to be away from him, even in her thoughts. Do you know what I mean? And the only reason I'm telling you this is because I want you to be prepared and able to help her. She's been through enough."

"I appreciate it. Tell me more."

"She's right in the car with you, correct?"

"You do have a way of putting things."

"Okay. I'll get to the point. This man is dangerous. Not Charles Manson dangerous—he's not crazy, and your lives aren't in danger. But Tess's emotional life is another matter. He can destroy her if she isn't careful."

"I understand. I'll be sure I check Sugar's food."

"Good. I don't want Tess to think we're talking about her."

"So how's Jack doing? Still seeing that doctor at Kaiser?"

"Of course. When has he ever stopped? Now, what have you heard from this man? Is he hounding Tess?"

"Yes."

"Is she going to meet with him? I'm getting a yes."

"You are correct, once again."

"Somewhere along the road, one of the towns you'll be going through—"

"Yeah, Las Vegas is one of my favorites," he said.

"He's meeting her there?"

"Absolutely."

"Don't leave her alone with him."

"I don't plan on it," Will said.

"It's a matter of pride with this man. He may not want her anymore, but he wants to be able to get back with her and then dump her on his terms. He can't stand being the one who was left."

"That I get loud and clear."

"Give both those furry girls a pat for me and we'll talk tonight."

Will hung up and glanced across at Tess. Her attention was on the road.

"Elaine?" she said.

"The one and only."

"I'm sure she was glad to hear about Sugar."

"And Toby. She wants to meet her."

Tess hesitated, then asked, "Does she do readings for animals?"

"Sure."

"I'm thinking—maybe I should do a reading with Toby to help explain to her what happened and what's going to happen."

"What is going to happen, Tess?"

"I'm not sure, but I do know one thing."

"What's that?"

"I don't think I want to go back to Illinois to live."

This came as a surprise. Will considered this and then asked, "When did you decide this?"

"In the shower this morning. Only I wasn't absolutely sure until I started driving."

"Any idea where you'd like to settle?"

"I think farther west. I haven't seen it yet, but I'll know it when I do."

"That sounds like a good plan," he said, then angled himself back in the passenger seat and closed his eyes. "Let me know when you decide." *And I hope to God it's Los Angeles . . .*

MADELINE studied the clothing she'd piled on her bed. What exactly did you wear for a trip to Las Vegas in which you had to convince your stepdaughter that she was making the mistake of a lifetime? On one level, she wished she could make this little trip on her own, without Paul. It would make it so much easier to knock some sense into Tess's stubborn head.

Madeline examined one outfit, then another, discarding them to one side of the bed as she found them wanting. She had to be ready. She couldn't afford to let emotion take over. She had to be cool, collected, and controlled. Tess would thank her in the end; maybe not in a year, maybe not in ten. But when she finally looked back on her life and realized what generous advice Madeline had given her, what practical advice for ensuring that her life continued on in its ordered way, Madeline was sure of one thing.

Eventually, Tess would thank her.

She took a deep breath and selected one outfit and then another. That is, of course, if Paul didn't let male pride and his considerable ego blow things apart for all of them.

TESS had wondered what she and Will would talk about today, but he seemed more than content to be quiet. And she really didn't mind. It gave her time to relax, to think and dream and watch as the van ate up the miles, bringing them closer and closer to Boulder.

She wanted to see mountains. She was tired of the same flatness she'd seen on this trip thus far. She wanted to see land and rock formations very different from her hometown. She wanted to know she was somewhere else, because she felt as if she were in an entirely different country emotionally.

As Will snoozed in his seat, relaxed, eyes closed, Tess thought about Las Vegas and what she was going to say to Paul. Of course she'd give him the ring back. It was an overblown piece of jewelry, and rather than keep wearing it on her hand, she'd put it on a chain around her neck for safekeeping and to be sure she didn't leave it somewhere or lose it. Subconsciously, it might be just what she wanted to do.

She'd give him the ring back. She'd tell him she had no interest in any sort of a relationship with him. And then—

Then what? Then she'd continue on her way to Los Angeles with Will, and when she got there and spent a few days seeing the sights—

She had absolutely no idea. The one thing she did know was that she didn't want to go home, ever again. Too much had happened, and she had no desire to run into Paul or have to listen to her stepmother go on and on about how she'd messed up her life.

Feeling the need to stretch, she snapped on her blinker and maneuvered the van to the far right lane, preparing to leave the highway.

That seemed to wake up Will. He stretched, yawned, and sat up.

"Hungry?"

"Just needed a stretch. And I'm thinking the dogs could use a walk. This looked like a good place."

"Good choice," he said, glancing around as the van took the exit ramp and started off the main highway.

THEY walked the dogs for almost twenty minutes, and Tess was amazed at how much clearer her head felt when they headed back toward the van. It was a strange stop. The walkways were covered with grasshoppers, as if they'd just fallen out of the sky. Sugar had barked at them, while Toby had almost eaten one before Tess caught her. So they cut their walk short and headed back to the van.

"Well, that was like something out of a horror movie," Tess said.

Will grinned. "Want me to drive?"

She thought for a moment and almost answered "no" reflexively. He probably wanted to rest some more. He looked tired, and he'd done most of the driving up until this point, so maybe he needed to rest—

"What do you really want, Tess?" he said softly.

"I—could you drive? I was thinking I'd love to dig out the sweater I'm working on and knit for a while."

"Sure." He walked away from her, letting Sugar sniff at one more tree, and Tess marveled that it actually was this easy. That there were men out there who didn't turn every single thing a woman did into an accusation that she wasn't spending enough time paying attention to him.

Wonderful.

Toby pranced along beside her as she gave her dog one more little run and then they all climbed back into the van and shut the doors. And as Tess reached for her knitting, she realized that these were the moments in which she'd remake her life, one decision at a time.

She just had to be careful that she didn't assume every new man in her life was going to be like Paul.

As Will started up the van and the dogs settled down in their crates, Tess took her sweater out of her tote bag and thought for a moment, looking at the stitches and remembering where she was in the pattern.

"That's a beautiful piece of work," Will said.

"Thanks."

"Something you clearly love to do."

"My grandmother taught me when I was eight, and I just never stopped. I think the first few things I designed were sweaters for my stuffed animals."

"I'm sure they looked very handsome."

"They were a lot of fun." She picked up her free knitting needle and got to work. She couldn't remember an afternoon she'd enjoyed more.

eleven

THEIR LAST FULL day in Nebraska came to a close at around eight that evening. Tess couldn't believe how gorgeous the sunset was and convinced Will to stop so she could take several pictures before they drove on. Brooke, thinking of everything as usual, had thrown a disposable camera into her tote bag.

Earlier in the day Will had used his laptop to find an animal-friendly motel and called ahead to reserve their rooms. When all four of them were settled in, Tess wanted nothing so much as to simply crash. Yet even as she lay in bed, Toby beside her, she was excited and couldn't really fall asleep. She'd be seeing Charlie tomorrow, and that made her happy.

She'd written to him for a while after he'd left home. For the first three years he'd been gone, he had no e-mail, so regular letters had been the way to go. He hadn't even had a regular phone—or electricity. Though her father had thought his second son was insane, Charlie had been perfectly happy in a cabin in the middle of the Colorado woods, compete with an outhouse and a huge fireplace as the only real source of heat.

When Tess remembered those letters she'd written and the sporadic notes Charlie had sent back, she recalled him telling her that he had decided to "do a Walden Pond," go into the wilderness and find himself. This had included living close to nature, being a ski instructor during the winter season, and working construction the rest of the time.

She'd forgotten the part about him finding himself, and remembering it gave her comfort. Maybe Charlie, at one time in his life, had been as confused as she was. Maybe her older brother would have some words of wisdom she could apply to her own life.

As excited as she was at the thought of seeing her favorite brother again, Tess finally found her eyes fluttering shut. She'd merely pulled off her clothes and put on a large, soft T-shirt. She hadn't even really washed her face or brushed her teeth. For some reason, this very ordinary day had totally exhausted her, and she didn't resist as she slipped into sleep.

•

WILL couldn't sleep.

He was waiting for Elaine's call, that was certainly part of it. And if she didn't call in the next thirty minutes, he'd call her. He was usually a man who let things unfold in the time that was needed, but he was finding that he didn't have a whole lot of patience when the subject was Tess.

He found himself wanting to know what was going to happen next, like the times he'd read the endings of books before even starting them. His mother and sisters had never understood that impulse, and he wasn't sure he could have explained it himself. There were just times when he needed to know.

The soft sound of his cell phone vibrating against the surface of the bedside table brought him out of his thoughts.

"Elaine," he said as he answered.

"The one and only," she replied. "How was the driving today?"

"Good. We covered a lot of ground. We should be in Boulder tomorrow afternoon."

"Then dinner with your friends?"

"Yeah, Brooke's brother Ron and Tess's brother Charlie. But we need to talk about Tess."

"You sound impatient," she said, a hint of laughter in her voice.

He sighed. He couldn't hide anything from this woman, and he didn't even know why he tried.

"How soon can I make a move on Tess?"

Elaine simply laughed, then said, "I knew it. I *knew* it!"

"I know I'm rushing things," Will said. "She's been through hell. But I don't want to be one of those guys who doesn't act and then finds out she's hooked up with someone else. I don't want to miss my chance!"

"You know my two beliefs about relationships," she said.

"Yeah. When in doubt, talk it out, and honesty is always the best policy."

"How well you remember. I'm impressed."

"How can I talk to her about this?"

He could hear her thinking over the phone and then she said, "I wouldn't say anything before the dinner tomorrow night. Let her have the time with her brother. I get the feeling that they were the two odd ones out in the family—do you know what I mean?"

"Yes."

"But he managed to escape and carve out a whole new life for himself."

"I know. He and Ron have done really well."

"And she didn't."

"It's a whole other world out there, Elaine, nothing like California. Men and women are still held to very different standards."

"And they don't do the same thing here in L.A.?"

"You know what I mean."

"Yes, I do. Expectations are a lot more relaxed out here. There's more freedom."

Will sighed and stretched out on his bed. "I get the feeling that she was pretty sheltered. I had that feeling about Tess when I was in high school. She'd come around the house to be with Brooke, and she always struck me as shy. But I liked her. And when I first saw her at the club, I felt like someone had punched me in the stomach."

"When it hits, it hits hard. Why do you think I got married four times?"

He had to laugh, but when he stopped, Will said, "Spoken like a true Aquarius. But we need to stay on track and talk about Vegas." Briefly, he told her what he and Brooke had discussed, including their idea for a Plan B should they need one.

"*That's* what I was picking up, the thing about your getting married. So it wouldn't be a real marriage?"

Will couldn't keep the smile out of his voice. "Maybe I could do a little negotiating with her."

"So you're sure she's the one?"

"It's always been that way with the men in my family— when we know, we *know*. And I know."

"She'll need a little time to catch up, but not much."

"That's good to hear. Anything else?"

"That stepmother of hers is dangerous. There's something in this marriage for her, something she gets out of it, and it has nothing to do with whether or not Tess will be happy. What I'm getting is that it will be what the father wishes. He wants this marriage to go forward. And she—the stepmother, I mean—will get points in her husband's eyes for making sure everything goes off the way it was planned."

"There's something else," Will said.

Elaine hesitated. "Will, I'm getting this feeling—what about marrying her before she meets up with Paul? Could you do that?"

"Do you really think Tess is going to cave that quickly?"

"They've got some pretty powerful and despicable ammunition—guilt, family responsibility. Tess is just getting out of the habit of pleasing everyone but herself. I don't know if she's strong enough to defy the two of them."

"The stepmother is coming along with Paul?" Will couldn't believe what he was hearing.

"She's not going to let him screw this up. The stakes are way too high for her. This is what I need you to be aware of, Will. These two aren't playing around. They want what they want, and Tess's happiness has nothing to do with any of it."

This new information was so foreign to Will's concept of family that he had trouble digesting it.

"So she's really nothing to either of them but a means to an end."

"Yes. Don't be misguided by thinking that they have the same emotions you and I do, or Tess does. Don't go there, and don't be naive—you can't afford it. They're coming out to Vegas with one thing in mind—to get Tess to go back on that plane with them and marry Paul. They won't even need the big blowout wedding—at this point, that woman would settle for a justice of the peace and total damage control."

"Unbelievable," Will said softly. "I have to be sure she's aware of this before we hit Vegas."

"That would be wise, Will."

"And as for how I feel about her?"

"That, you'll have to use your intuition."

"I'll marry her in Boulder," he said.

"It's easier in Vegas. But I wouldn't use the marriage as your Plan B. You can't wait that long. If I were you, I'd have it all locked and loaded before those two snakes hit the Strip."

"Really."

"Really. I have a very bad feeling about both of them. Please tell me you're hearing this, Will. I like Tess already, even though I've never met her. I like her so much because of what Toby's shown me. That dog simply adores her."

"I know." He thought for a moment, then said, "I'm going to call Brooke and tell her to fly in a day before they do. She can help me convince Tess to marry me. For her own protection."

"That ex-fiancé of hers is enough of a coward that he won't go poaching another man's wife if he thinks that man might give him trouble."

"And I would," Will said.

"And the stepmother might blow a gasket, but she'll have to respect the fact that you're married to Tess. If they take her away from you, you have legal grounds to go after them."

"You think they'd try it?" This whole thing seemed to be spiraling out of control. He was getting a definite sick feeling in his stomach.

"They both had a lot riding on this marriage. I'm simply advising you not to underestimate either of them. They're two spoiled narcissists who are used to getting their own way. They're not going to like the way this is going to turn out if you pull the wedding card on them."

"Got it."

"And Will?"

"Yeah?"

"Don't leave Tess alone. That stepmother has been getting inside her head, into her emotions, and messing with her since she was a teenager. Do not underestimate the power this woman has and how she'll use it."

"I hear you, Elaine."

"Now, how's my fluffy girl?"

"Snoozing on the edge of the bed, out like a light. She and Toby had some spectacular walks today along with their French toast."

Elaine laughed. "I'm glad those two girls are having some adventures."

They said their good-byes, and Will lay back on the bed and considered these new developments. He had no doubt Elaine was right in her assessments of Paul's and Madeline's characters. She'd never been wrong before in a reading, and from the little time he'd spent on the phone with these two con artists, he knew they were stunningly self-centered.

Knowing that he had to make plans, he phoned Brooke. She picked up on the second ring. Quickly, he filled her in with all the information Elaine had given him.

"I don't know how she does what she does, but she's dead on! Those two would sell their own mothers down the river if it meant they could make a little more money or get a little more status. It's like a sickness with them. And yes,

I think I should come in a day early. I can be one of your witnesses."

"Do you think Tess will go for it?"

"All we can do is lay it out on the table for her and let her make the decision. But I agree with Elaine—let her have the dinner with her brother and Ron. Let her have some fun. Paul kept her on a pretty tight leash. Maybe if she gets a taste of what the world is like without Paul, and what other men are like, she won't be in such a big hurry to get back to him."

"You think she would?" The thought had genuinely never occurred to him.

"Women have done crazier things. I'm with Elaine. I think those two have an emotional hold on Tess."

"Okay." Summing up, he gave her the date he thought they would arrive in Vegas.

"I still can't believe Madeline's coming with Paul," Brooke said just before they ended their call. "What will do those two in, and the reason they're going to lose, is that they don't trust each other. They're like a couple of reptiles, so cold-blooded that they'll end up turning on each other and tearing each other apart to get what they want."

"I couldn't agree more," Will said.

"COLORADO today," said Tess as they walked out to the van. "I'm so excited I can't stand it. I've never seen the Rockies."

Her excitement made Will smile. He'd traveled all over the world and had to admit that there were times he'd felt jaded. Seeing it all through Tess's eyes was fun.

They'd hit the road early, before seven, and had stopped at a convenience store for coffee and doughnuts—not the healthiest breakfast two days in a row, but a speedy one. Will could feel her impatience to get going, to get to the next bend in the road of their adventure. Her excitement was contagious.

The dogs were becoming regular road trip experts. They both bounded into their crates without protest, though they kept their eyes out for any bits of food that might come their way. And of course, their beloved rest stops.

"Nothing can top those grasshoppers yesterday," Tess said, scratching Toby's ear before she shut the steel mesh door to her crate.

"Oh, I don't know," Will said. "What about a cow? Or a buffalo?"

"We'd see something like that?"

"Maybe even deer. Or elk."

"Oh my God! Toby, Sugar, keep your eyes peeled."

"Or in their cases, their noses."

Will started the van's engine. He had only one thought on his mind, thanks to his talk with Elaine last night. Today was for Tess. They were going to have a completely fun day, culminating in a dinner with two of their favorite people in the world. There had been too much sadness on Tess's plate—it was time she had some fun.

"COLORADO state line," Will said and grinned as Tess craned her head to see the roadside sign. It was just before noon, and the sun was high in the sky.

"But it's still flat! It looks just like Nebraska! Where are the mountains?"

"You'll see mountains, don't worry." He glanced at the plastic bag full of candy and chips at her feet. "Stocking up like we're going through the Donner Pass—is there something I should know?"

"I just thought I'd be prepared so we wouldn't have to stop as much. I even got some dog biscuits."

Biscuits was the magic word, and both Sugar and Toby put up a racket, shamelessly begging until Tess gave each of them a peanut butter and molasses dog treat.

As the dogs crunched along, Will turned his attention back to the road, Tess got out her knitting, and the miles flew by.

THEY'D barely stopped for a late lunch, just some subs at a family-owned shop. The sandwiches had been incredible and enormous—both Sugar and Toby had shared with them. They'd eaten in the car as they'd continued to drive because Will had sensed that Tess wanted to get there in a hurry. Perhaps she wanted to talk to her brother about something. He probably knew her better than anyone except Brooke. The only thing they'd stopped to do was pick some burrs out of Sugar's and Toby's fur.

"Do you think people can change?" she asked him suddenly as she folded away the sandwich wrappings and put them in the large brown paper bag that had held their subs.

"Their basic characters?" Will replied.

"I guess so."

"I think character basically remains the same. If you're a decent person, you stay a decent person. But anyone can certainly change the way they respond to life."

She was silent for so long he wondered if he'd hurt her feelings.

"Tess? You okay?"

"It's just—I've been doing a lot of soul-searching on this trip, and—I don't really like the person I've become. The choices I've made." She lowered her voice. "I feel like I've been pretty stupid."

"We've all been there."

"You're not just saying that?" she asked.

"I wouldn't insult your intelligence."

"So you've gone through periods of your life when you didn't think much of yourself or the choices you'd made?" Tess insisted.

"Sure. The main thing is, can you see what you've done that's kind of—how can I say this—gotten you off your path? Most of the time, when I've felt I wasn't doing the right thing or making the right decisions, it came down to a feeling that things just weren't right, or a real sense of unhappiness. Emptiness."

"Exactly," she replied.

"So I always had to sort of do detective work, go backward and try to find out what had happened, where I'd gone wrong, where I'd taken that first misstep. There were a few times in my life when I had to go back years to understand certain patterns and how they weren't working for me."

She laughed, and he heard the shaky sound.

"Okay, what's up?"

"Try going back to your teens," she said quietly. He didn't like the tired resignation in her tone.

"What does that mean?"

She kept her gaze on the road unfolding ahead of them. "I think it was right after my parents got a divorce that I decided I'd always take the safe road." She hesitated and then said, "I just didn't want to hurt anymore."

"I can understand that."

"But I think that in making that choice, I've missed out on a lot."

"Every choice involves missing out on one thing or another. Making a choice, by definition, negates all the other things you thought you might do. It's hard. I always feel as if there isn't enough time in life to do all I want to do."

"I haven't done anything," she muttered.

"That can't be true," he said.

"I mean I haven't really done anything that mattered to me. On any level."

He hesitated, then said, "You seem to really enjoy knitting."

"It's just a hobby."

"I think it's more than that to you. It seems more like a passion, like collecting guitars is for me."

She considered this, but before she could answer, he said, "And you rescued Toby from a short and probably very frightening life. That's something you can be immensely proud of."

He glanced at her and saw tears welling in her eyes. He also knew she was trying not to let him see them. So he wouldn't. He'd give her that little bit of dignity, of personal privacy and respect.

"Does that make sense?" he said, focusing intently on his driving while he saw her, out of the corner of his eye, reach for one of the napkins from the sub shop. She dabbed at her eyes furtively.

"Yeah. There was never a doubt in my mind that I was going to rescue her."

"And you did," he said, keeping his tone mild. "And that's what I mean by character. You have great character, Tess, and it will see you through this difficult time. You're stronger than you think you are. And smarter."

"How can you say that?" The question sounded slightly strangled, as if she were trying to keep intense emotion out of her voice.

"Because you told me that the night before your wedding you sensed something was wrong. That's smart, listening to your intuition. Because when you discovered that Paul was with another woman, you didn't beg him to come back to you. You made up your mind and took action. That's smart and shows that you have self-respect. And because you were wise enough to decide to take this trip, to take some time out from your life, and try to figure out your next move."

She stayed silent, staring straight ahead, but he sensed she'd heard him.

"Sometimes, Tess, the smartest thing a person can do is to just realize they have a problem. You'd be amazed how many people don't even take that first step."

"I didn't. For a long time, I didn't."

"But you eventually did." He smiled, concentrating on the road. "Now, don't get mad at me, but you're actually at a relatively young age to make all these discoveries about yourself. Think of all the people in their fifties and sixties who wake up and realize that the life they lived wasn't the one they wanted."

She thought about this. He could tell.

"You're barely thirty, Tess. Believe me, you have plenty of time to put things right. But you need to trust yourself to know what's right for you. Don't ever give that power away to anyone, ever again. Keep it close to you, and really listen to what that little voice inside of you says. I know from experience that it never steers you wrong."

She took a breath, and he could tell she was still struggling with emotion.

"What if it's telling me nothing right now?"

"I've had those moments. They're damn frustrating. And the only remedy is just patience. I mean, there isn't any reason that you have to make all your decisions concerning the rest of your life right now, is there?"

He saw her nod her head out of the corner of his eye.

"I think you may be right, Will."

"It's one of the hardest things in the world, to get a

sense of inner direction. It's so much easier to just live on the surface, doing everything on a very superficial level. Skating along on the top, not thinking or feeling deeply, letting other people make your major decisions. You'd be surprised how many people choose to live that way."

"I feel so foolish, as if I just gave myself away."

"You're not a shallow person, Tess. Like I said before, you have an essentially good character. It wasn't a reluctance to feel emotion that led you down that path you were on."

"Then what did?" she asked him, and he could hear the little bit of challenge in her voice. It didn't seem as if she was looking for a fight, but he could sense the slight bit of defensiveness in her.

"Do you want my opinion?"

"I'd be curious, yes."

"I think you wanted to be loved. And it's not something a lot of other people don't do, every single day. Very few families give their members unconditional love. In fact, the masters of that sort of love generally have a furry body and a wet tongue, like our friends on the seat behind us."

Tess laughed at that, grateful for the diversion and scared she might cry at how close to the mark he was. And she wondered at the fact that, in a matter of days, she was talking with this man on a deeper level than she ever had with Paul. And it wasn't about whether she loved purple or green or how many children she wanted.

He understood her.

"That was exactly it," she said, her voice flat. She felt dull and lifeless and overwhelmed.

"Good for you."

"For what?"

"For seeing the truth and meeting it head-on."

"Yeah, like I was able to do that before."

"Don't do that to yourself, Tess." He hesitated and then said, "Do you mind if I ask you a very personal question?"

She thought of answering back, "Why stop now?" but then decided Will didn't deserve her bitchiness. He was being a good friend, a good sounding board, helping her through this difficult time.

"Okay," she said cautiously.

"What happened to your mother after the divorce? Why didn't she get custody of the three of you? Why did you all remain with your father and his new wife?"

She was in extremely dangerous emotional territory here. "He had the money. And he cut her off completely so she didn't. He had a powerhouse lawyer. She couldn't afford representation, so the court gave her a guy who was okay but no match for the team my father hired. They painted a picture of her as an incompetent mother, a hippie, and it stuck. By the time his team was done with her, anyone would have awarded him his children."

"My God," Will said softly, thinking of the total emotional wreckage of a family one man's need for revenge had caused. "Was your mother seeing someone else before the divorce?"

"No." The word came out of Tess's mouth in a short and bitter sound. "I knew my father was having an affair because I picked up the phone and heard him talking to Madeline. My mother—they weren't getting along at the time, but she had no idea that a divorce was imminent."

"And the three of you were used as pawns."

"I think my dad already had Brian pretty brainwashed. He was like my dad in a lot of ways, wanted to go into the same line of work, always interested in how things looked to other people. He desperately wanted Dad's and Madeline's approval. Charlie just marked time until he could get out. He left home barely days after graduation."

"You must have missed him terribly." He could picture the way it must have been for Tess. Charlie had been the one member of her family she could relate to. After he'd left, she'd been alone with the rest of them and like none of them. Adrift and alone, it must have hurt like hell.

"I did. I wanted to go with him. I wish I had."

They were silent for a time, and then Tess said, "I think the reason I despise myself the most is that it was easier to just go along for the ride. It was easier to say yes instead of fighting with my stepmother every step of the way. She was just a person who demanded complete control, complete capitulation. What you ate, what you wore, where you went, who you saw, how it looked—"

"Do you think she had Paul picked out for you from the start?" He had to plant this thought in her mind, had to make sure she saw her ex-fiancé and her stepmother for who they truly were. He had a feeling he already knew the answer. People like Madeline never left anything to chance.

Tess sighed, and he'd never heard such a tired and defeated sound in his entire life. "Oh, I wouldn't be surprised."

A flash of anger unsettled Will, but he kept his emotions firmly under control. He wanted to help her, but he was no help to her if he indulged in a fit of temper. So much for a fun day for Tess, so much for keeping things light. But he realized that she needed a sounding board. She was working out some pretty difficult stuff. And she was doing it all at once, after her life had blown up in her face.

"You're on the right path," he said.

"I hope so," she whispered. "In my heart—in my heart I wanted a big adventure, but I was always too much of a coward to go after one."

"Hey," he said, mock offended. "And what do you call this?"

"Oh, I didn't mean—"

"And who made the phone call at around four in the morning that started this whole thing—"

"I guess it was—"

"Yeah, I really had to wrestle your ass into this van, you were so dead set against going—"

And then Tess was laughing. The sound made Will surprisingly happy.

twelve

TESS SLEPT THE entire way into Boulder, truly exhausted. She woke when she felt the van slow and sat up, realizing they were pulling into a Sonic drive-in.

"Where are we?"

"Boulder. Just on the outskirts. You missed some deer, a buffalo, and some prairie dogs, but I thought you needed the sleep more."

"What?"

She must have had an outraged look on her face, because Will laughed and said, "I'm sure Ron and Charlie know where all the good wildlife are. We'll see more."

"What did the girls do?"

"Sugar barked at the buffalo—I'm surprised she didn't wake you. Toby just stared. But she liked the deer, and they both wanted to eat a prairie dog. Do you want anything? I thought it was time for a snack—plain hamburger okay for Toby?"

The look her dog gave her as she climbed into the front

passenger seat was so beseeching Tess had to relent. "And a chocolate shake for me."

"Oh ho, this really *is* a vacation."

"No comments from you."

"I know my place, and I stick to it," he said, grinning.

Will placed the order with that precise British accent, but the sounds coming out of the drive-in speaker were anything but audible. It sounded as if the woman speaking was part of a *Star Wars* movie and discussing their order in an alien tongue. It didn't help that Sugar heard the word *hamburger* and began to bark her approval.

Will finally gave up and said, "Fine, that's it," and then turned toward Tess and said, "I guess it's Sonic Surprise for us!"

She had to laugh. "Ah, it's not that bad a place to order a mystery meal. There's not much on the menu that's bad."

"True."

Amazingly enough, their order was perfect, just what they'd asked for. Will had ordered a huge hamburger with every condiment known to man on it, along with a jumbo order of fries and a Coke. Tess snuck a few fries dipped in ketchup, but only after asking.

"Charlie called. He's thrilled to death that you're here."

"He is?"

"Don't look so surprised."

"It's just—been too long. Did he remember I was supposed to be getting married this weekend?"

"Do men ever remember things like that?"

"Point taken. Okay, can we not mention the fact that I'm supposed to be on my honeymoon?"

"I think that can be arranged."

"I'm having more fun with you, anyway," she said, smiling up at him and wondering how she'd gotten the nerve to just come out and say it, just like that.

"I'm flattered."

His eyes were intent, his expression warm. She held his gaze as long as she could and then looked back out the passenger side window. A short silence reigned until Will said, "Help me give Toby her hamburger."

She broke it into bite-sized pieces for her dog and then they left the drive-in's parking lot and pulled over to the side of the lot where they walked both dogs on a very short strip of grass. The Keeshond stared up at Will with an expression of disgust on her furry face.

"Sugar's giving me a look that clearly says, 'So where are all those buffalo?'"

Tess had to laugh. After all their rest stop adventures, this small piece of grass had to be somewhat anti-climactic.

"But just think, Sugar, you got a hamburger."

On the magic word, Sugar barked once, then twice, and then wagged her curly Nordic tail and looked up at both of them expectantly. Toby, watching her friend, sat down next to her and gazed up at the two of them.

"Maybe a B-I-S-C-U-I-T when we—"

"No good," Will said over Sugar's excited barking. "That's one word she knows how to spell."

THEY stopped at a huge Barnes and Noble bookstore next to a Whole Foods Market. Will and the two dogs claimed an outside table while Tess went inside and bought them both fruit smoothies from the juice bar.

When she came out, she saw a stocky, middle-aged man dressed in khakis, a red plaid shirt, and a forest green apron next to their table, organic dog biscuits in hand.

"And this is Sugar?" he said, handing the Keeshond one of the biscuits.

"She'll love you forever," Will said and then he caught sight of Tess and winked.

"And here's one for Toby," the man said. "We love dogs at Whole Foods."

"And these two have died and think they've gone to heaven," Will said. "First hamburgers, then two biscuits in a row!"

"Thank you—" Tess glanced at the nametag. "Thank you, Rick. That was really sweet of you."

"My pleasure. Here's a coupon for a box of them—half off if you decide to try them today."

"Smart salesman," Will remarked as the man walked away. "Get the dogs hooked, and you've got your sale."

"You make him sound like a biscuit pusher!"

"My point exactly."

Tess leaned back in her chair, enjoying herself. Boulder had a distinct feel to it. Lots of dogs on leashes, people with backpacks and rugged boots, and all their clothing looked like they were ready for a hike in the woods. It was a living ad for Lands' End or Eddie Bauer. Boulder seemed to have that vibe of a college town and a very outdoorsy place, with all sorts of interesting stores, coffeehouses, and a young, vibrant population.

"I could live here," Tess said almost to herself.

"Wait till you see the Pacific," Will said.

"Oh, I don't know if I could afford Los Angeles."

"There are ways around it," he said.

He probably knew them all. Being a musician, playing in a band, he probably had to make every penny count. That whole starving artist thing was a lifestyle Will probably knew too well. But she found that she liked being with him a whole lot more than going out with Paul, who threw around his money in an attempt to impress anyone and everyone.

Will's cell phone rang, and he answered it.

"Hey, Ron!"

Tess sat back in the sun and simply relaxed. The last few weeks before the wedding had been so jam-packed with activity that she hadn't had a chance to just sit and do nothing. She'd forgotten how much she'd missed it.

"Sounds good," Will was saying. Both dogs had their leashes fastened to his chair and were sprawled at his feet after their biscuitfest, so Tess indicated that she was going to go next door to the bookstore. Will nodded his head and continued to talk to Ron. She gave both Sugar and Toby a pat on the head, told them where she was going, and headed toward the Barnes and Noble.

INSIDE the bookstore, Tess realized how long it had been since she'd had a day to browse, to look, to just play. Of course she glanced through the crafts section and found a wonderful hardcover book crammed with knit and crochet sweater patterns, one more beautiful than the next. Then she picked up a couple of paperback mysteries by a favorite author and glanced through the self-help aisle.

What she wanted was something along the lines of "Just Dumped—What Do You Do Now?" She ended up with a book that promised to relieve stress through a combination of biofeedback, massage, guided breathing, meditation, and visualization, with some yoga thrown in.

"Cover all my bases," she muttered as she brought them up to the register. She also bought the current CD from one of her favorite British bands, thinking they could listen to music while they drove. That and a couple of magazines finished her shopping spree.

She bought a decaf caramel latte at the coffee bar and a blueberry scone and then headed outside and back to their table in front of the Whole Foods Market.

Will was still on his cell. When he saw her, he wound up the conversation and ended the call.

"Ron said to go get our room, get settled, take showers, whatever we want to do. They're thinking dinner at around eight tonight. I got directions to the steak house."

"But we'll get off to a late start tomorrow," Tess said, suddenly worried. She was conscious of the fact that he would be much farther along on his trip if he hadn't allowed her to have her mini-breakdown back in Iowa.

He touched her forehead gently. "No furrows here, no frowning. I figured that because you haven't seen your brother in a while, we might stay in Boulder an extra day. Ron said something about a hike tomorrow after brunch and then we could go up to Charlie's cabin."

Perfect. She hadn't even realized she'd wanted more time with Charlie until Will had laid out the whole plan. But she knew that a hurried dinner wouldn't be enough.

A whole day was a gift.

"Thank you."

"Don't mention it."

"Do you have a place to stay in mind?"

"Just let me take a look at my trusty laptop, find something animal friendly." He glanced up at her. "Unless you want to risk spending the night at either Ron's or Charlie's bachelor digs."

She could barely repress a shudder at the thought of using an outhouse in the dead of night. Who knew what bugs and spiders might lurk in the small building? She loved nature, but not that much.

"Ah, no. Whatever you pick will be great."

AFTER some deep breathing, a few yoga stretches, and a hot shower, Tess felt like a new woman. Studying herself in the bathroom mirror, she thought she might go wild and have some highlights done when they reached Las Vegas. For some reason, she didn't want to look like the same woman who had left her small town in Illinois. She wanted to shock Paul and show him how far she'd come in just a few days. More than that, she wanted to let him know he was no longer the big boss.

"Almost ready?" Will called from outside the bathroom.

"Just about."

The only place he'd been able to find that allowed animals had only had one second-floor room with two double beds. Tess hadn't even balked. She felt safe with Will. There was something about him that was comforting, even if she did find herself studying him whenever he wasn't looking.

She knew he wasn't the sort of man to take advantage of the situation. The thought had never even crossed her mind. Well, it had, but if Will ever made a move on her, Tess would welcome his advances. She'd already had some extremely interesting daydreams about him. Both of them had had starring roles, and clothing had definitely been optional.

"Okay, ready," she said, opening the bathroom door. She'd dressed with care for this dinner, blowing her hair dry, applying her makeup in a more glamorous way, and wearing a rust-colored mid-calf-length skirt with an autumn-hued, multicolored hand-knit sweater and a pair of brown boots.

"You look great," he said, and she warmed to the knowledge that he noticed.

"So do you." Will had showered before her and now wore jeans, a blue chambray shirt, his leather jacket, and boots.

"Is the place we're going dressy?" she said.

"Ron said it's more of a local hangout. I'm sure what you have on is fine." He glanced at the two dogs. "Okay, guys, into your crates." When they were both safely inside, he turned the television on to the Food Network, the volume on low, and left just one of the bedside lamps on.

"That's thoughtful of you, to angle their creates so they can watch each other and the television."

"Why not let them have a night, too?"

The last thing Tess saw before she left the room was Toby's contented little face as she stared adoringly at Sugar.

DAN'S Steak House was a local hangout, with a rustic bar that wouldn't have been out of place on the set of the HBO show *Deadwood*. Their hostess said they could wait in the bar, and Tess was halfway through a glass of very good white wine when she looked up and saw her brother Charlie striding through the room toward her.

She put down her wine glass and met him a little less than halfway, hugging him tightly as he hugged her right back.

"Hey, you look great!" Charlie said, giving her a quick visual inspection.

"So do you. Sunburned," she said, touching his cheek. He'd always been tall, with hair the same dark brown as hers and light hazel eyes with eyelashes to die for. She could see where months of construction work had built solid muscle, but there was something more to her brother. He had a quality about him she couldn't quite define. Or maybe she could. It felt like a deep, deep contentment with life. She sensed that he knew his place in the world and was happy with it.

He'd found a real life for himself.

"Sunburn. An occupational hazard. I've gotta get one of those higher SPF sunscreens. Hey, Will!" Then he and Will embraced, clapping each other on the back.

"Where's Ron?"

"On his way. Oh, and he's bringing this girl he met. Terri. I think it may finally be serious."

"Ron?" Will said.

"I know, I know, the one who swore he'd never get hitched. I say the more they protest, the harder they fall. Why don't we go ahead and get a table?"

They'd ordered drinks and appetizers when Ron showed up. He had Brooke's same red hair and green eyes and was a tall, lean man with an easy smile. The woman with him was a petite brunette. One look at them together, and Tess knew this could be serious.

"Gotta get the steak," Charlie said. "It's what they're famous for. Unless, of course, you have a hankering for buffalo."

Tess wrinkled her nose. "They're too cute."

"And cows aren't?"

"*Now* I feel at home," Ron said and raised his glass. "Here's to old friends, best friends, and keeping in touch." He turned toward Will. "How'd you know where to find me?"

"I paid a quick visit to your mom and dad."

"And you just decided to come along?" Ron said to Tess. "Is Will going to drop you off in Vegas or L.A. and then you'll fly home?"

She opened her mouth to reply and heard Will say, "She's coming all the way to the Pacific, and I'm going to show her around the city for a few days."

Her heart sped up; her stomach started to flutter in a very good way. Tess didn't know why, but she'd thought that perhaps when they reached their final destination and handed Elaine her van and her dog, he'd want to be rid of her. And as she didn't really know anyone in Los Angeles, she would have had no choice but to fly directly home. Sightseeing on her own had never been one of her strengths or anything that she'd found appealing. It was so much more fun with a friend.

It would be so much fun with Will.

"Sounds like a plan," Ron said.

Tess talked with Terri and discovered she was a ski instructor, just like Ron and Charlie. She'd met Ron on the slopes, when they'd both been skiing on their off time and had literally crashed into each other.

"When men say that they meet a woman and see stars, they aren't kidding," Ron said, and Terri laughed.

"So what did you think of this guy when you met him?" Will said, ribbing Ron.

"Was I impressed with his technique?" Terri replied, and Charlie started to laugh. "Once we got up and dusted the snow off and he offered to buy me a Hot Toddy, I was extremely impressed."

"Right answer," Ron said.

The evening passed with much talking and laughter. As Tess covertly watched Ron and Terri, she got a real sense of what a good match they were—comfortable, but with a definite sexual spark. He treated her as if he cherished her and wanted to be with her, not as if he had to impress her in any way. And Tess realized, more than ever, what a poor match she and Paul had been.

In a strange kind of way, it made her relieved she hadn't married him. Less than a week after she'd thought her world had bottomed out, she found herself happy.

A steak house in the middle of Boulder, Colorado, with three men she'd known since grade school and one very interesting woman. A rowdy dinner, terrific food, and lots of laughter and good-natured teasing. It wasn't the planned-for honeymoon in the Barbados—this was so much better.

They stayed at their table for almost two and a half hours, from appetizers through the main course, then huge helpings of a spectacular dessert called Chocolate Suicide Cake. As Tess polished off the last bite, Charlie said, "Just like at home. She ate like a horse and never gained an ounce."

"Charlie!" Tess said and felt herself flush.

"I like a healthy appetite in a woman," Will said, immediately putting her at ease.

After paying the bill and leaving their waitress a generous tip, they walked out into the parking lot, turning up their jacket and coat collars against the cold night air. They discussed where they would meet tomorrow and what they would do. Charlie told them to bring the dogs; they could meet his black Lab, Sadie.

"This won't be one of those fifteen-mile, torturous endurance hikes, will it?" Tess asked Terri. The pretty brunette laughed and assured her she wouldn't let either Charlie or Ron make things too difficult.

Tess hugged Charlie tightly before letting him go and then watched as he got into his black pickup truck. He drove off into the night, and she turned her attention back to Ron and Terri, still talking with Will.

"No later than nine," Ron was saying. "We want to get off to a great start."

Tess stood by the van as Ron and Terri walked away. He put his arm around her and pulled her close, and her arm came up around his waist. Something in Tess's throat tightened as she wondered if she would ever experience what those two had.

"A good match," Will said softly from behind her.

"Yeah. I'm happy for him."

"Now we have to get to work on Charlie," he said.

"I wonder why he doesn't have someone in his life."

"How do you know he doesn't? Maybe he just wanted this evening with you."

"Hmmm."

They got in the van, and Will started the engine. After a few minutes he turned on the heat. "Cold?"

"I'm fine. You?"

"I'm one of those thin-blooded Angelenos, not tough like you Midwesterners."

"Oh, please!"

"It's true. I don't know that I'd ever want to live in a cold climate again. We get spoiled out on the West Coast."

"I can understand that."

"Fasten your seatbelt," he said. "We have two pooches to walk before we can settle in for the night."

THAT evening, quietly lying in bed, Tess played the entire evening over in her mind.

She'd loved seeing Charlie. And she wondered why it had taken her so long to get out to see him. Even Brooke had visited her brother Ron and come back with news from Charlie, how both men were doing, what they were up to. Brooke's parents made a point of going out there once a year for a week or so, and once in a while, Ron had come back for Christmas.

Charlie never had. She couldn't blame him. It couldn't be easy to contemplate facing both her father's and Brian's scorn. In their eyes, being just a ski instructor and supplementing that income with construction made Charlie little more than a bum. He probably hadn't wanted to come home for any holidays because he hadn't wanted to hear it.

He'd gone his own way, followed his own heart, and the

results had been fabulous. He looked happy. At peace. And Tess found that she wanted what he had. Not the cabin with the outhouse and the skiing, but the feeling, that sense of knowing you were doing what was right with your life. Not right in the eyes of others, but right for you. The perfect fit.

She sighed and, as quietly as possible, adjusted her position on her bed. Toby moved in her sleep, her little legs running for a moment as she chased something in her dreams. Tess could hear Sugar's soft doggy snores across the small space dividing her bed from Will's. She could hear his breathing, deep and even.

She thought about it all, how strange life was. That she and Brooke had gone out to their favorite bar and run into Will. That he should have given her his number. That she just chanced to stop by her church on the way home to ask for guidance, a sign, and had caught Paul cheating on her with Marti. That she'd had time to go to his house and rescue Toby, clear out all her possessions, and head over to Brooke's. And that when she'd reached for her keys, the scrap of paper with Will's phone number had come out with them.

Looking back, all those events, while seeming chaotic at the time, had followed each other smoothly, in perfect progression. Her only thought had been to get away, to find a private place where no one could find her where she could lick her wounds in peace. And amazingly, Will had afforded her that privacy, along with a wonderful road trip, a feeling of freedom, and now the time to see her brother.

It was enough to give her a little faith in the way the universe worked. She'd been on autopilot from the moment she'd seen Paul with Marti until she'd finished her mini-breakdown and they'd finally hit the road again. But she found that she didn't feel as jumbled, as blown apart. It

felt as if the pieces of her soul were slowly knitting themselves together again, taking a different form, a different
shape. And she had a feeling when all of this was over, she
was going to be at peace with the woman she'd become.
And would like that woman a lot.

IT was much harder sleeping in the same room with Tess
than Will had thought it would be. Yes, he considered himself a gentleman, a man who genuinely liked women. It
would have never crossed his mind to take advantage of
such a situation. But that didn't mean he couldn't have his
private thoughts.

He'd even dreamed of her the last two nights in a row—
some awfully vivid dreams starring the two of them, a bed,
and not much in the way of clothing. The dogs were somewhere else, in that convenient way of dreams, and it had
been just him and Tess, total intensity, getting to know each
other in the most primal way possible.

He'd thought about telling her how he felt after their
dinner tonight, but when he'd seen how happy she was with
Charlie, he'd decided he could wait. They had tomorrow
with her brother and Ron and Terri, then another evening
in this room, and then the open road and heading toward
Utah, then Nevada.

As long as she knew how he felt before they arrived in
Las Vegas, that would be good enough.

He'd watched her at dinner and was convinced she was
healing nicely. He'd bet whole evenings went by when she
didn't think about Paul. And she hadn't gone through the
standard, "Today we'd be on our honeymoon; today we
were supposed to be walking on the beach" and all that
other stuff. It was almost as if catching Paul in the act with

another woman had had a cauterizing effect—incredible hurt, but the wound had been cleaned, sealed, and allowed to heal.

He was nothing if not a patient man. Both his grandparents had been incredible gardeners, and he'd learned from them that certain processes couldn't be rushed. The same was true for Tess. He'd have to talk to her about the marriage plan before Las Vegas; he couldn't just spring it on her out of the blue. But he had a feeling she'd be strong enough and she'd see the sense in it. She had to let him be in a position to really help her if things got nasty.

He quieted his mind and listened to her gentle breathing and then a soft little moan from Toby. The little dog had been scrabbling on the bed in her sleep, probably chasing an imaginary squirrel. Strange, how terribly fond he'd become of both of them, to the point that after only a few days he couldn't imagine his life without them.

Patience. It had served him well all his life, from assimilating into an American high school when he'd been a teenager, to getting his band up and running and becoming highly successful. And when he'd wanted to move on and add other dimensions to his music, that patience had enabled him to compose songs and eventually write the scores for movies.

He was happy with his creative life, but he hadn't found the right woman until that night in the bar when he'd been looking for Brooke, wanting to say hello. Tess had been a complete surprise, and his reaction to her had first taken him by surprise and then delighted him.

At thirty-three, he was ready for a committed relationship. In fact, both his mother and his gran had long despaired and practically given up that he'd ever settle down and get married. He wasn't going to get their hopes up this time until he was sure how Tess felt. But once he knew, and if the answer was the one he hoped for, he'd fly to England with her and introduce her to the entire family. There were so many people he wanted her to meet—his family; his band mates; friends in Los Angeles, London, and New York. He'd traveled a lot with his band, grueling world tours, years in which he'd known it would be fruitless to even start a relationship.

But now that he was doing more composing than actual performances, the timing was perfect. And he'd met the perfect woman. The only thing standing in the way was finding the perfect time to tell her how he felt about her.

THE following morning they got up, walked the dogs, fetched coffee and some sweet rolls from the motel lobby, and then came back and took turns showering and getting ready.

"You guys don't have any practical jokes cooked up for today, do you?" she said as she walked out of the bathroom, toiletry case in hand.

"On my honor, I'll protect you," he said. "Today's a day for you and Charlie."

They fed the dogs and took them for a short walk. Then everyone got in the van, and Will exited the motel parking lot and started toward Charlie's cabin.

THE little log cabin felt as if it were perched at the end of the world, in a setting so gorgeous that all thoughts of spider-filled outhouses fled Tess's mind.

"Oh, Charlie," she breathed as she looked at it. A huge pile of firewood covered with a tarp was on one end of the wraparound porch, while at the other were a few rocking chairs and a small table between them.

"Your home is just—wonderful."

He beamed with pride, and with a sudden flash of insight, Tess realized that no one in her family had ever really praised Charlie for anything. No wonder he'd hightailed it out of town with Ron. Ron had probably given him more emotional support, as a friend, than his family had.

"You really like it?"

"I love it! I can't wait to see the inside!"

Charlie was definitely a minimalist. He didn't own a whole lot, if you discounted the enormous shelf of books that lined one wall. He had a radio and a stereo system—

"I thought you didn't have electricity!"

"Not for the first few years but then I put in a generator."

His kitchen was small and functional, his living room had glorious views of nature outside, but his bedroom was what enchanted Tess. A loft area, the views of the surrounding trees made you feel as if you were floating in an enchanted tree house.

"It must be beautiful when it snows," she said.

"It is."

They went out into his backyard, which he'd fenced for his Lab, Sadie. The dogs met, and there were no altercations, as Sadie immediately became the submissive one, on her back and exposing her belly. Toby quivered with excitement at the chance to have a new friend, while Sugar was totally regal, the alpha female in all her glory. Within minutes, all three dogs were playing together.

"Did you guys eat already?" Charlie asked.

"Just coffee, really," said Tess.

"Then I'll make you all breakfast and we can take our hike."

He was as good as his word, first frying up apple-smoked bacon and then whipping up a batch of blueberry pancakes.

"And there's eggs if anyone wants a little more protein."

"This is more than enough," Will said. "I don't remember you being this good a cook."

"A man has to survive," Charlie said, expertly flipping a pancake.

They carried everything out on to the back porch, where a huge wooden table and two benches on either side created an ideal outdoor eating spot.

Tess dug into her pancakes and couldn't remember when she'd felt happier. The dogs were playing out in the yard, Toby barking excitedly and running from both Sugar and Sadie. Birds twittered in the trees, and the sunshine felt good. The air smelled clean, scented with the green smell of the trees. Charlie had certainly found his own little piece of heaven.

"And I'm sure that the best news for you, Tess, is that I installed indoor plumbing about six months ago."

"Really?"

"Yeah," said Ron. "That outhouse was scaring off too many of the ladies."

Terri simply laughed.

THEIR hike wasn't that strenuous, just a long, lazy walk along one of Charlie's favorite trails.

"I like to get out here as much as I can," he said. "Whenever things get kind of confusing in life, if I just get quiet and go to nature, nothing seems that bad."

And it was true. Tess felt a great sort of peace as she walked along beside her older brother. Ron and Terri were a bit ahead of them, and Will had joined them, so Tess had some private time to talk with her brother.

"If you're going out all the way to Los Angeles, you should stop by and see Mom," Charlie said.

"She's still in Santa Barbara?"

"Yep. Still with Jim."

Their mother had remarried after the divorce from their father. Jim, a high school science teacher, had been her perfect match, and from all accounts, the marriage was a happy one.

"Charlie . . . why didn't she ever come and see us when we were growing up?"

Charlie stared straight ahead of him before he spoke, choosing his words carefully. "For a long time I was mad at her, leaving us with Dad and his new wife. But as I got older, I realized it wasn't that simple. Remember my senior year, when Ron and I went out to the West Coast on that band trip?"

"Yeah."

"We had a free day, and the two of us hitched up the coast and saw Mom."

"You never told me!"

"I didn't want to get you in trouble. I knew Dad and Mad wouldn't like it."

"What happened?"

"Well, we turned up on her doorstep, and I thought she'd be embarrassed. I mean, she hadn't seen us, written to us, bothered to phone—"

Tess's throat tightened. She'd never understood why, and after enough time had passed, she'd stopped hoping.

"Anyway, you've got to picture it. Me, all hot and sweaty, with all the cockiness and know-it-all of a typical seventeen-year-old. I was spoiling for a fight. Poor Ron and Jim, caught right in the middle. And then there was Mom."

"What did she do?"

"She took one look at me, started crying, and then hugged me—"

"What?"

"Tess, she was ecstatic. I couldn't even get all my words out, but I kind of pulled back and started shouting at her, at what she'd done, how could she—"

"Oh my God."

"She just stood there and took it all. I remember the way tears just kept filling her eyes. She let me get it all out, even when Jim would have stepped in and stopped it. She held up her hand to him and let me have my say."

"And?" Tess held her breath. Suddenly whatever Charlie had to say was unbearably important.

"Do you know that she wrote to us every single week? Sent pictures?"

Tess stopped dead in her tracks. She couldn't walk and take all this in at the same time. Ron, Will, and Terri looked back, but Charlie motioned them to go ahead. Toby, on a leash with Tess, sat down on the trail and looked up at Tess, her expression concerned.

"I don't remember—" She stopped. "Madeline."

"Got it in one. Did you know Mom wanted us to come out and spend summers with her?"

"Dad," Tess said quietly.

"Yep. She *begged* him, Tess, but I guess the gist of the conversation was that if she ever called the house again, he'd make life that much more difficult for us."

She stared at her brother, a horrible feeling spreading throughout her body.

"She told me it was the hardest thing she ever did, but she let us go. And you know what I saw in her living room?"

"Oh," Tess said softly before she started to cry.

"Pictures. You and me and Brian, all of our baby pictures. Our childhood. Practically a shrine."

Tess's throat was so tight she couldn't speak.

"You know Dad would have done it," Charlie said. "He would've made things hell for us if we'd contacted her. Tess, that was why I left the moment I graduated. I took off with Ron because I couldn't stand to spend another moment under his roof."

"That was why—" Tess cleared her throat. "That was why Madeline always went out of her way to portray Mom as such a—hippie freak. She even implied that she used drugs, that she would've been a totally unfit mother—"

Charlie laughed, and it sounded slightly bitter. "Sure, she sometimes wore those gypsy skirts, and she was always into yoga and natural foods, alternative medicine, that sort of thing. Hell, a lot of the people here in Boulder are into the same things. But it didn't make her irresponsible."

"Why did he do that?" Tess whispered, almost to herself. "Why did Dad do what he did? Did he hate her that much?"

"I have a theory, if you want to hear it."

"Sure, I—can we sit down?"

"Yeah."

There were a couple of large boulders with smooth tops. Charlie checked them carefully—"Rattlesnakes really like warm places like rocks"—and they sat.

"This isn't going to be pretty," he warned her.

"Oh, please. Like what I've heard wasn't painful enough."

"Here's the deal. Dad has to keep up appearances, even to himself. And he couldn't see himself as just another man who got bored with his marriage and went out looking for a little bit of action on the side. There had to be a villain, and it wasn't going to be him. So in a brilliant little bit of psychological craziness, he made our mother into the bad guy."

She nodded her head. It fit.

"Charlie, from the time Mom left, all I heard about her was how unfit she was. And they made sure to back up that story with their actions. I'm positive now that they intercepted her calls and confiscated any letters she might've sent us. So it looked to us as if she didn't give a damn, when all the time all she wanted was to be even the smallest part of our lives."

The two of them sat in silence for a short while, Toby in Tess's lap.

"Charlie?"

"Yeah?"

"You want to know the real reason I'm on this trip with Will?"

He smiled. "Sure."

Briefly, hitting only the main points, she told him. And he sat, quietly, taking it all in. She felt no sense of judgment from him. He asked a few questions but mostly let her talk. And when she finished, he reached over and took her hand in his, his palm big and rough and callused.

"Congratulations, Tess. You were smart, and you got out."

THEY went out to a Mexican place for dinner, and Tess couldn't remember the last time she'd had more fun. She'd never felt closer to her brother, and when they finally went back to his cabin late that night and prepared to say goodbye, he asked her to wait for just a second.

"I've got something for you."

As Charlie loped up the stairs to his loft bedroom, Tess stood watching Ron and Will talk while Terri sat on the couch and played with all three dogs. Sadie the Lab was so happy with her two new friends that Tess had promised

Charlie she and Toby would be out for a visit before another year passed.

"Here," said Charlie as he came down the stairs. He handed her a photo in a frame, and Tess's breath caught as she realized it was a picture of Charlie and their mother. Their arms were around each other, and they were out on a balcony surrounded by potted plants bursting with colorful blooms. And Tess saw an older version of herself, a happy smile on the face but a familiar sadness in the green-gold eyes.

"And this," Charlie said, handing her a piece of lined paper. Tess took it, knowing that their mother's address and phone were written on it in Charlie's bold handwriting.

"Thank you," she whispered and then threw herself into his arms. They hugged tightly, then hugged some more, and finally Tess stepped back.

"Okay, then," she said.

"Okay," her brother said and smiled. "Don't be such a stranger."

"I promise."

She walked out the door with Will and their dogs, and they all said their good-byes, then headed for the van.

"Good visit?" Will said as he started up the engine.

"More than I ever expected," she said.

thirteen

SOMETHING HAD HAPPENED back at Charlie's cabin, but Will didn't have any idea what. Tess had changed. It was as if an enormous weight had shifted off her. She looked happier, and her spirit seemed lighter.

They'd left Boulder early that morning, neither of them really able to get a good night's sleep. At five A.M., when Will had realized Tess was awake as well, he'd asked her if she wanted to hit the road. With so little traffic at that time, they could get a good head start.

Now, driving south for the last hour away from Boulder, he glanced over at his passenger.

"So you had a good time with Charlie?"

"Yeah." She hesitated and then said, "We talked about my mother."

"Good things, I hope."

"There was a lot of deception in my home after my parents got divorced."

"That's tough."

"My father basically pulled every string he could to make sure she never saw any of us again."

That shocked him. He'd heard of some bitter divorces, but to deprive your children of one of their parents? It seemed cruel.

"At the same time, my stepmother told us all sorts of lies about her. She intercepted her letters and calls, all the time telling us our mother didn't care for us and didn't want the bother of raising children. That she was too much of a free spirit and didn't want the responsibility."

He didn't know what to say. "I'm sorry" didn't quite cut it. And he realized the enormity of what she'd discovered during this trip. How a woman perceived her mother was a foundational part of who she was, and Tess had once again had her world rocked.

"Your stepmother did all this?"

"Yes."

"Unbelievable."

"I'm going to have a hard time forgiving her for this."

"To do that to a child," he mused. "What memories do you have of your mother?"

"I was thirteen when they divorced. I loved her. I loved being with her. Toward the end she cried a lot, and I was terrified by her unhappiness. And then she left. And then Madeline told us she didn't want us anymore. I felt like I'd been thrown away."

He stopped himself before he said *I can imagine*, because he couldn't. They would have been empty words. Though he'd left home soon after his time as an exchange student due to the combination of an independent nature and a curiosity to see the world and play music, he'd always known he had a safe and loving place to come home to. He couldn't imagine his life without a place to call home.

He tried to picture what she and her siblings had been through. To believe that your mother had walked out on you . . .

Will decided that this was not the time to tell Tess that she'd probably be seeing her stepmother at the same time she met with Paul in Las Vegas.

"Have you thought about the meeting with your ex-fiancé?" he said instead.

"Yeah. I just want to give him the ring back and get it over with."

"Do you want me to come with you?"

"No. This is something I have to do alone."

Not good.

"If you decide you need some support, I'm here for you."

"Thank you."

Thank God Brooke's flying out. She'll talk her into accepting support.

"So," she said, turning toward him. "What sorts of things are you going to show me in Los Angeles?"

He sensed she didn't want to talk about her mother, or Madeline, or even Paul anymore. And that was fine with him—for now.

"The Pacific, of course. It's one of the most beautiful oceans I've ever seen. There's this little shack on Highway One in Malibu that serves up the best fresh fish, right on the water."

"I'd like that."

"And Chinatown. I like to go there and just walk around, browse in stores. The atmosphere's great, it makes me feel like I'm in a different country."

"I love exploring things like that."

"Of course, we'd have to drive around Beverly Hills and

take a stroll down Rodeo Drive. Maybe do some shopping, the whole *Pretty Woman* thing."

"I agree."

"We'd probably have dinner with Elaine one night, and she'd bring along her friend Jack. They've never been involved, but they're closer than most brothers and sisters and consider each other family. I think it's because neither of them has much family in L.A., so they spend holidays together, things like that."

"I know Elaine's a psychic. What does Jack do?"

"He's a highly respected astrologer. He does charts for a lot of people in the industry. Some of his clients literally won't make a move without him."

"Is that healthy?"

"Jack doesn't think so, but he can't control his clientele."

She seemed to be getting into his vision of Los Angeles. "What else? All of this sounds good so far."

"You'd have to come hear my band."

"Absolutely."

"We'd have to take Toby to see the ocean."

"I wonder if all that water would scare her."

"I have a feeling that dog would face the entrance to hell if you were by her side."

"You're right." Tess glanced back to where both dogs were sleeping peacefully in their crates. "Would Elaine mind if I brought Toby over to play with Sugar?"

"She'd love it. She's one of those people who always has a house full of friends, jammed to the rooftop. I think she's even rented out a few of the rooms in her house on occasion. She's got one of the most generous hearts of anyone I know."

"I like her already, and I don't even know her."

They lapsed into a comfortable silence for a while.

Then Will said, "You told me that you used to design outfits for all your stuffed animals and dolls when you were a
little girl. Brooke's toys as well, Ron said. Have you ever
thought about trying to make a go of it as a knitting designer? Is that the right term?"

"I sold a couple of patterns to knitting magazines when
I was in school."

"That's fantastic! Is it something you'd be interested in
doing on a full-time basis?"

"I never thought about it, but I have a feeling I'd really
love it."

"I have a friend," said Will, shamelessly trying to find a
way to make her stay in the Southern California area, "who
works on a lot of sets. Movies, soaps, that sort of thing.
They're always looking for interesting designs for their ac-
tors and actresses. You'd have to make up some samples,
show her a few sweaters, things like that. If they're as great
looking as that sweater you're working on, I'm sure she'd
use some of your stuff."

"Are you kidding me?"

"No. Not at all. When you were knitting before, I didn't
see you looking at any sort of pattern the way my mother
and gran used to. Is it a Tess original?"

"It's one of my own designs, yes. I worked it out in my
head—"

"Great. If you just finished that sweater, I could take it
to her and it might be a way to make a little money until
you decide what it is you want to do. I know you haven't
even seen Los Angeles yet, so you have no idea if you're
going to like it or not, but when Ron told me about your designs—"

"How did he know?"

"He talked Brooke out of one of the teddy bear sweaters
you designed so he could give it to his girlfriend. He

bought another bear, put the sweater on it, and she loved it. Points for Ron."

"Brooke never told me that!"

"I think he was fourteen at the time."

Tess laughed. "Yeah, he was popular with girls at a young age. I should be flattered that he liked my work that much. And I'm not upset with Brooke for giving it to him. She'd do anything for Ron."

"They're a terrific family. They made my first year in America a great one."

"There's such a—a loyalty there. They'd all do anything for each other. I always kind of envied her that, because after Charlie left, I always knew that I had to—act a certain way, be a certain way, to fit into my own family."

"It's a strange way to show love."

"I agree."

"And speaking of Brooke," said Will, "She wants to fly in to Las Vegas when we arrive and spend some time with us."

He caught Tess's quick glance at him, as if she were attempting to size up what he'd just said and how he felt about it.

"She doesn't think I can get rid of Paul on my own," she finally said, her tone flat.

"I wouldn't be so quick to refuse her help. She loves you, Tess, and she's of the opinion that Paul isn't going to let you go without a fight." He took a deep breath, knowing that after he said the next words, there was no going back. "And from what I've heard about the guy, I believe she's right."

She opened her mouth. Closed it. Sat perfectly still for a moment. He would have given anything for a peek inside her mind at that time, for some idea of what she was thinking. But all he could do was wait until she was ready to talk.

"Will, what can he do? I'm meeting him in a public place, a Vegas buffet! I'm giving him back the engagement ring and telling him that we're through. He can't do anything to me in a public place. Do you honestly think he's that deranged?"

"I think he's a man who has to win, who has to come out of everything as the good guy. You've thrown a major wrench into that, Tess, with what happened between the two of you. So yes, I think he would go to drastic lengths to get you back into his life. I have a bad feeling about this man, and I wish you'd let both me and Brooke protect you."

SHE didn't know what to say.

An automatic denial rose to her lips, but she didn't voice it. Instead, she tried to look at things from Will's point of view.

How well did she actually know Paul? Not very, considering that he'd been having a fine old time with Marti on the side and she hadn't had a clue. Would *still* not have a clue if she hadn't taken that fateful little detour to her church. If she hadn't caught Paul, she'd be married to a cheater right now and not even know.

She shuddered and then felt sick. Could she honestly say that she knew how Paul was going to react when she broke off their relationship? From what Brooke had told her, Paul just thought her refusal to get married and the decision to take a road trip were little aberrations, tiny bumps on the smooth highway that was soon to be their married life.

If she told him this wasn't the case, that she wanted out for good and never wanted to see him again, would he fly off the handle? Turn violent? Demand that she get on a plane to Chicago with him immediately? Force her to?

Brooke and Will had a legitimate point—how well did she really know this man? How could anyone know the charming chameleon who'd ensured she thought they were soulmates? Now that she'd lowered the boom on Paul and denied him something he wanted, would the hidden, and possibly ugly, side to his personality come out?

I think he's a man who has to win, who has to come out of everything as the good guy . . .

Will's words caused her stomach to clench with a sharp pain as an emotional truth seemed to explode in her head, kicking her to life.

I almost married my father . . .

She couldn't breathe properly, and sweat was forming on her hairline as her stomach clenched even tighter. "Will?"

"Tess, are you all right—"

"I think I'm going to be sick—"

He managed to pull to the side of the road, and she barely had her head out the window before she was completely sick, upchucking everything in her stomach. They'd stopped at a diner for breakfast, so she had a lot to get rid of.

"I'm sorry," she muttered as he pressed a paper towel into her hand.

"Stop it, Tess. You have nothing to apologize for."

She wiped the towel across her mouth and sat perfectly still, trying to quiet her raging stomach. And she felt Will's hand on her shoulder, firm and reassuring.

"Could we—could we drive to a gas station? Someplace with a bathroom?"

"Of course."

Within minutes she was at a station, taking a fresh T-shirt into the bathroom, along with some baby wipes she had in her bag. Toby had scrabbled frantically in her crate the moment she'd been sick, wanting to get to her side. Will had the van parked in the shade where he could see the doors to the restrooms, and he had Toby in his arms and was reassuring the little dog.

Inside the bathroom Tess stripped off her messy T-shirt and stuffed it into a plastic bag she'd brought along. She rinsed out her mouth, splashed water on her face, and wiped the baby wipe down her neck. When she felt relatively cleaned up, she pulled on the new T-shirt and glanced up into the cracked mirror.

She looked like a wreck, especially the dark circles beneath her eyes. Her skin looked pale and felt clammy, though she knew it was only because she'd recently been sick. The emotional truth of her relationship with Paul had been so overwhelming. Not only had she been ready to marry Paul to please her father and stepmother, but she hadn't realized that he was *exactly* like her father—a cheater and an extremely vengeful man.

Now she didn't feel at all confident about meeting Paul in Las Vegas. She closed her eyes for a moment, thoughts whirling through her brain. Then she decided that she had to face this like she'd faced everything else so far on this trip, this trip that had started when she'd looked through that window in her church's door and her whole life had exploded into bits.

* * *

WILL observed Tess carefully as she came out of the bathroom. She looked about as whipped as a human could possibly be.

"No more driving today," he told Toby, who rewarded him with a lick on the chin. "Mind if I tell a white lie about you?"

Toby whined.

"I'll take that as a yes."

When Tess reached the van and swung open the passenger side door, he said, "That's it for today. I think we should get a motel."

"But we've only been driving for a couple of hours."

"I think Toby needs a break. She just doesn't feel one hundred percent. It's pretty cold today, and the van's heater seems to be laboring, having trouble keeping the dogs warm. If we stopped at a motel, you could stay with them while I find a good mechanic. I don't want it to get any worse."

"Oh," she said, and he watched as she decided it wasn't because of her. He also knew she would do anything for her dog, and for Elaine's. One thing about Tess—her facial expressions were so easy to read, she was so open. "All right. Yes, of course."

"I'll just get out my laptop."

HE found a cute little motel barely twenty minutes away and got them adjoining rooms. Then, while Tess stretched out on her bed with the two dogs, he went to repair the van.

"You can reach me on my cell if you need anything," he said. "Don't hesitate to call."

"Okay," she said, and he estimated she was asleep by the time her head hit the pillow.

He didn't go to a mechanic. He went to a car wash and cleaned the van, inside and out. Then he found the local movie theater and bought a ticket to the current feature, figuring that would kill some time. Tess wouldn't believe his mechanic story if he wasn't out for a while.

When the show finished, he headed back to the motel with a large pizza and some bottles of soda. He didn't think Tess had anything like flu. She probably didn't need to go back to her diet of chicken rice soup and toast. She'd just been overwhelmed by all of it, and she'd probably be hungry by now.

Less than a week of her life had passed and she'd been cheated on, cancelled her own wedding, had her entire perceived future destroyed, hit the road, seen her long-lost brother, found out that her mother hadn't abandoned her, and discovered the true nature of her father and stepmother.

Pretty heavy emotional work for less than a week. As far as Will was concerned, she was holding up beautifully. And thank God for the dogs—when life went to hell, an unconditionally loving friend with a wet nose was a great comfort.

He let himself into his motel room quietly, surprised the dogs didn't bark. Setting the pizza and sodas down on the table in his room, he walked quietly to the adjoining door and peered into Tess's room.

She was sprawled out on the bed on her stomach, fully clothed, none of the covers pulled back, sleeping the sleep of the truly exhausted. Both Toby and Sugar glanced up, and Sugar gave him a look that quite plainly said, *You didn't think we were going to wake her up, did you?*

He patted his leg, his signal for them to come, and both dogs jumped quietly off the bed and padded into his room.

They jumped on his bed, nostrils flaring as they took in the scent of the pizza.

"Just a taste," he said, opening one of the bottles of soda. "We have to leave some for Tess."

"HEY," she said from the adjoining doorway, and he looked up at the sound. She looked absolutely adorable and breathtaking at the same time, her hair all rumpled, her eyes still heavy-lidded with sleep.

"Good nap?"

"Yeah. I guess I needed it. Pizza?"

"I thought I deserved it after my day at the mechanic."

"Everything fixed?"

"Good as new."

She walked over to the table and lifted the lid to the pizza box, took a piece, and began to eat. He was pleased to see she had her appetite back.

"I'd like you to come with me when I face Paul," she said quietly. "And Brooke, too."

He took a minute to digest this. Then he finally asked the question he had to ask. "What changed your mind?"

"I guess I realized that I don't know Paul at all. Our courtship was all superficial. We never really connected. It's obvious that he was marrying me to find a way into my family, to get in with my father and possibly his business. So Paul did whatever he could to look good in my eyes. I don't know the man. I never did."

He considered this, then realized he could give her no less than the truth. He had to be honest with her if there was any hope for her to come out of this whole mess unscathed.

"I think you're right. I think your ex is a real con man,

used to telling women what they want to hear. Tess, if you'd married the bastard, you might have gone along for a few years before you finally realized who he was and what he was capable of."

"I feel so stupid," she whispered. "I feel like I was one of those women so desperate to get married that I didn't look at the whole situation the way I should have."

"Don't go there. You had a father and stepmother who set you the standard, showed you the hoop they wanted you to jump through. And you wanted a family, and love, and acceptance, which is all anyone really wants at the end of the day. Anyone in your position would have done the same thing."

"You really think so? You're not just saying that?"

"I really think so."

She hesitated and then said, "You don't mind helping me?"

"I'd be honored."

She considered this, took another bite of pizza, chewed, and swallowed. "I should call Brooke tonight."

He might as well go for broke. "There's one more thing you should know. Brooke and I have discussed this in detail, and only because we've both been worried about you. Neither of us believe Paul is going to take defeat graciously."

She'd been reaching for another piece of pizza, and her hand stilled. He could feel she was still overwhelmed. Too much had happened in too short a time. But he felt he knew the real Tess, the woman who had once been the slender, shy girl who had stood slightly apart from all the noise and laughter at the Matthews' home.

She'd had a crush on him then, and he had a feeling she

liked him now. He'd liked her then, and he liked her now. And he was veering into feelings that were deeper, that had everything to do with like and a whole lot more.

They'd gotten to know each other in a very strange way. Not cautious dating, where you could keep the relationship on a superficial level for quite a few weeks if you wanted to. She'd hit the road with him on shaky legs, with a desperate desire to change her life. She'd done the classic one-hundred-and-eighty-degree turn, and he admired her courage more than she'd ever know.

No hanging back on the edges now. Tess was up to her knees in this mess, and continually moving forward.

"Tess?" he said quietly. She was staring at the pizza box.

"I feel like I can't trust my judgment anymore."

"You know what I think?"

"What?"

"I think you got hoodwinked by one of the best. And I think if Paul had come to me with some business scheme, the only thing that would have saved my financial neck is that I would have checked with Elaine first and she would have smelled a rat. He's a good con, your Paul. He might have even taken Brooke in."

She hadn't considered this, he could tell.

"So maybe I'm not that stupid after all."

"You're not stupid at all, and stop thinking that way. I want you to think about something else, something that could help you get out of this entire mess in a brilliant way. A way that Paul couldn't touch you, couldn't get to you ever again. A way that you'd be protected from him. It's something Brooke and I have talked about, and we both believe it would be for the best."

"Okay." She leaned back in the chair. "I'm going to

have a completely open mind about this whole thing. Hit me with it."

He couldn't believe his luck, just as he couldn't stop the grin he could feel on his face.

"Tess, I want you to marry me."

fourteen

"MARRY YOU?" SHE could barely get the words out of her mouth. And for some insane reason, she felt as if she were an adolescent again, mooning around in her room and imagining going out with Will, going to a dance, getting married, the whole nine yards, even down to the damn white picket fence . . .

And here he was, offering her a marriage. One in name only, of course. And for her own protection. But *marriage . . .*

"Yes. That's the general idea, Tess. I think even Paul would give up if you were married to another man and that man was by your side."

"You'd do that for me?"

"Of course." He cleared his throat as she stared at him and said, "Tess, I always liked you, from the moment I met you. But these last few days on the road with you—I'd have to say that we've gotten to know each other in a pretty profound way.

"I've been a witness to your changing your life completely, and I've admired your courage and your—your *heart*, every step of the way. You did what needed to be done, even though your heart was breaking. And even though you may have had enormous emotional difficulty and stress, you didn't complain. You grieved, you mourned, but you didn't try to change what couldn't be changed."

He took a deep breath, looking as if he was as surprised by the length of his speech as she was. Trust a Brit to sum things up so beautifully. She'd always admired Will's command of the language. And of course, that accent.

"Thank you," she said quietly. It helped to know that he thought she had heart, when *she* thought she was a stupid, clueless, and spineless jellyfish who had merely jumped into his van and let him take charge. The biggest favor he'd ever done for her was getting her out of town before the wedding.

No, she thought tiredly, rubbing her aching temples. The biggest favor he'd be doing for her was marrying her.

"Headache?"

"It's a lot to take in," she said quietly. "This feels like one of those movies where the woman buys an escort to a wedding or marries a guy to quiet her family's nagging."

"I know what you mean. But this marriage we're talking about is for a much more important reason—to protect you from Paul. He's a bad one, Tess, I can feel it. I've never met the man, but what he's done to you so far—I just can't stand the thought of him getting his hands on you again. I hope you'll forgive me for overstepping any boundaries—"

She glanced up at him and felt her eyes fill.

"Do you know what it feels like to have friends care for me this way?" she said, hating the fact that her voice broke. "Do you have any idea what it means to me when my own family was perfectly content to let me marry him? It felt like they just wanted to get me out of the way! Poor dumb

Tess! Poor little ineffectual Tess! Let's marry her off to
Paul and be done with it!"

That he didn't contradict her told her that he probably
saw things the same way.

"I've never felt a real part of my own family, Will. I've
never even felt like they liked spending time with me, let
alone helping me see to my own best interests. It's like, this
last week on the road with you, all this truth has come
crashing down on my head."

"It's okay, Tess."

"Has anything like this ever happened to you?"

"I've had my moments."

"Not as bad as this."

"Tess, everyone has moments when the life they had no
longer works. The only question is, do you have the
courage to change things for the better, or do you try to
cover things up and go on as if nothing happened?"

"You think people do that?"

"I know they do. I see good friends do it. It's part of human nature. People delude themselves all the time. But you
chose not to. And that makes you, in my opinion, one of
the bravest women I know."

Tess stared down at the open pizza box. It seemed an
eternity since she'd grabbed a piece and eaten it. It had to
be progress that she was having this conversation with Will
and didn't feel like upchucking her meager lunch.

"Okay. Can we make a compromise?"

"Whatever you want." But she could tell he was hoping
she would go along with the marriage idea.

"How about if you and Brooke come along with me to
the meeting with Paul, and if anything goes wrong, we tell
him we're engaged and one of the reasons I ran off was that
I realized I couldn't marry him when I was in love with
you."

Will grinned. "Paul should love that." He looked at her for a long moment and then said, "You're in control, Tess. I'm just here to help in any way I can."

"Thank you," she said quietly, then glanced away. She reached for another piece of pizza and sat down at the small round table by Will's queen-sized bed. Both dogs jumped into alert begging mode, and she had to laugh.

"It's good to see you laughing, Tess."

She hesitated before biting into the slice and then said, "I'll be so glad when this whole thing is over."

"Just a few more days, and it will be."

WHEN Brooke called late that night, Tess was in the shower so Will could talk freely. He filled her in on their conversation.

"We'll just have to play it by ear," Brooke said. "I'm going to come in a day earlier than I planned, scout the place out, the buffet and everything. And I'll meet you both at the Hard Rock, okay?"

"Sounds like a plan," Will said. They said their good-byes and hung up, and as he placed his cell on the bedside table, he caught Sugar glaring at him with an accusing look on her doggy face.

"And what's up with you, Miss?"

Sugar whined.

"You think I should've been more forceful with Tess, more aggressive, is that it?"

Sugar whined and came closer, butting her head beneath his hand for a pat.

"Sugar, darling, I think this woman's had all she can stand of forceful. The man's a bloody beast."

He scratched her softly between her velvety ears, and she closed her eyes in total bliss, leaning into his touch.

"I know it wasn't the road trip that either Elaine or I promised you—"

She opened her eyes and looked at him as if to say, *Oh come on, like I would have done it any other way!* and Will laughed.

"We should be in Los Angeles the day after Las Vegas. It's a one-day drive. You'll see your mum soon."

THE rest of the trip, on their way to Las Vegas, passed without incident. Driving through Utah was one of the most visually stunning drives Tess had ever experienced. The rust-colored rock formations towered over them as they drove along the highway, making her feel somewhat small and insignificant.

"But maybe that's healthy," she said as she and Will shared sandwiches they'd bought earlier on the side of the road. Both dogs had had a walk and their treats, and now Toby lay with her head on Tess's foot while Sugar was sprawled out beneath the picnic table in the shade, snoring softly.

"Feeling that you're a small part of the entire big picture? I suppose it is."

She considered this, chewing. The scenery around them was breathtaking, so raw and primeval, and the air was fresh and cool, crisp and clear. Sweater weather. Leaves were turning, and Tess had the feeling that as the earth was preparing for a new phase of life, a new season, so was she.

"I never wanted more than that," she said quietly. "A small, but significant role in my family's life."

"You wanted what mattered, Tess. What's always mattered, down through the ages. People, and the warmth and love of a family. I don't consider that stupid, and I don't consider you a stupid woman for wanting it. The only thing that went wrong was that your love for your family blinded you to the reality of who they all were. And anyone could understand that."

She studied the sandwich in her hand as she felt all the shame at her supposed ignorance and stupidity seem to fall away. And as it did, she felt lighter, as if her heart were opening up to further possibilities. She did have family. She had Charlie in Boulder, and she had the promise of a relationship with her mother after she discovered what had really happened.

She couldn't condemn her mother for not trying harder to contact them. God knows what her father and stepmother had told her. Also, she knew her mother had never had the financial resources her father had possessed. If she'd fought him, the reality was that she would've been squashed flat.

"My father saw us as things," she blurted out. "Nothing more than an extension of his property."

"It had to have been a horrible way to grow up," Will said.

"Everything, all the emphasis, was on things, on possessions, on how things looked, on what the neighbors would think, on how to get further ahead and acquire more status—it was awful."

"And one good storm would wipe it all away, and your father would be sitting on a heap of rubble and wondering what had happened to his life. My gran told me once that the only thing we take with us when we die is the love we've given to others and the love we received back."

"Is she still alive?"

"Alive and going strong in her eighties. Everyone in the village loves her. She never has time to dwell on aches and pains, she's so busy helping others. That's what I grew up with, Tess, and I'm truly sorry that you didn't have the same."

"She sounds like a wonderful person."

"We love her."

"Does she ever come to visit you?"

"She was out last summer. She loved the ocean, and she took Sugar for long walks along the beach."

"I'd love to meet her."

"Stick around out west, and you just might."

Tess swallowed the last of her sandwich and folded the paper wrapping up carefully before putting it inside the brown paper bag. It would have been sacrilege to have littered this area. "I'm almost done with the sweater."

"Excellent. You'll have to model it for me, and I'm sure Brooke will want a look."

"Were you serious about showing it to that friend of yours?"

"Yes."

She took a deep breath. "I don't think I want to go back to being a dental hygienist."

"Is that what you did?"

She nodded her head.

"A safe way to acquire a lot of things, right?"

She smiled.

"But not a lot of passion."

"Yeah," she said. "It was all right, but I never loved it the way I loved my knitting. I'd just never considered there might be a way of making a living doing what I loved."

"I think you have an excellent chance."

"Will," she said suddenly, taking his hand it hers. "I think things are going to happen really quickly once we reach Las Vegas. And I want to be sure you know how much I appreciate all you've done for Toby and me. I just wanted you to know how much I—I wanted to thank you for everything you've done."

"You're welcome." He smiled at her, and her stomach did funny little flip-flops as she looked into his beautiful gray-blue eyes.

THEY cleaned up their makeshift lunch area, and Will watched Tess as she walked over to the trash can and deposited the rest of their litter.

"Ah, Tess," he said softly, his words caught up on the soft fall breeze. "I've got to be every kind of fool to be thinking what I'm thinking, but Gran also told me that being optimistic never hurt anyone. Hope for the best, and you'll often get it."

"Did you say something?" she said, coming toward him. The dogs were waking up, standing, stretching, and yawning.

"Nothing," he said quietly. "Let's take these two for a short walk and then get back on the road."

THEY stopped at another small motel that didn't mind animals, and Tess realized she was at peace.

"It's a nice feeling," she told Toby as she sat in a tub full of bubbles and simply relaxed. Toby lay stretched out on the bathroom rug, watching her nervously.

"You're not getting a bath, Toby. You can relax."

Toby stretched and grinned her doggy grin, her good eye almost seeming to twinkle.

"We'll be in Las Vegas tomorrow."

Toby whined.

"I won't make you see him. I'll protect you. He never really liked you, Toby, but you knew that before I did." She rubbed the scented soap between her palms and began to scrub her forearms. "Hell, he never really liked me."

Toby barked softly as if to say, *You got that right!*

"Whatever happens, we'll stick together and get through it."

She went to bed early, determined to get a good night's sleep and be ready for whatever the following day would bring. But when Tess woke, she'd been dreaming, and she lay still in the motel bed, trying to recapture the bits and pieces.

She'd been six years old and with her mother. They'd been out in the yard, and her mother had been laughing with her, daring her to climb higher in the tree out back. Brian and Charlie had a tree house up in the arms of the old oak, basically just a small platform that hadn't hurt any of the branches. And Tess was way out on a limb, laughing down at her mother, climbing higher and higher—

Tess rolled over in the warm bedclothes, smiling. She'd loved trees when she was little, used to hug them and couldn't wait to climb them. She'd been a grubby little girl, always outside, always in nature, and if she found a kitten or a frog, well, they would come home with her.

And as she lay in her motel bed, she realized that she'd always picked the colors of nature in her yarns, never the bright synthetic shades. She'd received so much inspiration from the natural world, and some of her problems had started when she'd been too busy to spend time in it.

This trip had opened that up for her as well. She thought of the flat cornfields of Illinois, with their vivid green, shiny leaves. She remembered the sunrises and sunsets in Nebraska, the colors of the mountains and the trees in Colorado, and the rusty red rock in Utah. The sight and sounds of the small brook running along the side of the highway, the sunlight glinting off it. The smell of the air as fall arrived; the sense of anticipation for what was to come—

Quietly, not knowing if Will was up yet in the room next door, she got up and changed into a pair of jeans and a soft green sweater. She washed her face, brushed her teeth, brushed her hair, and packed up her small carryall.

Then Tess drew back the curtains of her room and looked out at the glorious rock formations all around them. She sat down in an overstuffed chair next to the bed and faced the outdoors.

"Toby," she called softly, and her little dog lifted her head from the warmth of the bedcovers. She got up, stretched her legs until the stiffness left them and then trotted over to the edge of the bed and carefully jumped on to the chair and into her lap.

They sat in silence, looking outside as the sky slowly lightened. Tess knew they would reach Las Vegas late today and she would see Paul the following day. She would deal with the man and put the entire relationship behind her. And she knew she would never trust an excess of superficial charm in a man, ever again.

"We'll make it through this, Toby," she whispered, hugging her dog to her. Toby wriggled in her lap until she could lick Tess's face, her little stump of a tail wagging furiously. "We'll be stronger for it. It was a gift, my coming across Paul and Marti that way. It was a gift, and it enabled both of us to get out."

Toby snuggled closer.

"I don't know what we're doing or where we're going or how things are going to turn out, but I think we just have to go to the edge of the unknown and jump, you know what I mean?"

Toby butted her head against her hand.

"And I think it's okay for us not to know for a while. I'm just going to give Will that sweater and start another one. And we'll rent a car and go see my mom. And we'll find a place in California and hang out there for a while. I have enough in my savings to keep us going for at least six months, and I could always get some kind of part-time job in the meantime. And we'll see the Pacific." She couldn't even begin to imagine the color and design ideas she'd get from that vast body of water.

Toby looked up at her, total canine trust in her face, and Tess felt humbled by that trust.

"And I'm so sorry I ever made you live in that house with that man, Toby."

Toby licked her hand softly as if to say, *Ah, all is forgiven, okay?*

"We'll be fine," Tess said softly. "In forty-eight hours, he'll be out of my life forever and we can go on with our own. Deal?"

Toby snuggled closer and rested her head in Tess's lap and looked up at her, her dark eyes filled with love.

THEY arrived in Vegas early that evening. It seemed a magical city to Tess; they saw it sparkling in the distance, out in the middle of the desert. She knew it wasn't really out in the middle of the desert, that there were suburbs all around and even a university, but the Strip still glittered in the night and it was a glorious sight to see.

They drove right to the Hard Rock Hotel and checked in. Will had made a reservation as soon as he'd known they were headed there, and when they had their suite, he went down to the registration desk to leave a message for Brooke.

They were both unpacking, the dogs sprawled on their

various beds in the suite, when a knock sounded on the door. When Tess raced to open the door, both Brooke and her cousin Kim stood there, grinning from ear to ear.

"You both came!" Tess said.

"After what I put her through," Brooke said, indicating her cousin with her thumb, "I thought she deserved some R and R. How about a morning at a spa?"

"Sounds great."

"Hey, Will," Kim called out as he poked his head around a bedroom door. "Long time no see."

"Kim!" He strode forward and enveloped her in a bear hug, rocking her back and forth. Brooke glanced at Tess and said, "I hope you don't mind that I brought her."

"No, not at all."

"I *love* your hair!"

"Thanks."

"Where's the Tobester? There she is!" Toby bounded enthusiastically up to Brooke, and for a short while pandemonium reigned.

After things calmed down, Will said, "I think room service would be wise for tonight. Once the whole thing with Paul is over, we can hit the streets and do the town."

"Sounds like a plan," said Tess.

They ordered in what seemed like the entire room service menu—pizza and sandwiches, a few appetizers, the works. And they sat around the large suite's living room, sprawled out, talking and laughing. It reminded Tess of the past, when Will had lived at Brooke's house. That easygoing camaraderie was still there, and she began to forget about what had to be done the following morning.

Until her cell phone rang.

"Uh-oh," said Brooke.

Tess checked the number. "It's Paul."

"Pick up," said Will. "Let's see what he's up to."

She did.

"Tess? Is that you?" Paul's voice sounded abrasive and loud in her ear. How had she ever thought she could marry this man?

"Hi, Paul. How are you?"

Brooke covered her mouth with her hand to silence a snort of laughter.

"*How* the *hell* do you *think* I am?" he demanded. "Are you in Las Vegas yet?"

"Just about. When do you arrive?"

"I'm already here. Listen, we have to talk—"

"Are we still on for breakfast at the buffet tomorrow as planned?" she said, injecting an authoritative tone into her voice.

"Yeah, but there are a couple of details that I want to go over before—"

"I'll see you then, Paul. Don't call back—"

"Listen to me, you little *bitch*. If you think you're going to get away with *dumping* me, you've got another thing coming! When I see you tomorrow, I'm going to knock some *sense* into that head of yours—"

She hung up, shaken. Will and Brooke had been right. Paul was not a man to cross. She'd never gone against anything he'd wanted before, so she'd never seen this very ugly side to him. Suddenly she was so glad Will and Brooke and even Kim were all here with her and would be with her tomorrow.

Will had been on one side of her during the phone call, Brooke on the other. She had no doubt that both of them had heard what Paul had said to her, and the way he'd said it. No respect, no regard for her feelings. Threatening her. Silencing her.

That would have been her marriage. That would have

been her life had she gone through with the wedding. She shuddered.

The silence stretched until she glanced up and saw her three friends looking at her with nothing but concern.

"I think," Tess said quietly, "that we'd better go to Plan B. The wedding."

"I don't even think we should leave our suite if that man's in town," Brooke said quietly. They'd ordered in a bunch of desserts and were sitting around, having finished them all off while making plans. "The two of you can get married right here."

"Let me call the concierge," Will said, "and get a few options."

"I'm going downstairs to see what I can find. Maybe they have a wedding boutique," Kim said. "What size are you, Tess? Around a six?"

"But we shouldn't go to all this trouble," Tess began.

"We'll need to make the wedding as convincing as possible," said Brooke thoughtfully. "Otherwise Paul will know it's a trick."

Tess glanced at Will. "I'm certainly willing to put on a tux for a good cause," he said.

"Think of it as planning a party," said Brooke. "Hey, I'm in my element now." She turned to her cousin. "You handle the flowers and dress. Will, you talk to the concierge about all the technical and legal details, and rustle up a suit. I'm going to arrange for the dogs to get a bath and Toby a trim. And then I'm going to get both Tess and I a full-body massage, and afterward we're going to watch a couple of feel-good DVDs until the witching hour tonight!"

"Brilliant," said Will. "You are *so* like your mother."

"Thanks," said Brooke. "Tess, are you with me?"

Overwhelmed by the show of love and support she'd just received from her three friends, Tess said, "You bet I am."

And the race was on.

ONE thing Tess learned from the evening before her wedding was that with enough money, anything could be arranged.

A French woman, an expert dog groomer, came to the room and began to wash both Sugar and Toby in one of the suite's bathrooms. She could have taken them to her twenty-four-hour salon, but Tess didn't want to take any chances that Paul might spot Toby. She wanted her dog to be safe from that man.

The full-body massage left her feeling lovely, relaxed, and weightless. Brooke found someone who came right to the room. She also ordered up a pitcher of margaritas, so by the time the DVDs were playing, Tess was feeling no pain.

"*Sense and Sensibility.* Always a good one," Brooke said, sipping her drink. "That Emma Thompson is a genius. And you know how much I adore Kate Winslet."

They never made it to the second DVD. Kim burst into the room with what looked to Tess like perhaps one of the most beautiful wedding dresses she'd ever seen.

"And shoes and everything," Kim said. "Boy, this place has the shops, let me tell you!"

Toby and Sugar came out of the back bathroom to choruses of "Ooohs" and "Ahhhs." Both dogs looked stunning, Toby with her cute cut and Sugar with her glorious fur poufed out all over in a silvery, shimmering mass.

"Lovely dogs," said the French groomer, and Tess made a point of tipping her lavishly.

Will arrived within the hour, a suit bag in his hand, with all the arrangements made for close to midnight that very night.

"We have the use of a luxury suite on one of the top floors," he said. "Very posh. So now all you have to do is pull yourself together. I even got a photographer on short notice. The concierge told me he's one of the best. And I bought a digital camera so we can print out some pictures in the business office before breakfast tomorrow to show Paul."

"We are good," Brooke said.

"I feel like I didn't do anything," Tess said.

"We couldn't have you out of the room, in case Paul's staying here," Kim said.

As if on cue, Tess's cell phone rang. She checked the number.

"Paul."

"Give it to me," Will said. "Hello?"

They all heard an ear-splitting, furious dialogue come out of the small cell. Will merely held it away from his ear and waited for the tirade to stop. After a few minutes, he answered.

"I understand you're upset, but you had your chance and you blew it. Now, let the lady meet with you tomorrow, and everything will be settled." A pause, then, "Who am I? Well, you'll find that out tomorrow, won't you?" And he disconnected the call.

"Turn off the cell, and don't go near it," he advised Tess. "The man's deadly."

She did, setting it in one of her dresser drawers.

"The last four hours were amazing," Brooke said, leaning back in her chair. "I can't believe we all got as much done as we did."

"Except for you," Kim said, teasing her. "Where's my margarita?"

As her cousin poured her a generous glass, Kim said to Tess, "Want me to do your makeup?"

AT eleven-thirty, the entire party made their way up to a luxury suite on one of the top floors. Will, Tess, Brooke, Kim, Toby, and Sugar. There was a minister there, and flowers at one end of the room by the floor to ceiling windows. A CD player played soft classical music, and lots of white candles had been lit.

"This is beautiful," Tess whispered. She glanced up at Will. "You shouldn't have gone to all this trouble!"

"No trouble at all," he whispered.

AS the two of them moved forward toward the minister, the dogs at their sides, Kim leaned over and whispered to Brooke, "You should see the ring he bought her."

"Are you kidding me?"

Kim shook her head. "I think," she whispered quietly, "that something happened on the road."

"Sex?"

Kim shook her head again. "Not that simple, and not that easy. I think they really bonded or something. I think he really cares for her. He's fallen for her. And Tess is just about ready to get it. She's been busy with all this other stuff, getting through the pain that bastard put her through. But she's going to wake up and see what a good man she's had by her side the entire time."

Brooke linked arms with her cousin. "God, I love you. You're such a friggin' romantic!"

"Hey, it's my job. I create illusion and glamour. And speaking of glamour, I think I outdid myself tonight."

"She does look stunning. And I love the way you put up her hair."

"Thanks."

Both women watched while the minister asked Will and Tess to stand in a certain area and then he nodded at them all that the ceremony was about to begin.

"I hope I don't cry," Brooke said as they approached the couple.

Kim sniffed delicately.

"Not you, too?"

"Yeah." Kim grinned. "But I have to say, even this wedding won't hold a candle to the one we pulled off. You were *such* a lovely bride."

Brooke stifled a giggle and then said, "Oh my God, what if Paul had seen you downstairs—"

"But he didn't, and we're here, and Will and Tess are getting married. So enjoy this wedding, Brooke, and go ahead and cry."

fifteen

WEEKS LATER, TESS might look back at her Las Vegas wedding to Will and see it for the turning point it was. But at the moment, she was so nervous about what had to happen later that same day that she merely clutched Will's arm and answered the questions put to her automatically. And before she knew it, she was married.

Married. She was married. About a week later than her original plan, and to a different man—but she was married.

"You may kiss the bride," the minister said, smiling.

For a moment, Tess panicked, wondering what was about to happen. Then Will leaned over and kissed her gently on her forehead. He smiled down at her as if to say, *It's going to be all right.* She was so grateful to him that he'd seemed to sense she was flustered and not in the mood to be swept off her feet with a fake kiss, a show for the minister.

The thought of facing Paul at the buffet had her stomach in knots. But she felt a lot better, knowing that there was nothing he could do now. She was a married woman, and he would be in trouble with the law if he pulled any of his macho crap.

Kim and Brooke opened the champagne, and flutes of the sparkly stuff were passed all around. Even the minister had a glass and wished them all the best life had to offer for the rest of their marriage. He was also obviously a dog lover, as he gave both Toby and Sugar fond pats on their furry heads.

All in all, it was a good time. They retired back to their suite, and Kim and Brooke finally had time to unpack. No one was really tired, and Tess sat on one of the queen-sized beds in a bedroom off the main area that had been turned over to her two friends.

"You did the right thing," Brooke said, hanging up another dress and reaching for a small pile of underwear and throwing it into one of the drawers. "He can't touch you now, Tess, even if he wanted to."

"He won't go up against Will," Kim said, placing the last pair of shoes in the bottom of the generous closet. "Bullies never fight with their physical equals."

"Or their superiors," said Brooke.

"Are you both coming with us to see Paul?" Tess said.

"If you want us to. If you just want Will there, we'll understand."

"I'd like you there—but maybe at a different table."

"Fine with me," Kim said. "I don't think Paul is going to be that thrilled to see us, what with what we did to his dream wedding."

"You mean Madeline's dream wedding," Brooke said. "And don't be surprised, Tess, if she shows up with him. Sharks seem to like to swim in pairs."

"Madeline? Here?"

"She might be," Brooke said as she took her small, quilted bag of toiletries into the bathroom and then came back out. "Think about it—they work together for their mutual benefit. I'm sure she had something invested in pairing you up with Paul."

"God, the whole thing sounds so—Machiavellian," Tess mused.

"Yep," Brooke replied, as she sprawled on the bed across from the one Tess was sitting on. "Some people only seem to be able to act out of their own self-interest, and those two are champs."

"Hey, guys," Kim said, coming out of the bathroom, her vivid red hair pulled up into a high ponytail off her face. She'd just washed off her makeup and now pulled some pajamas out of one of the drawers. "We need to get some sleep, or none of us are going to be any good tomorrow—I mean, today. It's almost two in the morning, and when's the bomb-dropping breakfast scheduled for? Eight?"

"Right as usual," Brooke said, getting up as Tess did.

Tess looked from one woman to the other. "Thank you. For everything. Thank you so much. It's been—you're like—"

"Fairy godmothers?" Kim said.

"Mischievous elves?" Brooke suggested.

"The best of friends," Tess said. "The very best."

"Our pleasure," said Brooke, giving her a fierce hug.

TESS didn't sleep the rest of the night. This was it, meeting Paul at the breakfast buffet would finally end the emotional nightmare that had started when she'd looked in that church window and seen her fiancé bonking another woman.

By the time this breakfast was over, she'd be a free woman. And that felt wonderful.

Not able to sleep, she dug out her knitting and sat down in one of the overstuffed chairs in her bedroom after turning on the floor lamp next to it. Toby glanced up from the pile of sheets and blankets on the bed, let out a doggy yawn, stretched, and then burrowed back into the covers. Within seconds, she was breathing deeply and fast asleep.

Tess relaxed. Knitting always calmed her. As the stitches flashed across her bamboo needles, the process became repetitive and soothing, like a meditation. And she thought of all that had happened since she'd climbed into Will's van and decided to leave town.

To the untrained eye, not a lot had happened in the past few days. But there had been a seismic shift in her interior landscape, a series of discoveries that had rocked her world. She couldn't look back now and try to make the old life work, not with the new knowledge she had. She simply had to pick up where she was and build a new life for herself, one a lot more healthy and authentic than the one she'd planned with Paul.

There were always moments in life you looked back on as crucial turning points, and Tess knew that the last week was that sort of moment for her. She remembered a song that her high school choir had sung at her graduation, the lyrics from the well-known Robert Frost poem. *Two roads diverged in a yellow wood . . .*

I'm definitely taking the one less traveled by . . .

The vividly colored sweater was swiftly taking shape beneath her hands, and now she was in the home stretch. She worked nonstop, as the city outside the large glass hotel window slowly lightened as the sun began to rise. And just as the desert sky was being washed in shades of pink and peach and gold, she fastened off the last stitches and looked at the last piece of the sweater in her hands.

It could be the start of something wonderful. Tess was lucky Will had suggested she think of knitting as more than a hobby and was willing to go to bat for her, generously giving her the necessary contacts. A person could have all the talent in the world and be totally prepared, but if that talent never met with a great opportunity—

There was a gentle knock on the door, and she went to answer it, still in her pajamas. They were simple, soft pink striped flannel with a darker pink piping around the edges—men's pajamas, actually, with a feminine twist.

She opened the door and saw Will, Sugar by his side.

"Just taking Sugar out for a long walk. Want me to take Toby?"

"Thank you." For just a moment, she considered going with them.

"Better not to," he whispered. "We're this close. We don't want to blow it and have Paul see you before breakfast."

How he could read her. "Right." She walked back inside her bedroom, then found Toby's leash and jingled it softly. Toby shot bolt upright from the bed and came hurtling down to her side. She let Tess fasten the leash on to her collar and hand the leash over to Will.

"I thought I'd tire them out so they'd stay in their crates and sleep during breakfast," he said. "And if I see Paul and he should recognize Toby, we'll all make a run for it."

"Good plan, but I doubt he would. Toby wasn't high on his radar screen, if you know what I mean."

Will glanced down at the Schnauzer mix, straining against the leather leash in her eagerness to take her walk. "His loss," he said softly.

After he'd left, Tess headed into the bathroom, stripped off her pajamas, and hopped into a hot shower.

* * *

SHE dressed with care. After all, this was a showdown, and
she wanted to have every feminine weapon possible at her
disposal.

She wanted Paul off balance, so she decided to deliberately play off what he'd expected of her. He'd wanted the
quiet little mouse of a stay-at-home corporate wife, with
her black velvet Alice headband, her long straight hair, Peter Pan collars, ballerina flats, and preppie-style fashions.
Things so tastefully tailored and so neutrally colored that
she might as well have been dead. Sort of a washed out
Bree Van de Camp look from *Desperate Housewives*, prim
and proper to the max. Clothing that shouted both tailored
and trapped. Whipped. She was only twenty-nine, but
she'd been wearing matronly fashions.

Tess was having none of it. What she was going for was
more of a Gabrielle Solis approach—fabulous, young, flirty,
and sassy. Independent and with a fiery Latina spirit. What
she loved most about the television character was how inap-
propriately she often dressed, but how she dressed *for herself*. Whether mowing the lawn in an evening dress or going
to her mother-in-law's funeral in a revealing little black number and sky-high heels, Gabrielle was a force to be reckoned
with. And Tess wanted some of that force to rub off on her.

She'd taken Kim aside before she'd run out to shop for
her wedding gown and asked her to pick up a few things for
her if she saw them in a boutique. Tess had wanted clothing
that was completely the opposite of what she'd worn before. When she'd explained all this to Kim, her green eyes
had lit with pleasure.

"I love to shop!" she'd told Tess. "In another life, I
would've loved to work as a costume designer." She'd

grabbed Tess's arm, squeezed it, and said, "I think I have exactly the idea of the look you're going for!"

When Tess had opened the various boxes and bags Kim had left in her room, she'd agreed.

The outfit was stunning—totally unlike anything she'd ever dared wear before. But now she didn't have her long hair; she had her shoulder-length style with rock star layers and wispy, sexy bangs. And Kim had agreed to do her makeup, something a lot more daring than what she usually wore.

Out of the shower, Tess quickly made her bed and spread her new outfit on top of it. She sighed with pleasure as she looked down at it and had a moment of total, gleeful anticipation as she thought of how Paul would react. Because if ever an outfit screamed at him that she didn't give a damn what he thought, this was it.

The form-fitting capri pants were a vivid turquoise, designed to hug a woman's butt and make a statement. Even the subtle stitching down the side would enhance her figure. It was a pair of capris that screamed *Look at me* in a way that all the sexless Peter Pan collars in the world failed to achieve.

The top was pure white, sleeveless, made with a bit of stretch so it would emphasize her curves, and with the sexiest little baby doll ruffle around the arm openings. The underwear (which Paul would never see but which she would know was there) was La Perla, for God's sake! Gorgeous wisps of silk and lace, European in design, and sexy as hell, surely created to give a woman nothing but confidence. And the shoes . . .

The shoes were her favorites. Those heels had to be at least five inches, if not six. And white. Sexy, white strappy sandals. If Madeline really did come along with Paul to this breakfast, her stepmother might actually have a stroke, seeing as how Tess was about to actually wear white shoes after Labor Day . . .

Totally satisfied with her outfit, Tess dropped her hotel towel and reached for the exquisite lingerie.

WHEN Kim was done with her makeup, even Tess didn't recognize herself.

"Wow," she said softly, staring into the hotel mirror.

Kim had styled her hair in a way Tess never would have thought of, a high ponytail that emphasized her cheekbones and looked wild and sexy after she'd put a few hot rollers in her hair and then swept it up off her face.

Her makeup was just as dramatic a transformation. The emphasis was on her eyes, with black liner and mascara, and a sparkly, very sheer lavender shadow Kim assured her would make her hazel eyes pop. She applied a blush she'd actually called Orgasm and a pinky-beige lipstick just slightly darker than her own lip color that defined her lips perfectly and let her eyes take center stage.

She was ready. Tess slipped on her sky-high white stilettos and walked out into the main living area of the suite.

Will and the dogs were just coming in the door, and he was carrying coffee from Starbucks for all of them. But he stopped dead when he saw her.

"Tess?"

His jaw dropping did wonderful things for her ego.

"The one and only."

He was smiling now, a deep smile that reached his eyes. He set down the coffee, unsnapped the dog's leashes, and came toward her. Toby and Sugar stayed where they were, both dogs staring at her.

"You," he said softly, giving her a very appreciative once-over, "are a little vixen."

"Thank you." Her pleasure was complete.

"Paul won't know what hit him," Will said, handing her one of the coffees. "I take it that was the idea?"

Tess took a small sip of her coffee and smiled. "Got it in one."

THE buffet they'd picked had three vital criteria. It was always packed with people—including a fair share of off-duty cops. It was brightly lit. And most important, the food was fabulous. As if things couldn't get any more perfect, the price was right as well.

Will had showered and shaved in record time, dressing in a pair of well-worn jeans, his boots, and a scruffy rock 'n' roll T-shirt. He looked incredible, the T-shirt emphasized the very nice muscles in his arms. Tess asked him to leave his shoulder-length hair loose and not tied back, and he complied.

As they approached the buffet, she held on to his shoulder, squeezing his bicep. His arm felt hard and warm and strong beneath her fingers and offered some comfort.

"Showtime," Will said softly. "Don't worry, Tess. I'm not going to leave you alone with the bastard."

"Thank you."

The gorgeous diamond ring Will had slipped on her finger last night, along with a platinum wedding band, felt so conspicuous on her left ring finger. Tess found that she wanted to hide it at first, not give away the game, so she slipped them both into a ring box and into her turquoise clutch bag.

As they entered the buffet and paid for their breakfast at the register up front, Tess saw Paul and Madeline sitting at a large table by one of the windows. Bright autumn desert sunshine spilled over the blond wood of the table, and Tess noticed that they had already had breakfast.

Probably think they're going to take off with me right from here, to the airport, and back home. Think again . . .

She looked right at them, and they looked right past her. Tess realized with a start and then with a feeling of glee that they literally *couldn't see her*. They didn't recognize her. If she didn't fit their little preconceived package of how she should look and behave, she simply didn't register with them.

Astonishing.

She whispered this to Will, and he said softly, "It's always amazing how people don't see what they don't want to." He gave her arm a reassuring squeeze and then said, "I have a feeling this won't take that long. It could even be fun."

I wouldn't take it that far, she thought as they headed toward the table.

PAUL looked up in passing as they paused at their table, and Tess was deeply gratified as he did a classic double take and said, "Tess? Jesus Christ, is that you?"

Before she had a chance to respond, he said harshly, "What the *hell* have you done with your hair?"

The old Tess would have crumbled. Wilted. The new Tess gave him a huge smile, fluffed her bangs with her newly painted nails, and said, "You like it? I think it's the most flattering cut I've ever had!"

He looked as if he were about to say something else but then his jaw snapped shut.

"Why don't you both sit down?" Madeline suggested, her voice smooth and melodious, trying to make peace as usual. Make peace before she moved in for the kill. The old iron fist in the velvet glove.

The table was rectangular, with the short end up against the large window. Madeline and Paul were sitting across from each other in the seats closest to the window. Will took the seat next to Paul, while Tess slid in next to Madeline.

"You don't want to sit next to Paul?" Madeline said, sounding hurt, like a little girl who had been denied a piece of candy.

Oh, what a little manipulator. "Nope," Tess said. "Can we get on with it?"

"What's *he* doing here?" said Paul, eyeing Will with distaste. The long dark hair, the rock T-shirt, the jeans and boots—it all combined to create a type of person Paul particularly abhorred.

"I'm with the band," Tess said and then turned to Will. "What are you going to have? I'm starving! Those made-to-order omelets looked fantastic—"

"Tess!" Now Paul sounded angry. Frustrated. Pissed as hell.

"Yes?" She turned toward him.

"Don't you think you have more important things to do than eat?"

"Paul," she said, leaning forward and looking him directly in the eye, "how easy for you to say when you've already eaten. Now I want both of you to be polite and let Will and I get our breakfasts. Try not to make a bad impression."

And with that, she got up from her chair and turned, giving Paul a spectacular view of her butt in her turquoise capris, and sauntered over to the buffet.

Tess grinned as she heard Madeline's audible gasp. She'd finally seen the shoes.

* * *

WHEN they were back at the table with their breakfasts—a spinach and cheese omelet with a side of home fries for her, and for Will, pancakes and sausage with a side of fried eggs—Tess dug into her omelet with obvious relish. Will had gone back to the buffet one more time and brought back coffee and freshly squeezed orange juice for both of them.

"Cream and two sugars, right?" he said, handing her a coffee.

Tess didn't miss the glare Paul shot toward Will. He was obviously pissed that they were close enough that Will knew how she took her coffee. Paul had never bothered to remember. As Will had said just that morning—his loss.

"Isn't Vegas the *best*?" she said between mouthfuls as she reached for her glass of freshly squeezed orange juice.

"Tess," said Paul, his patience clearly wearing thin and speaking patiently, as if to a child. "We did not come all this way to discuss Las Vegas. Now, you have to listen to—"

"Paul," she said softly, a piece of her omelet dangling from her fork, "don't talk to me as if I'm a dimwitted child. I know exactly why you and Madeline are here, but I want to discuss this after I have my breakfast. That's what I assumed we were doing this morning—meeting for breakfast and then discussing this entire mess. Only you two went ahead and anticipated the breakfast. How rude! Now please, let me have mine and then we can talk."

"Mess?" Madeline said, hurt in her voice. "Oh, Tess, how can you refer to this as a mess? Why, I—"

"Because it is one," Tess said before eating her bite of omelet. She chewed, swallowed, and then said, "Let's talk about inconsequential things while Will and I finish our meal. You know—small talk. You're both so good at it." She turned to her stepmother. "So how's Dad?"

Madeline lowered her eyes, looking hurt. "So very disappointed in you."

Tess took another sip of her orange juice. "So you didn't tell him Paul was having sex with another woman the night before our wedding day?"

"Didn't tell him!" Paul said, practically exploding out of his seat. "Those two *friends* of yours told *the entire congregation*! I don't understand your vindictiveness, Tess. It's not like you."

Tess lowered her fork, the last third of her omelet forgotten. "Were you planning on telling me about Marti before we got married?"

Paul looked dumbfounded. Clearly this was the last question he'd thought she would ever ask him.

"Well?"

No answer from Paul, just goggle-eyed shock.

Madeline pleated her paper napkin and said, "Tess, please . . ."

"Tess please nothing. I want an answer, and I want it now."

"I don't find this manner of speaking particularly attractive," Paul said quietly, having gotten his emotions back in line.

Tess marveled at the man. A week ago, a month ago, his words would've crushed her. She would've scurried around, trying to make things better for him. She'd thought her sole job on the planet was to make Paul's life better, at any cost to her own. But now—

"I don't particularly care. I want an answer. *Now.* Or I'm leaving this table and never speaking to the two of you again."

"Have you been giving her drugs?" Madeline said to Will.

"Just coffee," Will said easily, taking another sip of his. "You know what they say about some people and caffeine."

"You think this is funny," Madeline said to him, narrowing her eyes.

"That's where you're wrong," Will said quietly. "I think this is all dead serious."

"Will," said Tess quietly. "You'd better finish up your food, because the shit's going to hit the fan."

"Tess! Such language!" Madeline said, her tone scandalized.

"Yeah, well—whatever," Tess said, taking a small velvet box out of her purse and sliding it across the table toward Paul.

"What is this?" he said, not picking it up.

"I think you know," Tess replied. "This is the part where I say, 'I regret to inform you that my heart is simply not engaged in the way it should be for a relationship of such magnitude to take place.' Got it?"

"I am not taking this diamond ring back!" Paul said, setting his jaw, his entire manner mulish.

"Well, that's true," said Tess quietly. "What you're taking back is a very good fake—a cubic zirconium incredibly well fashioned to fool me into thinking it was a two-carat diamond engagement ring."

"*What?*" Paul reached for the box, but Madeline was quicker. She grabbed the little black velvet box and snapped it open. "Paul, this is the same ring!" She turned to Tess, splotches of angry color appearing on her cheeks. "What kind of nonsense are you making up now?"

"There's a jeweler I met in Vegas, a very nice man named Henri. I asked him to come up to my room and provide me with a box for my former engagement ring, but when he took a look at the ring, he asked me if he could examine it a little closer. Turns out the ring was as fake as you were," she said, directing the last sentence to Paul.

"*Paul?* Is this *true?*"

This time Tess had the distinct feeling Paul wasn't going to get out of answering the question. It looked like the two sharks might turn on each other.

"Madeline—you know how careless Tess is with things! Look how thoughtless she was about her own wedding day! I thought she could wear this one and then keep the real one at home, bring it out for special occasions." Reaching into his jacket pocket, Paul pulled out another ring box.

He'd come prepared. In case everything else he'd planned hadn't worked, he'd been willing to appeal to Tess's supposed love of things. He was betting on the fact that she felt the same way he did about material possessions and needed them as badly as he did to shore up his shaky sense of self.

His beliefs about women seemed so narrow to Tess. The classic, didn't every woman on the planet love a huge diamond? A gigantic ring to wear on her finger and a man to have in her life, because God forbid she should be alone long enough to figure out what she really wanted.

But she'd never really wanted lavish gifts. She'd wanted love. Paul was smugly convinced he could reel her in using the same bait that would have worked for him.

"Willing to take that one to a jewelry store and have it appraised?" Tess said softly.

Both Paul and Madeline leaned in at the same time. It was clear they thought their work here was almost done.

"Of course, darling," Paul said. "Anything for you."

"Willing to give up Marti and be a faithful husband?" Tess said, her voice dead cold.

Paul hesitated and then said, "If that's what it takes, then yes, I will."

Madeline sighed and then said, "I knew we could find some common ground—"

"Finished?" Tess said to Will. He nodded, setting down his fork and reaching for what was left of his coffee. His blue eyes sparkled with suppressed mirth.

"Well," said Tess, "I've got to blow this pop stand." She turned to both Paul and her stepmother and said, "It doesn't matter what the two of you do or say, because what you think has nothing to do with me." She unsnapped her turquoise clutch and extracted another black velvet box, opened it, and slipped the two rings inside on her left ring finger. Then she lazily, casually, let her hand drop to the blond wood surface of their table.

"What is this?" Madeline said, her voice rising, panicking.

"Just what it looks like," Tess said. "I got married."

"What the hell?" Paul exploded out of his seat once again, reaching for her, but Will stood and effectively blocked him before he could touch Tess.

"No," he said quietly, but his voice had a quality that brooked no interference. "You will not touch her, Paul. You will *not*. Sit."

The commanding British accent did the trick. Paul sat, and Tess marveled at the fact that the man who had been so quick to bend her to his will, to physically enforce her obedience, would not go up against another man. Paul was a bully, plain and simple.

"This one's real, Paul," said Tess softly as her diamond winked and sparkled brilliantly in the desert sunshine coming in through the tall window. "As is the relationship." She glanced at Will. "He'll never lie to me or make my life a living hell the way you would have."

"Oh my God, this is going to kill your father," Madeline muttered, a last gasp at getting in the guilt.

"No, it won't, Madeline. He barely notices me as it is. The wedding was for the two of you, and Paul. It was a business merger, pure and simple. And there are easier ways to do it than sacrifice your stepdaughter's life." Tess glared at both of them. "You should both be *ashamed* of yourselves."

And to her absolute astonishment, they both looked rather subdued.

"Now," said Will, "a few ground rules if you don't mind, Tess?"

"Not at all, darling," she said, touching his arm and immensely enjoying the way a muscle worked in Paul's jaw line.

"You will never contact my wife again," he said, looking at Paul. "You will never call her, write to her, touch her, or get within a couple of hundred yards of her. Am I making myself perfectly clear?"

Paul glared at him. Will turned toward Madeline.

"You don't have to like this marriage, but you do have to respect Tess's decision and stop with all the guilt trips. She's not a child you can manipulate. She's a woman."

Madeline looked away, her mouth pursed tightly. She was angry.

Will turned his attention back to Paul. "And for you to have a chance in hell of happiness, you have to understand that a wife is not a piece of property. She's a gift, a gift given to you to make your life so much better than it was before. She's a full partner and deserves to have both dignity and respect within the relationship.

"And until you can understand that, Paul, you'd better stick to women like Marti who know what you're up to, who know the score, and who don't mind being treated like slabs of meat. And even with her so-called acceptance of what you're doing, you get no respect from me for what you're trying to do to her. But leave Tess out of all of this, or you'll answer to me. Are you perfectly clear about this?"

Paul was angrier than Tess had ever seen him, the emotion almost radiated off of him. He looked at her, his pale blue eyes icy with rage, and Tess had a horrible, sinking feeling that she was finally seeing beneath the slick facade once and for all.

This was the man she could have married, and she would have seen that look within the first few months of their marriage, perhaps even weeks. And at that point, she would have been trapped, with a web tightly spun around her made up of her father and brother and stepmother and community and—God forbid—perhaps even a child on the way . . .

"Let's go," she said quietly to Will, and he came around to her side and helped her to her feet.

He glanced at Paul and Madeline. "I won't say it's been fun, because it hasn't, but I hope the two of you have learned something from all this."

How she loved that accent. Crisp and no-nonsense, Will sounded like the ultimate headmaster at a tough boarding school.

They turned and began to walk away, but Paul yelled out, "That's right, Tess, shake your little ass and dress like a whore, and let's see how far this marriage of yours gets—"

Will turned in a flash and was at Paul's side before he even had a chance to finish the sentence.

"Did I forget to mention that you don't even get to talk to my wife that way? *Did I?*" He stared down Paul, absolutely furious, and to Tess's amazement, Paul backed down—sort of.

Will started to walk away when Paul glanced at Madeline and muttered, "Goddamn whore." Barely a whisper, it had been meant for Madeline's ears alone.

Will glanced up at the ceiling as if asking for patience and then said, "Oh, sod it!" He turned around, stalked over to Paul, and slugged him.

Patrons barely looked up from their plates as Paul went crashing down to the floor with the one punch and Madeline screamed. This was Las Vegas, after all.

Tess glanced over at two cops who were finishing up pancake breakfasts, both with coffee cups to their lips. They smiled and one winked at her.

"Can't say he didn't warn him," one said.

"He had it coming," the other replied. "My sister's married to a grade A asshole like that one. No respect."

"My condolences," said Tess, then she reached for Will's arm as he strode toward her, shaking his hand ruefully.

My hero, she thought as they made their way out of the buffet and back to the hotel.

"WE saw it all!" Brooke said as she and her cousin burst into the hotel suite. "Did you see us? We were about three tables over—"

"Hidden behind the proverbial potted plant," Kim finished. "Wow, Tess, you really told them! And Will, I was so glad when you punched out that idiot! The way he treats everyone he comes across, the man's a total—"

"Jerk," Brooke finished.

"Thank you," Will said quietly. "I'm going to lie down for a while. I didn't get much sleep." And he left the main area of the suite and headed for the balcony that overlooked the city.

Stretched out on a chaise, Will closed his eyes but didn't sleep. He kept remembering what he'd said to Paul about a wife being a gift. And he realized that this was how he truly felt about Tess. She was a gift that had been practically thrown into his lap, given to him, and the time they'd spent together had been some of the best of his life. And now they had a day of their journey left.

Los Angeles was only a day's drive from Las Vegas. When they reached the City of Angels, their trip was over. Oh, he could postpone things by getting in a couple of days of sightseeing on the Strip, or they could take in a show, but in the end, the way things were going, they would part company when they reached Los Angeles.

The only time they would see each other again would be when they discussed the annulment. And that wasn't what he wanted.

But how could he make her understand? *I married you to protect you from that bastard, but also because I thought there was something between us, and if we could make it work, make it a real marriage . . .*

It sounded lame, even to him. He took a deep breath and opened his eyes. Both Toby and Sugar were at his feet, in the shade, looking up at him, their dark doggy eyes uncertain.

"It's too hot for the two of you out here," Will said. "Let's go back inside."

As he slid the sliding glass door aside and let the two dogs in, Will decided one thing. It was time to make his move. Paul was out of the picture, he and Tess were officially over. He couldn't hurt her anymore. Bullies generally gave up the game when they were confronted by someone their own size and strength.

If he was ever going to have what he wanted with Tess, he had to make his move. Damn the timing, damn the details. Life was too short, and when something this good was presented to you, when you felt in your heart that it was right, you had to do something about it.

That time, for him, was now.

sixteen

WHAT WILL HADN'T counted on was anything beyond his own feelings and his own impulses to change things, to say what needed to be said, to start over. When he walked across the suite's main living area toward Tess's bedroom, he felt the absolute quiet in the living area.

Brooke and Kim had settled in for a nap in their room, because later they wanted to do some shopping and take in a show. And they'd also said it would be fun for the four of them to have dinner at a fabulous place, so there was no noise or movement from their room.

As he approached Tess's bedroom door, the quiet almost unnerved him. He'd put out the *do not disturb* sign earlier—they'd barely had time to rumple sheets or use most of the plush towels before racing through the wedding, so housekeeping wasn't a problem. Now, with Tess's door slightly ajar, Will hesitated as his hand came up to knock.

He peered inside, just enough so he could see Tess, still dressed in her blue pants and white top, on her bed, face buried in one of the soft pillows. Toby was curled by her side, asleep as well. The white shoes with their impossibly high heels had been kicked off and lay scattered on the carpeted floor.

She looked exhausted.

Will sighed. He'd waited this long; he could wait some more. He had always gone with his instincts, and that night in the bar outside Chicago when he'd first met the grown-up Tess, he'd known something deeply and emotionally significant was happening in his life. She was no longer the little girl who'd followed him around like a shadow.

He'd always believed it when his father had told him how he and his mother had met and within minutes "just knew." It had seemed the most natural thing in the world, so when it had happened to Will when he first looked at Tess, he had been in quiet despair at the thought of her marrying another man.

It wasn't that he thought love couldn't happen more than once. It did. But he'd secretly mourned the fact that he wouldn't get to explore what he and Tess might have had together if she hadn't been planning on getting married the next morning.

Then emotional disaster for Tess had struck. And then the road trip, and all that had happened, and the days with her on the road had only made that first feeling stronger. No man wanted to protect a woman, to help her, to see her get the very best life had to offer unless there was genuine feeling toward that woman, whether romantic or friend-ship. He wanted Tess to have the life she'd always dreamed of, and at this point, he only hoped it included him.

You've got some time. Give her some time.

But not too much, he answered himself impatiently. Taking one last look at Tess and smiling at the peaceful-ness the picture presented, Will backed away from the bedroom door and headed for his room. He found Sugar sprawled across his bed, snoring gently.

"Shove over," he said good-naturedly and then had to grin as the Keeshond got up, gave him a look, walked with great dignity to the far side of the bed, circled three times, and lay down with a sigh.

"It's not that I don't love you, darling dog," Will whispered, scratching Sugar behind her ears. She leaned into it and stared at him with pure love in her dark brown eyes. "But it's just that—there was someone else I was hoping to share some naptime with, and she isn't covered in fur."

Sugar whined softly and then licked his hand.

"Ah, who am I kidding," he said to the dog. "I'll give her all the time she needs."

"SO should we just leave?" Kim whispered from her bed. The suite's bedroom was shrouded in darkness, the heavy curtains drawn against the brilliant desert sunshine.

"My gut tells me we should give the two of them some space. Now that they're married and all."

"And that jerk's out of the picture," Kim said.

"Precisely," Brooke replied. "But if we leave too soon, it might look awkward, as if we were pushing them together. The problem is, their trip is almost over and I want them to have some time alone."

"You think they'll get together before the end of the trip?"

"Nope," said Brooke. "Not that way. Tess isn't all that impulsive, and she just went through this whole breakup. If Will's smart—and he is—he'll give her some time, but he'll be really honest about how he feels and let her know he'd like to take things further as soon as she's ready."

"You know, it's funny," Kim whispered. "I remember

them both from school. Will was so yummy, and Tess was always sneaking looks at him. She was so attracted to him, she could barely speak when he was in the room. I always thought that, in another time and place, and maybe not when she was so young, they could've been a great couple. And here they are."

"What are the odds?" Brooke said. "It almost makes you have faith in the fact that if something's meant to be, it's meant to be."

Kim yawned. "So what's our plan?"

"How about dinner tonight and a show. Then tomorrow, we fake some reason to get back to Illinois, but in reality move over to Caesar's Palace and do some serious shopping and sunbathing, leaving them more time to get to know each other."

"You are the master," Kim said, laughing.

EVERYONE straggled into the suite's main living room around four in the afternoon, looking much better for their down time.

"Vegas at our feet," said Kim, sprawled out on one of the couches, going through one of the tourist magazines. "Hey, how about a show? Maybe some standup?"

"Who's here this weekend?" Tess said.

Kim began to read off names until she got to the name of a famous standup who had had a top-rated television show for many years before leaving the small screen.

"I love her," Brooke said.

"A very funny woman," Will added.

"I'm good to go," Tess said.

"Me, too," said Kim.

Will stood up and stretched. "I feel like a walk, so I'll go down and see what I can do about tickets. Dinner before or after?"

"Before," said Kim. "You don't want to see Brooke drinking on an empty stomach. It's not a pretty sight."

Brooke threw a pillow at her cousin, and Tess laughed.

"You three figure out what type of food and where, and I'll be right back."

WILL couldn't remember a more fun time. They ate at an Italian place and then walked down the Strip to the hotel where their show was being performed. And they laughed and laughed until their sides ached as the comedienne shared her wry take on the world and all its foibles.

Afterward, they walked down the Strip, admiring the lights, and bought ice-cream cones.

"And so everything turned out happily ever after," Brooke said as they sat at the small café tables and enjoyed their dessert. "Tess, what are your plans now? Are you headed back home as soon as you reach Los Angeles?"

Will hoped no one saw the slight start of surprise his body gave when he heard what Brooke said.

"I don't know," Tess said. She proceeded to tell Brooke and Kim about his offer to show her sweater to a woman he knew who was a costume designer on a major sitcom.

"Oh, Tess, that would be so cool!" Kim said. "Can you imagine turning on the TV and seeing one of your sweaters on an actor or actress?"

"I'd like that a lot," Tess admitted, and Will decided then and there that he would move heaven and earth to get her some sort of deal.

"You're at a funny point in your life," mused Brooke. "Where you can kind of start over." She took a deep breath and said, "I wouldn't be in any hurry to get home. I think I'd take some time and get to know a different city, see what sort of opportunities it presents."

Thank you, Brooke, Will thought. He smiled at her, and he could've sworn her eyes glinted with mischief. What was she up to?

They went in and out of various hotels, walking and talking, taking in elaborate window displays, occasionally going in and looking at some of the merchandise. But before long, they all headed back to their suite at the Hard Rock.

"Any plans for tomorrow?" Brooke said, her tone bright. "Are you guys staying a few more days?"

"Up to Tess," said Will. "I've been here before."

"I'd like to," she said.

"Then we will," he said.

"OKAY, what's the crisis?" Kim said from the depths of her bed in the darkened bedroom. "And nothing with disease or death, because I don't want to tempt fate!"

"I know what you mean." Brooke rolled over in her hotel bed and propped herself up on her elbows. "Okay, how about something with Matt and Alicia," she said, referring to her cousin and his wife.

"Nah. It won't sound right. I mean, we stayed with them when we were hiding from Paul. We have to use someone else."

"You're right," Brooke said, and Kim could practically hear the wheels turning in her cousin's head. "We need something with a different tone, totally."

"Maybe something job related?" Kim suggested.

"Perfect! How about if you suddenly get a wonderful

opportunity to audition for a film that's shooting in the area, something like that—"

"Yeah, and they have to see me in the next two days because they want to get started fast, and—"

"What film?"

Silence.

"I know," said Kim. "My agent's getting all the details together, and he'll fill me in when I get home, but he thinks this is a tremendous opportunity for me!"

Another short silence.

"Do you even *have* an agent?" Brooke said.

"No, but—"

"Okay. My brother Ron was the master fib teller of all time when we were kids, and one of the main things he impressed upon me is that if you're going to tell a little white lie that doesn't really hurt anyone—"

"*Ron?*" said Kim incredulously. "You *are* talking about my cousin Ron?"

"Okay, if you're telling a whopper, the less detail, the better. So come up with something. Your job is more glamorous than mine."

"How about if a girlfriend called me and told me about this independent film looking for a makeup artist and she thinks I would be perfect and it would be a great opportunity for me and I really want to try to get it?"

Brooke started to laugh. "The gift of Blarney must run in this family. Perfect. That's it. We'll go with that tomorrow."

"SO even though I really wanted to see Vegas and spend some time with all of you, I really want to do this! And Brooke said she'd come back with me and offer moral support," Kim said, looking from Will to Tess anxiously. "Don't be too mad at us, okay, guys?"

"I'm not mad," Will said. "I understand completely."

"I do, too," Tess said.

Bags were gathered and good-byes were said, then Tess offered to walk them down to the lobby and their shuttle to the airport.

"You're both so full of it," Tess said as the elevator started to make its descent.

"Whatever do you mean?" Brooke said, obviously trying for a casual tone.

"I know exactly what you two are up to and—thanks. I really appreciate it."

Kim glanced up. "Are you going to go for it with him?"

"It's kind of confusing—"

"No it's not," said Brooke as the elevator reached the lobby and all three women walked out, hauling luggage and headed toward the main lobby. "You were nuts about the guy in school, he's still hot as hell, and I think you should just kiss your worthless father and stepmother good-bye and ride off into the sunset in Los Angeles with Will!"

Tess tried unsuccessfully to repress her laughter. "Tell me how you *really* feel."

"Tell *me*," said Brooke, suddenly dead serious. "I think things happen for a reason, Tess, and there was a reason you saw Paul doing the nasty with another woman and didn't marry him. And there was a reason Will was in town and heading west. Things couldn't have worked out more perfectly."

"Do you think it's too soon after Paul?" Tess said.

"Nope. That relationship was dead in the water for at least four months before you caught him red-handed."

"I feel like I could just walk into this relationship so easily, but don't I need some time alone to figure out who I really am and what I really want? I feel like I've spent so much of my life trying to be what I'm really *not*!"

"But Will's not like that," said Brooke. "He's easygoing, he has his own life, and he's more than happy for you to have yours. Trust me, he's not the kind of guy to put a woman in a box and demand that she stay there."

"Why don't we have a quick cup of coffee somewhere and talk for just a bit?" Kim asked. "We have time before our plane."

"What time do you guys leave?"

A short silence ensued. Brooke and Kim were careful not to look at each other.

"Let me try that again. Are you really leaving?"

"Oh shit, Tess, we're just going to Caesar's Palace. We wanted to give you and Will some time alone. There'll be plenty of time for fun when you invite us out to Los Angeles when you're living there with him." Brooke had the grace to look a little bit guilty.

"So the movie back home is—"

"—a total fabrication," Brooke said. "But it was a good one, don't you think?"

"One of your best. Let me tell Will we're going to sit and have coffee for a while, and then we'll just hammer this whole thing out."

"HIGHLY overrated, that time alone thing," Kim said, taking a sip of her venti vanilla latte. "I mean, think about all those men out there, those awful men, who you could be dating and trying to have sex with—*sex that isn't even very good*. And you have Will, all to yourself, in a suite at the Hard Rock, and you're wondering what to do?"

"I say," said Brooke, gesturing with her pumpkin spice latte, "that you've lived too careful a life. Go up to that suite, and jump this man's bones." She took a sip, laughed, and then said, "And call me tomorrow at Caesar's and give me a full report. I want *details*."

"It's been that long?" Tess asked.

"Don't ask."

"Here's the thing," Kim said. "Whenever I'm faced with a decision, one of the things I always consider is if I'm going to regret *not* doing something. And I think, in the long run, that you might regret *not* seeing if things could work out with Will. But the minute you get out to Los Angeles, you're going to be figuring out your life and he's going to be going back to his life, and there may not be that moment. And right now, you've *got* that moment."

"It's like this trip has been a little window out of time," said Brooke. "So I say take that window and enjoy it for all it's worth."

"And let me ask you this," said Kim. "Did Paul ever really make you feel like you were wonderful in bed? I mean, like a goddess or something?"

Tess set down her tall vanilla latte and considered this. Almost at the same moment, she shook her head. "I think I was always so—amazed that he chose me. My stepmother kept hammering home the point that he was such a good catch and we made such a good couple. The sex was—not very good, but I thought it might get better with time."

"Huge mistake. *Huge*," said Brooke. "Like thinking you can make over a man. My mother basically told me that, with minor modifications and a little domestication, what you see is what you get."

Tess's cell phone rang, and she answered. "Will," she said to Brooke and Kim.

"I thought," said Will, "that because we were staying a few more days, we could move to a smaller suite. What do you think?"

"Sounds fine with me."

"I'll have them leave you a key at the front desk."

"Okay."

She hung up the phone and told Brooke and Kim what was going on.

"My money's on Will!" said Brooke. "Smaller suite means more romantic and cozy. The man's smart."

"But what about that damn British reserve?" Kim said. "All those manners they have across the pond! What if he thinks that Tess needs more time and he decides to let her set the pace? This relationship could be doomed before it even gets out of the gate!"

"She has a point," Brooke said. "I mean, Tess, do you really need a whole lot of time to get over Paul?"

Tess thought for a moment and said, "I'm kind of embarrassed to say this, but no. I was so sick of always being on my toes, always having to do things a certain way or be a certain way. It was *exhausting*. Suffocating. Then I hit the road with Will, and he's seen me cry nonstop, be totally depressed, forget to wash my hair, not be able to carry on a conversation, lie in bed for days at a time, not eat, throw up down the side of the van—"

"Hey, look at it this way," Brooke said. "Sex *has* to be an improvement after all that!"

Kim almost blew some coffee through her nose, which made Tess laugh even harder.

"I'm not trying to make light of your whole situation, Tess," Kim said. "But in the end, it's only sex. I mean, it could work out, it could not work out. With all you've done and learned on this trip, you could go on either way, couldn't you?"

Tess felt a sense of calm come over her, and she reached for Kim's hand. "Thank you. You're right. Even though I'd like to see something happen with Will, if nothing happened beyond this trip, I'd still feel as if Will kind of liberated me from the whole mess with Paul." She hesitated. "But I still don't know if I'll sleep with him while we're in Las Vegas."

"Why?" Brooke said.

"Why not?" said Kim.

"Because I came to terms with myself on this trip, and I know what I want in a relationship. I want the whole thing. I want the romance and the chase and the courtship and all the feelings and taking the whole thing step by step. I want that first kiss, and I want to hold hands and laugh together. I want all of it, every little bit, so that by the time we do hit the sheets, it's going to mean something to me and to him. And if not acting on this trip dooms the whole thing, well then, in my opinion, we didn't have much to begin with."

Brooke and Kim just stared at her.

"Come on, guys, he'll have my cell number. Do you honestly mean to tell me that if he can't even get it together to ask me out for a hamburger that I should jump at a chance to be with him in case he's that incompetent? And for the record, I think Will is extremely competent!"

They simply stared.

"Am I being clear here?" Tess said.

"Yeah," Brooke said. "Yeah, and I love it! I guess I was a little impatient and wanting things to happen so I could—"

"—live totally vicariously through you," said Kim, "but that's another whole discussion. You," she said, turning to Tess, "do whatever feels right for you. I think everything you've been through has been absolutely amazing. I mean, how many people get a chance to redo their entire lives?"

Tess leaned forward. "Los Angeles. Swimming pools. Movie stars. Television and movie sets. Lots of makeup people needed, especially good ones like you. I'm going to get a little place out in L.A. and give designing knitwear a real chance. And along the way of the rest of my life, I think I have more than a good chance of having a great relationship with Will!"

Brooke leaned forward, batting her eyes as if they were misting up. "Oh Kim, our little Tess is all grown up!"

"Will you stop!" said Tess.

"Honey," said Kim, draining the last of her latte, "you're just sparkling, you're so full of that joyous vibe. I'll tell you this, Los Angeles isn't going to know what hit it."

SHE saw Brooke and Kim off amid much laughter and a few ribald suggestions. Once they were on their way to Caesar's Palace for a little R&R of their own, Tess checked with the registration desk, got her new key, and started to head up to the suite she would be sharing with Will.

And stopped.

What did she want? If ever there was a chance for her to rearrange her life to suit herself, this was that moment. Was she stepping from one relationship into another with barely a break in between?

It wasn't as if she was that experienced in relationships to begin with. Paul had been her first real boyfriend, aside from one or two relationships in college. She hadn't dated much in high school; she'd been shy and always felt she was somewhere in the background, fading in with the wallpaper.

But not now . . .

Now she felt free and even sexy. Amazing what hair and makeup could do, but even more, attitude.

She'd hesitated in the middle of the lobby, but now she turned and went back to the same coffee shop where she and Kim and Brooke had sat and talked. Finding a small back booth, Tess ordered another coffee and sat back and thought.

Within minutes, she knew what she wanted to do. She reached for her cell phone and dialed Charlie in Boulder. He picked up on the third ring and was happy to hear from her. Within a few minutes, Tess laid out what had happened in the past twenty-four hours and told him what she wanted.

"Do you think I have a chance?" she said and waited anxiously for his reply.

"I think," Charlie said, "that first of all, I have to tell you that I'm so damn proud of you for throwing off Mad Madeline and that bastard Paul! I'm so glad you didn't make any excuses for his cheating and just got out of town. Do you know how many women might have taken him back?"

This stunned her. "The moment I saw him with her I knew that wasn't an option." She closed her eyes as she remembered how both Paul and Marti had laughed about her, talking as if they were going to keep their relationship going strong after the wedding and beyond.

"Yeah, but Tess, you've just kicked his ass to the curb and made him realize that he can't treat you like that! That took guts, and I'm so proud of you!"

"I couldn't have done it without Will."

Charlie was silent for a moment and then said, "What do you think of Will? I mean, not that high school stuff. We all knew you had a major thing for him—"

"Oh God, was I that obvious?"

She could hear the smile in her older brother's voice. "Yeah. You were. But don't evade the question, Tess. What do you think of Will?"

Tess took a deep breath and said, "Promise me, promise me you won't make fun of me or say anything for just a moment after I tell you."

"I promise."

She swallowed hard, then said, "I think I may be falling for him."

"Falling for him as in you want to jump his bones, or falling for him in the way that means the white picket fence and a few kids and the whole thing?"

"Oh, Charlie . . . the whole thing. Big time."

Silence on his end.

"Charlie? Say something? Please?"

"I think it's great. He's one of the good guys, Tess. He's not at all like that piece of crap Paul. I can't think of anyone else I'd rather see you end up with, 'cause I want you to be really happy."

"So what do I do?"

"He's a good guy. He's not going to push for you to do anything you might not be comfortable with. I mean, you've just gotten out of a relationship, so you might want to take this one slow—"

"I had doubts about Paul for a few months before the wedding."

"Were you thinking of breaking it off with him?"

"No, I was stupid. I just thought it was pre-wedding jitters, you know, the kind everyone says they have."

"But were you already kind of out of the relationship before you hit the road?"

"Charlie, I was having serious, serious doubts." Tess had to smile as she remembered how she'd asked for a sign while she'd sat in her church. Boy, had she gotten one . . .

"So it's not as if you were madly in love with Paul and now you're madly in love with Will—"

"No, but—I really like what I've seen of Will on this trip."

"And you are married, after all," Charlie said, teasing.

"That was only to stop Paul," she said.

"*That* is where you're wrong," he replied. "No man goes to all that trouble with a woman if there isn't some kind of feeling there. Tell me the truth. Think back, now. When you first saw him, where were you? What did you feel? Honestly."

"I was at a bar with Brooke, and he came in the door. Mrs. Matthews had told Will where to find Brooke, and when he came up to our table—"

"Tell the truth, Tess, especially to yourself. It's crucial."

Tess stared down at her coffee as a small smile curved her lips. "Charlie, the first thought I had was regret that I was getting married because I—I felt like I wanted to go off with Will and—I don't know, talk and see why I had such a strong reaction to him. Does that sound too stupid?"

"Not at all. I think your heart was speeding along and your brain was having a hard time catching up. Happens to all of us."

"But I don't know what to do now," Tess said quietly. "Brooke and Kim have left, and Will and I have a suite together with the dogs, but it's different now because Paul isn't in the way. You know what I mean? It's like his presence isn't between us anymore."

"Got it. Okay, Tess, and here's where you have to stand up for yourself and really go for it. If you could call all the shots, and if it could go exactly the way you wanted it to go, what would happen right now?"

She considered his question carefully.

"Take your time, Tess," he urged.

"You're a good brother, Charlie," she said softly.

"Ah, not that good. I shouldn't have run off and left you all alone with that woman. I didn't really check back and see how you were getting along."

"But you're here for me now."

"Now and in the future, kiddo. Always. Okay, what do you want?"

Tess took a deep breath. "I want to start over with Will. But I think he has to finish his part of the trip as well. He has to deliver the van and Sugar to Elaine and then we're both done with the trip. And at that point, I'd like to—oh, I know this may sound dumb—but I want to start over. I want to go out and hold hands and walk along the beach and go to movies and eat dinner at little restaurants and—all that stuff people do when they're just getting to know each other."

"Tess, any man who's worth anything, and any man who cares for you, shouldn't have any trouble doing what you just told me. If I really cared for someone, I'd walk along the beach with her. I'd take the time to get to know her. Will's a good guy. Do you think he has the same feelings for you?"

She told him about the way Will had given her his cell phone number that night in the bar in case something happened and the wedding didn't go as planned.

"You've answered your own question there. No guy would do that if he just felt sorry for a woman. He's attracted to you. He likes you."

Briefly she filled him in on some of the details of their trip, even up to getting sick down the side of the van.

"Yep, I know he likes you now. Will's not into guilt. He's a solid guy, Tess. I say go for it."

"You think so?" She already had her mind made up, but she wanted just a little more reassurance. It felt so good, so right, to be talking to Charlie like this.

"Yeah." He hesitated. "I think you have a real chance for happiness here, Tess. And I have to admit I like the idea of having you on the West Coast and a little closer than you were before. I think we make our own lives and that happiness and greatness come to people who dare to go after what they really want. So if you want this guy, I think you should go for it. Let him know what you need, and I think everything's going to work out fine."

"You really think so?"

"Hey, life has no guarantees. I can't promise anything. But I do know two things."

"What?"

"One, that Will is the real deal, and he's one of the few men I'd consider good enough for you. And two, let's say everything blows up and it doesn't work out. You just have to pick up the phone and call, and I'll come down and help you out of anything that may make life suck."

She had to laugh at that.

"Thanks, Charlie. It helped a lot, talking with you."

"It helps me, too. I missed you after I left home. I'm glad we got reconnected."

"Me, too." She took another breath to ease the tightness in her chest and then said quickly, "I love you a lot, Charlie, and I missed you terribly when you left. But I never blamed you. If I'd been a lot stronger, I would've walked out myself."

"Hey, Tess, it's never too late to start over with your life, especially when you finally realize that you know what you want. Now get up to that suite and talk to Will. And ditto on that love thing."

seventeen

WILL HEARD THE main door of the hotel suite softly opening and closing. All his nerves seemed to tense. Tess had finally returned after seeing Brooke and Kim off to the airport, though he hadn't really believed that either woman was headed home. He hadn't bought their hastily fabricated story any more than he suspected Tess had.

Brooke had always been a sensitive individual, and she probably saw her and her cousin's departure as a way of letting him and Tess have the time they needed. If he knew those two women as well as he thought he did, they were probably close by in another casino taking a well-deserved vacation after the craziness of the last week. And hoping for the best for him and Tess.

Now he was finally alone with Tess, and Paul was no longer in the way. He was out of her life, and Will was as impatient as hell to get on with what he wanted.

He knew he had to let Tess set the pace. He wasn't the one who'd been practically dumped at the altar, when was it, about a week or so ago? How fast would she rebound?

Would she even want a relationship? Would she want to go out to Los Angeles and find herself before even thinking about any relationship? Perhaps concentrate on a career she really wanted?

He couldn't blame her. What little he'd managed to glean about her life in the Midwest had led him to believe that she'd never really lived the life she wanted. But now that Paul was officially out of the way, maybe he could find out what she did want out of life.

He only hoped that the life she wanted now would include him. He was willing to fight for her, and fight hard, but she had to want it, too. He would do anything in the world, but it would all come to nothing if she didn't want him.

It had been frustrating as hell, being this passive, surrendering to his fate. Letting things happen instead of *making* them happen. But he would've had to be an incompetent nitwit to thrust himself and his feelings on her when she was barely out of what had clearly been a horrible relationship. And he'd known from the start that his role on this trip was to support her, to help her, to get her out of town and on her way to a new life.

Once again, he knew she had to set the pace. He could only let her know what he wanted to have happen and take it from there. He could be honest and authentic in his desires, and that would be it. The rest was up to Tess.

She came into the main living room, and her gaze locked with his. She looked a little nervous, and that was all for the good as far as he was concerned. It didn't look as if they were going to engage in any more small talk. He couldn't take another dinner without feelings worked out between them. He was too impatient a man when he wanted something—or someone.

"Tess?" he said quietly.

Those beautiful hazel eyes looked directly at him, and he felt their effect in the pit of his stomach.

"We have to talk," she said quietly.

SHE felt as if her stomach were coming apart as she walked over to the comfortable sofa where he was sitting and sat down next to him. Toby and Sugar were sprawled out on the carpet in the sun from the sliding glass doors. They both looked totally spent, and she suspected Will had taken them for one of his marathon walks while she'd been out with Brooke and Kim.

"Will," she said softly. "I want to thank you for everything you've done for me on this trip—"

His eyes narrowed a fraction, but he stayed perfectly still. For just a moment, she thought he looked worried.

She had to find a way to let him know what he meant to her. What everything he'd done for her had meant to her. She'd never felt as cared for or as cherished.

At this moment, words seemed so inadequate.

"No one's ever cared for me the way you did," she began. "No one's ever seen me at the absolutely lowest point I've ever been in my life. You did. You did and you stuck around, and every single thing you did was so I could feel better."

He started to say something, but she held up her hand, palm out. "I have to get this all out, and I'm scared that if I stop I won't say it all."

He hesitated, then nodded, but she could still feel the slightest spark of frustration coming from him. Not anger, but a quiet feeling of frustration.

"I know you kind of invited me along. You gave me your cell number that night in the bar. But I thought maybe you believed there was no way I'd contact you. But then everything fell apart. I wanted to get out of Dodge before the wedding, that was the main lure, but then maybe I've—I think I've—I've been lying to myself all along."

She saw comprehension dawning in those gorgeous eyes, then the slightest of smiles, and she knew it was going to be all right. Her heart started speeding up.

"Go on, please," he said, and she felt from the way he was looking at her that she was the entire focus of his world.

"I—I don't know how to say this." She hesitated and then said, "Did you know I had a huge crush on you in school?"

He was smiling now. "I suspected as much. Charlie told me that if I even thought about it—well, he made it clear what he'd do."

"He did?" she said, surprised.

"Someone had to look out for you. But you were too young, Tess. We both knew that."

"Yes." She cleared her throat, suddenly desperate not to look at him. "Well, when you came into that bar, I found that—I was—what I felt was—I was suddenly having all these regrets about marrying Paul. And they had nothing to do with Paul." She hesitated, her tongue coming out to nervously moisten her lips. "And," she said, her voice suddenly a whisper, "they had everything to do with you."

She felt him move on the sofa, closer to her, and then he had both her hands in his.

"Tess," he said quietly. "Am I to understand that you have feelings for me?"

She nodded, unable to speak. The moment of truth was upon her, and she didn't know what to do. She was flying blind, without a safety net, but it felt good to have finally said what she needed to say, what she'd wanted to say from the beginning.

"Would it help you to know that I have those same feelings?"

A rush of joy so intense surged through her body that her eyes filled with tears. Pulling one of her hands away from his, she covered her trembling mouth with it as she stared at him, at his blurry visage before her.

"Darling, it's okay," he said, his voice so very gentle. "I think we're finally on the same page."

She nodded her head, and he eased her into his arms, into his lap, and it felt so very right to be there. She rested her cheek on his chest and could hear the rapid beating of his heart. They sat like that for a while as she struggled to pull herself together.

"You can cry, you know," he said finally. "I'm not one of those men who goes all to pieces at the sight of tears. Wouldn't have worked with two sisters."

She laughed as he handed her some tissue from the box on the low coffee table.

"You were all prepared," she said, after she blew her nose and wiped her eyes.

"I figured we'd be having a discussion like this after Brooke and Kim left. They were pretty obvious about why they were leaving."

She laughed again, then snuggled closer.

"Tell me what you want, Tess," he said, his voice low as he held her close.

"What do you want?" she said.

"Ah, no, we won't go there just yet. I need to know what it is you want from me. You've been through a lot in the last week or so, and we both need to honor that."

"Okay." She took a deep breath. "Could we just sort of start from the beginning? Like as if we just met?"

"That can be arranged."

"Because I think—I think I need to take things slow because I want to really be sure that we aren't going to hurt each other or that it might be wrong—"

"Do you just want some time to get to know me to find out if I have any really horrible secrets or habits you simply can't stand?"

She let out a long sigh and said, "Yes, that's it exactly."

"So when do you want to have our first date?" She felt him kiss the top of her head and then say, "I have to warn you that I'm a very impatient man. But for you, and only you, I'll make an exception."

"Could we finish the trip, deliver the van to Elaine, and then figure out what it is we want to do? I mean, I know I'm going to stay out in Los Angeles because I want a new start and I want to start things up with you—"

"I'd like that a lot."

They were silent for a while, just content on the couch, until Will said, "So I take it you don't want to go out and do the town. You'd rather have an early night and get to L.A. as soon as possible."

"Yes," she said. "And I might ask you for some help finding a place. Maybe you could recommend a good motel or something—"

"I'll think of something."

"Do you want to go out?" she said, twisting gently from his embrace just so she could see the expression on his face.

"Oh, no," he said quietly. "Like I said before, I've been to this city many times. But here with you," he said, smiling down at her, "it's all uncharted territory."

THEY made it to Los Angeles in record time.

Neither of them slept well in their separate bedrooms. When Tess got up and walked out on to their suite's balcony in her pajamas and looked out over the early morning light just beginning to touch the city, she wasn't surprised to hear Will join her. She could feel his presence even before he spoke, and she wondered if it would always be that way between them.

"I'm ready to pack up and leave if you are," he said, joining her at the railing.

"Can we come back someday?" she said. "I'd like to see more of this place."

"Absolutely. Sometimes my work takes me here."

She thought of his work, his music and his band. And Tess found that she could easily accept his starving-artist lifestyle. So long as basic bills were met and they were able to have some standard of living, she realized that the whole emphasis both Madeline and Paul and even her father had put on material possessions, on status and money, was so not her.

Will might not make as much money as Paul or her father, but she sensed he was the sort of man who would always provide for the people he loved. She knew that was true. And she could certainly learn to get along with less. None of the stuff Paul had given her had filled up the emptiness their relationship had been.

"I'm glad we'll be coming back." She turned toward Will and saw that he looked tired. Cupping his cheek with her hand, she whispered, "I'm so glad we found each other, Will."

Those eyes. The way he looked at her thrilled her down to the tips of her toes.

"Get in there and get dressed," he said, and although his tone was playful, she sensed there was something else beneath it. "Before I forget all my good intentions and don't give you the time you need."

*   *   *

THEY left so early that they reached Los Angeles right around noon. Will called Elaine on his cell and let her know he was back in the city and could drop off her van. And Sugar, of course.

"I'm going to miss that furry face so much," Tess said, glancing back at Sugar's crate.

"I'll make sure Elaine brings her over for play dates with Toby."

"I'd love that."

"It's hard to forget that dog," Will said. "She's such a little diva, but she has a real heart. Sugar and Toby make quite a pair."

They drove flat out on Interstate 10, all the way to the city limits and then toward the Pacific. And it looked so fresh and new to Tess, the palm trees and the mountains and the high rises and the sprawl. It was much greener than she'd thought it would be, and the sky was so blue and clear, with just a few clouds.

"Don't get used to this," Will teased her. "Eventually you'll see smog. It must have rained right before we arrived. It's much clearer in the fall and winter than during the summer."

They drove until they went into what looked like a small tunnel, and suddenly the highway eased to the right and they were traveling north, with the Pacific Ocean to their left. She could see people lying on the beach and surfers and swimmers farther out in the vivid blue water. The bright sunshine sparkled off the surface of the ocean, waves crashed against the sand in a ceaseless rhythm, and Tess couldn't stop looking. She'd never seen the ocean, and now she truly understood the meaning of the word *vast*.

"It's so—it's incredible!"

Will couldn't seem to stop smiling. "I love it. When I came here from England, I spent almost every weekend I could spare at the beach."

"Do you surf?"

He looked somewhat shamefaced and said, "I actually had a surfing teacher."

"Why do you seem so embarrassed?"

"Because it's so L.A."

She had no idea what that meant but found she was dying to find out. Glancing back, she could see that both Toby and Sugar had come awake from their naps and were smelling the distinct ocean breeze.

"I wish I had a dog's nose for just one day. What they must smell!"

Will laughed, but not at her. Tess knew he would listen to her and feel that what she thought was important. He wasn't the sort of man to relegate her to a small part of his life. She would share all of his life, and the thought made her happy.

Within a short time they reached a gated community along the coastal highway, and Will pulled off to the left. The man in the small gatehouse let him in, and Will started down toward the large houses and veritable mansions situated on the beach, their decks right on the Pacific.

My God, Elaine must make a good living as a psychic, Tess thought as she leaned out the passenger side window of the van, taking in everyone and everything. The sunlight seemed to make everything seem so vivid and intense: the smell of the ocean, people walking around in bathing suits and carrying surf boards, bright pots of brilliantly colored impatiens and geraniums.

The van continued along until they came to one of the larger, more impressive houses and Will pulled into the small parking area in front of a two-car garage. A silver Porsche was parked to the side.

"We're here," he said, but the announcement was unnecessary as Sugar began barking excitedly. Clearly the Keeshond was home.

"Hey, you two!" said a female voice from the deck that ran around the side of the house, and Tess saw a woman headed toward them. "You made great time!"

Elaine. She was exactly as Tess had pictured. She was a petite woman with dark brown hair and brown eyes, with an alert, cheerful face. It was the sort of face that would have been incredibly cute during her twenties and thirties, even her forties, but had matured into something even better. Tess guessed she was in her mid-fifties.

Elaine was clearly interested in life—the energy in her eyes told Tess that. She had a kind, inquisitive expression, and Tess had the feeling she'd seen and heard quite a bit during her career as a psychic. Dressed in a pair of jeans, a bright orange top, and sandals, she had the energy and verve of a woman a couple of decades younger.

"Will!" She hugged him tightly, clearly delighted to see him. Then she came around the van and said, "You must be Tess," and gave Tess one of the warmest hugs she'd ever received in her life. "A good trip?" she said, her brown eyes twinkling, and Tess had the feeling that she knew a lot more about their trip than she was letting on.

"The best," Tess said. Elaine grinned.

Will opened up the sliding side door of the van and reached in to open Sugar's crate. The silvery Keeshond launched herself out of her crate and headed toward Elaine like a furry, heat-seeking missile. She almost knocked the petite woman over in the enthusiasm of her greeting.

Then Elaine was kneeling on the cement, her dog in her

arms, looking up and thanking them both for bringing her dog home to her, safe and sound.

"Our pleasure," Will said.

"Well," said Elaine briskly, "I'd love to stay and chat, but I have a reading in about an hour and I'd like to get Sugar settled before that. But I insist on having you both over to dinner later in the week. I want to hear all about your trip."

Tess didn't feel as if she'd been dismissed at all. In fact, she had a feeling that she was going to be seeing a lot of Elaine in the future. This woman simply didn't know a stranger. It felt good to have made her first friend in Los Angeles.

"Can Elaine give us a ride to your house?" she asked and then heard a quickly muffled snort of laughter from the older woman before she turned away.

"What?" She turned toward Will, then glanced at Elaine. They'd returned Elaine's van and her dog, and she had to get Toby out and let her stretch her legs for a bit and then unload all their stuff—

Suddenly she took it all in, and the whole thing, the whole picture, seemed sharper. The house at the edge of the Pacific, the silver Porsche, the way Elaine had been waiting on the balcony—it all clicked into place with stunning clarity—

"Oh my God," she said quietly, then looked up into Will's eyes. "Is this your house?"

He nodded his head.

She turned toward the Porsche and then back to him.

He nodded.

Her cheeks burned with embarrassment. Here she'd thought he was a struggling musician, a songwriter barely making ends meet! The image of the starving artist had always been one her father had drilled into his children's heads, over and over again. He'd been so sure of his opinion that people in the arts never made any money. You had to be an excellent businessman to make any sort of decent living, according to his worldview.

"We need to unload the van," Tess said slowly. She realized she had to figure out where she was going to spend the night.

"Elaine," Will said suddenly. "Take the Porsche."

"Really?" she said. Her dark eyes lit up with excitement. "You know how I like to speed, Will."

"Just don't get in trouble. I'll drive the van over later tonight, okay?"

"That's fine. Now let me meet Toby before I take off."

Tess felt numb with shock as Will got Toby out of her crate and Elaine fussed over the little dog. And Toby stood there, strong and sure, basking in the attention. As Tess looked at her dog, she realized she wasn't the only one who had changed over the course of their trip.

"Well, I can't fit the dog crate in the Porsche," Elaine was saying, "and I don't trust Sugar to be loose in a seat—"

"Though her silver fur would look stunning in the car," Will teased.

"That's true," Elaine said. "Dashing as it blew in the breeze." She looked at her dog. "Sugar, would you stay with Will and Tess and Toby just a little bit longer? Will can drive you to the house in the van tonight, how about that?"

Sugar barked sharply once, then twice. Elaine looked up at Will. "She's asking me to make sure you're bringing her home this evening. No offense to any of you, but she wants to sleep in her own bed tonight."

"I promise," Will said.

Elaine got into the silver Porsche, started the motor, smiled brilliantly at both of them, and called out to Will,

"If I'm not home when you get there this evening, I'm just taking this beauty on a little ride."

Will laughed and said, "We'll wait for you."

THEY locked the van without unloading it and went inside the beach house—or rather, mansion—with the dogs. Will offered her some juice, and Tess accepted. Both Sugar and Toby pranced out on to the huge deck that faced the Pacific, and Toby started to bark at the seagulls that were circling in the clear blue, cloudless sky.

Will indicated that they should walk out on to the deck, and they sat in chairs, facing the ocean. Tess knew he was waiting for her to speak.

"The house?" she finally said.

"Yep."

"And the car?"

He nodded his head.

"And the band?"

He named a name that was known worldwide, whose albums had sold in the millions.

"How did I miss that?" she wondered.

"We're a little better known in England."

"Not much!" She hesitated and then said, "So you're filthy rich?"

He nodded. "I stand accused."

"You made it big with your music."

"Oh, we all went through the requisite years of struggle."

She didn't know what to say.

"Does this make a difference in your feelings toward me?"

She still didn't know what to say.

"I'm the same old Will," he said softly.

"I feel like I'm a little out of my league," she said.

"Not at all. But I have something in mind that should set yours at ease."

THEY dropped off Sugar and the van at Elaine's spacious house in Encino early that evening, after her reading. Her friend Jack, the astrologer, was there as well. They were in the midst of a friendly discussion, trying to decide what to order in for dinner. Tess met Jack and realized she'd made yet another friend in the funny, intelligent, and very charming man.

Then she and Will headed straight home, where they'd left a disgruntled Toby in her crate.

"I'll fix up the Porsche with a harness or something so she can ride in the car with us," Will said. "You know, one of those dog seat belts. And never on the freeway."

"That's your only car?"

"Why? Do you think I need another one?"

"Something to haul more than two people around."

"We'll go shopping," he assured her. "Now, about tonight—"

"I need to find a place to stay," she said.

"I have it all worked out," Will replied. "I called my next-door neighbor right after we talked in Las Vegas. He's a bachelor, and his beach house is something of a bachelor pad, but he's filming in Vancouver for the next four months, so he said you could certainly use his house while he was away."

"What?"

"Of course, he'd love it if you would water his orchids and feed the fish so he could let the orchid and goldfish nanny go—"

"Surfing teachers? Goldfish nannies? Have I fallen down the rabbit hole or taken a tornado to Oz?"

"Yes," said Will. "You have. And the best course of action is complete surrender. Accept your fate. You can't fight it." He grinned down at her. "God knows I tried."

SO she moved into the house next door and was out on the balcony with Toby when she saw that her dog was staring at the large deck on the other side of the house from Will's. On this beach house's deck stood a striking black Schnauzer, staring fixedly at Toby. His stump of a tail began to wag, and he gave a friendly bark.

"Max!" said a very clipped female voice from inside the house. "You'll disturb the neighbors!"

The large black dog, his glossy coat shining in the sunlight, gave Toby one more very interested look and trotted inside his house.

Toby looked up at Tess, grinning in delight. She yipped once, then twice.

"My advice?" Tess said, picking up her dog and letting Toby wriggle in delight and frantically, happily lick her face. "Play hard to get."

HE'D asked her to meet him at a little bar and restaurant just down Pacific Coast Highway. It was easily walking distance, so Tess locked her new temporary beach house door behind her and took off as the sun slowly set over the ocean, a sight that truly took her breath away.

She'd left lights on inside the house in the living room and the master bedroom and Toby asleep on the enormous bed. She'd found clean sheets and changed the bed earlier that day, in that surreal space whose windows looked out over the ocean. "What a sight to wake up to," she told a prancing Toby as she helped her make the bed.

Tess let herself in the door of the restaurant and turned toward the bar. She walked in, glad that Kim had also bought her a couple of stunning dresses along with a pair of dressy shoes. The dress she had on was simple and black, a sleeveless knit with a V-neck that hugged her body, a dress made for a night of mystery and magic, dinner and dancing.

She approached the bar and sat down. The bartender came over, and she ordered a glass of white wine.

Within minutes, the bartender was back. "That gentleman over there would like to buy you another glass of wine," he said.

She glanced up and saw Will sitting much farther down the bar.

"Thank you," she told the bartender, accepting the drink.

Will slid into the seat beside her.

"Thank you for the wine," Tess said.

"My pleasure. I haven't seen you here before."

"I just got into town."

"Where are you staying?"

"Just down the road, at a beach house."

"I live that same way. What a coincidence." He took a sip of his drink. "Are you having dinner tonight?"

"Yes."

"Then you must let me join you. I can't see a woman like you eating dinner alone."

"I've eaten many dinners alone," she said, trying for the manner of a woman of the world.

"Now that," said Will, "is something we're going to rectify right now."

*   *   *

THEY had a long, leisurely dinner, during which time they talked about everything and anything. She found out that he had two older sisters in England, along with his parents and his grandmother, and that he'd traveled extensively. She told him all about the traveling she wished she'd done in the past and intended to do in the future. He answered all her questions about his band; she asked him about composing music. He made her open up about her love of knitting and design.

They talked of politics and recent news, movies seen, books read. When their table was ready, they went into the dining room and enjoyed their meal, seafood prepared excellently by the chef. Tess even splurged on dessert, a chocolate soufflé still warm from the oven. And she insisted that Will share some with her.

He offered her a ride in his Porsche, and they took a leisurely drive up the coast, the Pacific dark and black and glittering mysteriously to the left of Pacific Coast Highway, the stars sparkling in the sky. Thirty minutes later Will walked around to her side of the silver sports car and opened her door to let her out at her new, temporary home. He walked her to the door of the beach house.

"I had a wonderful evening, Tess," he said.

"I did, too."

She knew he was going to kiss her good night, so she wasn't surprised when he took her in his arms and lowered his head toward hers. What did surprise Tess was the rush of emotion she felt when their lips met, so effortlessly, and she knew they fit. She knew they belonged together. She knew she had a future with this man and was so thankful he understood her need to take things step by step.

It was all starting with a kiss, the kiss she'd been waiting for her entire life. And it didn't matter that she'd been kissed before, many times, because this kiss was different. She knew it, and she treasured the moment. A first kiss, never to come again. And she found herself hoping Will would be the last man she'd ever kiss, her one and only.

He kissed her again, with slightly more intensity, and then stepped away. She could feel the tension almost humming between them, the attraction palpable. Very thankful that she had her own house to retreat to, she wished him a breathless good night and slipped inside her new home.

When the door closed behind her and Toby was winding around her legs demanding a pat, Tess found she couldn't stop smiling. She sat down on the tiled floor just inside the door and let Toby jump into her lap.

And she just couldn't stop smiling.

SHE woke up before sunrise, happy and surprised that she'd slept as well as she had with the sound of the ocean outside. Both the smell of the sea and the hushed roaring of the waves were so different but had become so restful. The feel and sound of the wind was so sensual. As she'd drifted off to sleep, Tess thought she could live by this ocean for the rest of her life. It was as if she'd found a beautiful kingdom by the sea, the perfect place to spend her life.

She turned on the lights and walked downstairs, fed the fish, checked the orchids, and made a mental note to water them later in the day. She was in the beautifully appointed, very modern white and silver kitchen, trying to figure out how to make some coffee when she heard her cell phone ring.

Smiling, she ran upstairs.

"So," said Will when she answered. "I saw the lights go

on. Can I tempt you and Toby into coming over with doughnuts and coffee?"

"Where did you find doughnuts at this hour?"

"There's this little twenty-four-hour place up the road, a real hole in the wall, but the doughnuts are fantastic. I'm actually making the coffee myself."

She almost laughed—this from the man who had constantly bought her coffee on the road. Who would've thought he'd know his way around an actual coffeepot?

"You couldn't have slept that much," she said, thinking of him out on the road picking up those doughnuts.

"Actually, no."

"You really made coffee? I'm impressed. You're such a talented man."

"You have no idea. Coming over?"

"I'll be right there."

It was fun, stepping off the deck while it was still nighttime and into the soft sand, Toby in her arms. Her little dog had gotten as far as the deck, but the actual sand and the waves still gave her a moment of trepidation. So Tess carried her feisty little dog, all sixteen pounds of her, and then set her down after she walked up the steps onto Will's large deck.

They sat at a small round table, Toby at their feet, and Tess fed small bites of her first doughnut to her ecstatic dog.

"Not too much—you'll get sick," she warned her.

Will took a sip of his coffee. "I thought of calling you last night."

"You did?" The idea gave her great pleasure.

"I wanted to talk to you about our evening."

"What about?" she said, wanting to hear.

"About how the minute I walked into that bar and saw you, I knew something special had happened."

Tess stilled completely, another doughnut halfway to her mouth. She set it down on the plate in front of her, ignoring Toby's pleading expression. She knew Will wasn't talking about the bar they'd been at last night. She knew he was referring to the bar back in Illinois, outside Chicago.

"I knew it the moment I saw you. I remembered you from school, but my first thought was that you'd turned into such a beautiful woman. I felt as if my heart was going to come right out of my chest, it was beating so fast."

She couldn't stop looking at him. What was it about Brits? They had such an effortless command of the language that they could take human emotion and make it simply take flight. She also knew he was being totally vulnerable with her, telling her this.

"My father saw my mother at a dance and he told me that he just *knew*. I heard that story so many times while I was growing up, from both of them. I wanted it to happen to me."

Tess sat perfectly still, fascinated.

"I'd just about given up. Then I walked into that bar and saw you. And you had that damn ring on your finger and were getting married. So I took a chance and gave you my number. And Tess, even though you came on the road with me, I didn't think I could tell you how I felt, I didn't think I could touch you, I didn't even think I could want you the way I did."

She could feel the last few bits of her reserve breaking away, shattering like brittle glass. Leaving her forever. The more she looked at him, the more she listened, the more she thought the world was the most magical and mysterious place. There were so many things there were absolutely no explanations for, and that was the way it should be. She didn't want to think too much about the total ele-

ment of chance, of fate, that had brought her together with
Will.

What were the odds . . .

"Your heart was breaking, Tess, but the more I traveled
with you, the more I admired you. The more time I spent
with you, the more I knew you were a woman worth loving. You were hurting like hell, but you didn't call him, you
didn't try to break into his phone messages, you didn't
leave him long rambling messages. You were so brave."

"I was in shock," she said quietly.

"You were also brave. Your heart was breaking, and
your entire future had gone belly up, and you were polite to
me. You didn't take it out on me. The more I learned about
all the circumstances that had brought you to this place in
your life, the more I thought you'd conducted yourself with
such grace."

"I didn't know what I was doing," she protested.

"You handled the whole thing with such class. You
didn't get drunk as an excuse to dial his number and sob to
him over the phone. You didn't talk about him endlessly
and wallow in the whole thing. There were whole parts of
our trip when you simply looked out the van window and
thought."

"I—" But she stopped. What he was saying was true.

"You didn't let your grief overshadow a reunion with
your brother. You didn't let your pain ruin the entire drive
out here, about two thousand miles. You always did what
was best for the dogs and best for the trip because that's the
kind of person you are."

She simply couldn't speak.

"You didn't turn to food or booze, you didn't shop yourself sick or talk about getting revenge. You didn't go for rebound sex, or drugs, or whatever your poison. You didn't

delay the pain, Tess. You just felt it and let it go through you and then you let it go. And when the time came to meet up with Paul, you cut things off cleanly, quickly, elegantly. And you didn't look back."

She looked at him, speechless.

"You didn't whitewash the past and try to pretend he was something he wasn't. And you didn't make him out to be some sort of monster, either. You refused to be a drama queen. You simply shouldered your share of the responsibility for the whole thing and took a long, hard look at your life and saw the choices you'd made that had landed you in the entire experience. And you worked on yourself. You made so many discoveries on this trip, and it was like your whole attitude was, 'Bring it on! Even more!' You had nothing to lose and nothing to fear, so you ended up gaining an entire new life."

She reached over and took his hand, feeling the warmth of his fingers and his palm as she made contact and linked her fingers with his. She needed to hold on to him, to ground herself in what he was saying. She'd known, about halfway through their journey, that this road trip was going to save her life, but hearing him actually say the words was having a profound impact on her.

"Breaking up with anyone is hard and takes courage. You trusted yourself, and you faced up to what your relationship really was. Although you felt like you were falling apart on the road, I saw a woman who was absolutely courageous and had the guts to take her life into her own two hands and mold it into something she wanted to have.

"You didn't obsess over what he was thinking. You didn't try to stay friends. You were involved with a man who, to put it mildly, didn't wish you well at all. But you didn't indulge in a pity party. You saw that hard work was needed, and you got on with it."

She was holding on to his hand so tightly now, as if it were a lifeline.

"I'm so proud of you, Tess. Every little step along the way made me sure you were the woman I truly wanted to spend the rest of my life with. That was why it was so easy to marry you when we finally reached Las Vegas."

"But I thought—"

"I could have handled Paul. I didn't need to marry you to protect you."

She didn't know what to say.

"You can't run away from pain. You have to feel it, walk through it, face it head on. I've been there and done it. And I've seen so many people in the business I'm in avoid their pain and end up ruined, or worse. The more time I spent with you, the more I knew my heart had been right. Something, somehow, had been recognized that night in the bar. I knew you were the right one before I even had any conscious reason to believe it. Tess, I think we know things on a deeper level than rational understanding, and when I first saw you, I knew I'd finally found what I had always been looking for."

She knew from the expression on his face what he was about to say, and her throat closed with emotion.

"I just need you to know that I want to make this marriage a real one. I want to spend the rest of my life with you, Tess. I know we're right together, and I want to spend the next few weeks or months or whatever it takes proving it to you."

She could feel the lightest of emotions filling her body, a spiraling happiness, and it was as if something that had been out of focus was suddenly thrown into sharp relief. Drawing her hand away from his, she touched his arm.

"It's over. It's done. I'm ready."

He looked at her in disbelief.

"I don't need to know anything else. I feel it, too, Will. I don't think I'll ever want to be with any other man the way I want to be with you."

He seemed to struggle with her sudden change of heart as he said, slowly, "But what about long walks on the beach? Taking things slow? Being absolutely sure—"

"I *am* sure. For the longest time, when I was a girl, you were my ideal of everything a man should be. But the man I discovered as we traveled together eclipsed the man of my dreams. Reality was so much better than any daydream. Will, I don't know why or how we came together the way we did, but I want you to know that, as far as I'm concerned, I don't want to get this marriage annulled either."

And to illustrate her words, Tess got up and started for his door.

She was halfway up the stairs to where she thought his bedroom was, early morning sunlight pouring through the large windows, the sound of the ocean outside filling her senses, when Will caught up with her and lifted her high into his arms. She laughed with happy surprise, putting her arms around his neck as Toby pranced around his feet, barking and wagging her stumpy tail happily.

"I love you, Tess," he said, right before he kissed her, a kiss filled with so much emotion she was actually shaking when they broke apart.

"Me, too," she whispered. "You, I mean."

"I know." He smiled down at her as he started up the rest of the stairs. "Welcome to the rest of your life, Mrs. Tremere," he whispered in her ear. "Starting right now."

Elda Minger is the bestselling and award-winning author of dozens of romance novels, including series, contemporary, and historical. She is also known in the world of romance for her inspiring and entertaining workshops on writing. Her books include *Embrace the Night*, *The Fling*, and *The Dare*, along with several novellas. *The Kiss* was inspired by a road trip she took with a friend. Elda lives in California with her family, both two- and four-footed, and is currently at work on her next novel.

Also available from
BERKLEY SENSATION

Duchess of Fifth Avenue
by Ruth Ryan Langan
The *New York Times* bestselling author of
"heartwarming, emotionally involving romances"*
brings the Gilded Age to life.

0-425-20889-3

The Penalty Box
by Deirdre Martin
From the *USA Today* bestselling author, a novel
about a hockey heartthrob, a stubborn brainiac,
and a battle of wills that just might end in love.

0-425-20890-7

Dead Heat
by Jacey Ford
Three beautiful ex-FBI agents have founded a security
firm—and their latest job uncovers a fatal plot against
America's top CEOs.

0-425-20461-8

Library Journal